COLOSSEUMS
FOR DINOSAURS

THE RUNNING OF THE TYRANNOSAURS
NYOTA'S TYRANNOSAUR
THE SCREAMING OF THE TYRANNOSAUR

STANT LITORE

Westmarch Publishing | 2019

MORE FROM STANT LITORE

THE ZOMBIE BIBLE

Death Has Come up into Our Windows
What Our Eyes Have Witnessed
Strangers in the Land
No Lasting Burial
I Will Hold My Death Close
By a Slender Thread (forthcoming)

ANSIBLE

Ansible: Season One
Ansible: Season Two
Ansible: Rasha's Letter

OTHER TITLES

Colosseums for Dinosaurs
Dante's Heart

&

The Dark Need (The Dead Man #20)
with Lee Goldberg, William Rabkin

&

Lives of Unforgetting
Lives of Unstoppable Hope
Write Characters Your Readers Won't Forget
Write Worlds Your Readers Won't Forget

Colosseums for Dinosaurs

Stant Litore

Westmarch Publishing

2019

CONTENTS

for the young women
of this generation—
no matter what a magazine cover
might tell you,
you are each beautiful

THE RUNNING

OF THE

TYRANNOSAURS

1

WATCH ME. I stand tall on the red sand and breathe deep. Inside me, the nanites are rapidly at work, increasing my oxygen intake, quickening my metabolism, honing the chemistry of my adrenal glands. I can hear the snorting breath of the tyrannosaurs, can you? They don't like the chill air. Neither do I, but in a few moments we will all be running, we will all be slick with sweat, we will all be fiercely alive. And you, every one of you, will be screaming my name.

This is my day. The garland will be mine. The other runners are stretching or singing their low prayers to my left or my right. I must be faster than them. I must be smarter than them. The hooks are strapped to my wrists, their ropes wrapped around each of my arms, ready to be uncoiled quickly when needed.

Like the others, I stand naked, my skin dusted with glitter, my head back, my back straight. Today I am Liberty's daughter. Today I am a goddess. The crowds far above us and to the sides watch in a hushed silence, waiting for the trumpets—I can feel you, the immense pressure of your millions, your gaze like the beat of the sun on my skin, almost sexual in its intensity. Today every woman among you wishes she were me; every man wishes he could fuck me, and some of the women do too. Rotating screens in midair project my face, hundreds of feet tall; floodlights of all colors wash past from the hovers filming me and filming all of you reacting to me. Pennants stream in the air, bearing the athletes' sigils. My own, an egret in flight, spreads its wings wide on ten thousand waving banners and is tattooed on my back and belly for you to see, its head toward you, its white wings cupping my breasts, embracing me with its feathers, its thin legs pressed together and extending down toward my vagina, declaring to all of you that I am a woman, the most desirable of women: an athlete, a sacrifice, Liberty's daughter. Somewhere outside this orbital spin-gravity cylinder burn a billion billion stars, but I burn brighter.

Breathe deep, stand tall, knees slightly bent, my weight on the balls of my feet. Let the nanites do their work.

I have never been so aware of my own body.

Almost I can feel each vein, each rush of blood. Every sense is heightened; I can smell the blossom-scent in my short hair and the heavy musk of bull tyrannosaurs; I can feel each grain of sand under my toes. The air is still. I sing the Liberty Prayer softly as the others do.

The only one of the others I fear is Alicia, who has run the tyrannosaurs before. She has often been cold to me, and I know she expects to be first today as she was on the last Patriot Day. But I will be better than her. Parents will name their infants after *me* this year.

One of the tyrannosaurs lifts its head and screams, and the sound is terrible, like the shriek of rending metal, but I do not flinch. The gasp of the crowd is like the sigh of the sea. The tyrannosaurs are to be respected, not feared.

Liberty is light on her toes; Liberty dances with what would consume her. Liberty springs over the back of the bull and lands on her feet.

The others have finished stretching and singing, and stand as expectantly as I, though Alicia looks bored. Fuck her. She is seventeen and old. Last year's sensation. But suddenly, and with a tiny smirk at the corner of her lip, she sets her hands to her hips and tosses her head, flipping back her long, golden braid. That braid is stupid for a runner, but she is very skilled and her hair has become her sigil every bit as much as the prancing figure tattooed in gold ink on her body. Seeing her proud stance, a lot of you thunder your feet against the hull and scream her Patriot Day name, *Gazelle! Gazelle! Gazelle!* – and I flush with fury. You will scream louder than that for *me*. I will *make* you scream louder.

There are two kinds of people on this cylinder world: competitors on the sand beside me, who I will destroy, and you on the platforms, whose worship I will earn.

I must do something to steal your attention from Alicia, and quickly. An egret flies above a gazelle. Always. You must see that. I must do something bold, even if I risk looking ridiculous. I cannot see your faces except for brief glimpses on the rotating screens interspersed with shots of the tyrannosaurs and images of me and the other sacrifices, but that doesn't matter; I will *hear* you. I take a few steps across the sand, turning in a circle, drawing your eyes. Smiling proudly, I lift my right arm, miming Liberty holding her torch.

It is an audacious gesture from a runner, and you break into a scream of joy and adulation that nearly deafens me;

my ears ring. Yet I grin back, my breast hot with pleasure. A brief, disdainful glance over my shoulder shows me Alicia, her face rigid, her eyes seething. Good. I face the screens, facing all of you, my hand high in the air. There you all are, all of you, all my worshippers. You women who have been discussing every publicized detail of my life for weeks, you men who tonight will hire tattooed courtesans glittered like cheap imitations of me, you young lovers who have betted on the outcomes of this run, with the winner of the wager acquiring the other as a passion-slave for a night or a week. I do know that among your millions a few of you do not cheer. A few of you, a very few, sit silent and robed in black, in protest, but you few are pathetic. I am alive and I will run. Watch me.

2

YOU ARE IMPATIENT with waiting; I can hear the stir of you. But I love this moment; I hope the Master of Rites will prolong it. I want your appetites whetted, I want you desperate to see me in motion. I want to hear the gasp when I finally leap from the sand. You have never seen me move, though so many of you wave my pennant, hoping I will be the best. I will leave you all breathless. Watch me.

Victory will be sweet; I will stand on the red sand and I will stand alone, apart from the whole world, and the whole world will be there for *me*. I live to hear you scream my name. Live to hear you love me. Only this matters. And for it, I must be perfect, absolutely perfect.

The nanites help with this. Since my periods started they have been reshaping me, day by day, making my breasts heavy and full yet keeping them high on my chest, enlarging my lips, rounding my hips. It is strange when I see a mirror, for I change so quickly, as the criteria for perfection change. When I look in a mirror, I see myself looking back out of a strange body.

I ignore the mirrors.

My trainer is Mai, and she is relentless. She only trains the best. She has trained thirteen champions over the past twenty-four Patriot Days, and I will be the fourteenth. We each have a training implant in our left wrist, and when Mai is displeased, it spreads fire through our skin, every nerve in the arm burning. Mai is often displeased. It is not easy to be a first runner, she says. It is not easy to be the best. We train from before lights-up to after lights-down. Physical training, mostly. Honing our bodies. The nanites can only do so much to augment us; we have to be fit. Millions of credits have been spent on our muscles, Mai tells us. Use them!

My diet is strict. If I eat too much, I must vomit it up into the silver ewer I keep for that purpose. Mai has the ewer inspected regularly. She has me inspected regularly. No surplus carbohydrates or sugars, no alcoholic beverages, no vids she hasn't approved, no open channels to outside the temple school, no failure to take sleep induction once I am in my bunk. And no boys, absolutely no contact with boys, because boys all want to fuck me, and my virginity is as important to what I am as the sigil blazoned on my back and below my breasts. My body has to be perfect and pure. Girls have cheated this rule before, but now doctors check us the morning of to be sure, and Mai says if they catch you, they bury you alive beneath the red sand as an example. Once, when I was twelve and furious with her over a punishment, I shouted at her that I'd loved to be buried and hidden under quiet, dark sand, where no cameras could see me and people wouldn't be watching me all day and I could rest. She slapped me and then sealed me inside my own capsule where I keep my clothing, emptying it first so that I was locked inside a tube of cold metal. It was dark, and it was silent, and I beat on the sleek surface above me and screamed. I tore at it with my nails but could find no line or crack or anything, and I have never been so scared *in my life*. It was forever and forever. When Mai let me out, her face was cold. I let her dress me, and followed her silently to physical training, and I have never suggested again that I talk to a boy.

It was humiliating, having a doctor's gloved fingertip inside me. If being with a boy is anything like that, I want no part in it anyway.

You up there, you fuck whoever you want, you can eat whatever you want, as much as you want, and be fat and lazy if you want, but not us. We have to be perfect. We have to be the dream you want to hold and never can, the unattainable. Every one of you women will be cutting your hair in my style by the end of this week, dieting and buying corsets to try and force your body nearer to my measurements. Every one of you men will jerk off later to vidcasts of me standing triumphant and sweaty at the end of the run, or you will try not to say my name by mistake when you're fucking tonight.

I have to be perfect for you.

Ten years of training, each morning checking my body's measurements and my stats for speed and agility against Alicia's, and Cora's, and Rai's, and I *am* the best. I am Egret, born Livia Nigeria Tenning, and I am proud of my training.

And yet, sometimes, in the dark of night, I wake groggy from the sleep induction yet shaking from dreams of my mother running after me, chasing the car that came for me when I was six, men in white taking me to be an athlete, to train, to be taught how to truly, truly live. In my dream, I watch out the back window as my mother falls behind. No matter how red her face is from running, how wide her mouth with screaming for me, she is always too slow. She is not an athlete, not Liberty's daughter. Her mascara runs with her tears.

As I sit up in the dark, wrenched from my dream, panting, her tears unsettle me, a pang near my heart. But I also flash with anger. She should have been proud of me. She should have smiled and told me how wonderful it would be. She should be up there with you, somewhere, even now, waving an egret banner and screaming for my victory, her face flushed with joy because her daughter, *hers*, is today's sacrifice. She should be happy for me, so happy.

Why was she crying?

3

TRUMPETS SHATTER THE AIR, ringing from sleek, silver hovercraft that drift high above us, flooding us with light and color and noise. Over your shouting and the music and the thunder of my own heart I can't hear them break the gates, but I feel the ground shake as the tyrannosaurs charge. Then I see them burst through the ribbons that separate the sands from the stables, and they are rushing toward us; they are swift and brutal, leaning their heads forward, nostrils flared, driven mad with hunger at our scent. As they pant, their ribs stand prominent against their skin; they have been starved in preparation for this day. My day.

They avalanche toward us, and the reek of them hits me like a wall: yet I keep my feet. I uncoil the rope about my left arm, drop the cold metal hook into my left palm. You up there, you see the tyrannosaurs huge on the screens but you have no idea just how *massive* they really are. You can't begin to understand that until they are charging at you, explosions of sand about their feet. Nor can you even imagine how deadly, how lethal they are, if you have never looked closely in their eyes, as I have.

Today is my first Patriot Day, but I have practiced mounting many times with Mai's harsh voice barking out directions, and many times I have looked into the tyrannosaur's eyes. Darker than dark and deep as time, and alien like a bird's eyes.

They are pack hunters, and fierce. Early in my training, I watched them stalk elephants in the jungle on Orbital Conservatory Station IX-C. They leap on their prey; they are incredibly powerful animals, worthy to run for the goddess. Each of these has a white ribbon tied about its tiny left foreclaw, belying the fixed, hungry regard of their eyes; they are consecrated. These bulls will run the sixty kilometers of the sand road down the length of Liberty Cylinder, a narrow path enclosed between tall walls of steel. We will run them. At the road's end, at the Liberty Shrine, Madame President will kiss the first runner and hang the garland at her neck. These once fierce predators that ruled a planet, these fast, birdlike creatures have been resurrected by human science and reshaped to meet human ends. They exist, as I do, for the goddess' glory and for your entertainment and approval. Today I run the tyrannosaurs for you. Watch.

They are upon us, and I am running before them, breathing evenly. Watch me dodge the snap of one bull's teeth, then duck beneath its body as it charges over me. I can never be caught or eaten. I will never lose my balance. I am the best. One of the other athletes—Cora, I think, that is the lion on her back—dodges a little too slowly, a little too awkwardly (when you run the tyrannosaurs, grace is *everything*, the one thing they and the goddess respect), and the tyrannosaur catches her in its teeth and tosses its head back. I haven't time to look or think about it, the tyrannosaurs are rushing by, the sheer *mass* of them, as though they are planets and I a ship falling in. I leap and sprint. I swing the hook, chopping it deep into one's feathered flesh just below the knee, and then I am swinging up, catching its rump with my hand, flipping onto its back near the tail, landing with my legs wide to balance myself. There is sand everywhere in the air, grit and dust and I am striving not to cough in it, striving to see clearly, and I can feel the thunder and heat of the beast beneath my feet, its powerful body moving, and I am *on* it, riding it, precariously, and you all *wish* you were, all of you, you up there in bright clothes with your lovers beside you, you who have freedom *from* so much, from poverty and hunger, from the fear of being bombed, from the fear of being eaten, from even the fear of being solitary; a suitable lover might be engineered for you. You have freedom *from*, but you don't know what you have freedom *for*. You have forgotten. That is why you watch me. That is why you roar. Because I, your sacrifice, your athlete—I and this tyrannosaur—know what we are for. We are for breathing, for running, for the sweat and the heat and the cry of the crowd. We are free to live. These few moments, these brief few moments. You envy me.

I cannot stay by the tail. The tyrannosaur's run will throw me; I can barely balance here. I tug on the line, ripping my hook free and flipping it up, catching it in my other hand, and I have to leap, *now*, higher on this beast's back, to some steadier perch, but even as my legs tense a larger beast careens past, larger and faster, brushing by the young bull I ride. An instant's decision, an impulse, a breath, and I spring through the air to the other bull, taking the risk. But my feet glance off its left shoulder and I flip through the air over it with a startled cry. Its head slams into me from the side and I hurtle away through a blurred world of flesh and heat and dust and all of you screaming, whether you scream my name or some other's, so loud, a glimpse of the lights above me, then a glimpse of the steel wall. Then I hit the sand, and I hit hard.

4

MY EYES FLY OPEN after a darkness that must have lasted only a second; the tyrannosaur has turned and its head is darting toward me, cobra-quick, but I am already rolling, then leaping up and sprinting, *fast*, the nanites repairing my body as I dash. Having already shut off my pain and jolted me awake on adrenaline, now they repair a snapped rib, seal closed my ruptured lung, smooth out the abrasions and tears in my skin, all in the time it takes to draw a few quick breaths. I see my hook half-sheathed in the sand before me and I dive for it. The tyrannosaur's jaws snap closed just behind me. Snatching up the hook, I spin on the balls of my feet and slam the metal into the soft flesh above the creature's right nostril. It whips its head back, throwing me into the air but I have the hook in my hand and the rope in my other and as it screams I loop the rope about its upper jaw. Then the hard impact of my knees as I come down on its head, my teeth clacking shut, cutting my tongue. Rush of hot blood into my mouth. I spit it out, entrusting the repair to the nanites, just keeping myself from choking on the bitter, metallic fluid. All of you are wild above me and someone is laughing hysterically and I realize it is me. I can feel your worship in every beat of my heart, every pulse of my blood; I am hot with it, I am alive with it. As the tyrannosaur turns and stampedes, I am riding its head, laughing, my arm lifted again, Liberty's torch. You are screaming my name now: *Egret, Egret, Egret!* The very ground shudders with your shouting; I can feel it through the bones and flesh of the tyrannosaur. Standing, I pay out the rope, dancing nimbly up the bull's head and down along its spine, leaping and using the rope to pull myself in, again and again, Liberty dancing on the back of the beast. *This* is what you want to see, *this* is what you lust for, and I give it to you, as you have never seen it before, my body spinning high in the air, glittering like diamonds in the floodlights, wet with my sweat as though I am oiled for sex or bathed in the goddess's wine. My laughs become shrieks of joy; I revel in the light impact of the creature's skin each time my feet touch before I spring again. No one can do what I do. No one has a body like mine. Only I am dancing this beast, only I.

5

OUR TYRANNOSAURS are in full stampede now, carrying us down the long red road, creating wind in our faces. Liberty's daughters have danced with violence and have not only survived but gentled and bridled these most vicious of beasts; now we careen across the world on their backs, lifting our voices, one after the other, in song. Only one of us lies bleeding and broken behind; the goddess is pleased. And you are pleased; how your feet stomp! How your screams fill the cylinder! Scream for me!

Something swerves into the peripheral view on my left. Glancing, I see Alicia perched high on her tyrannosaur's head. Her tyrannosaur is in full charge beside mine. My gaze at her is hot with hate. She smirks at me, taking her second hook in her left hand and tapping its blunt end against the beast's eyelid. The beast's eye snaps shut and it leans its head sharply toward me and veers suddenly, slamming its body into my own bull's shoulder. My beast stumbles and I am in the air but I flip quickly and swing in on my rope, catching the beast's knee painfully with my hip, forcing a cry of pain from my throat. The nanites are on it, and the pain fades almost instantly, but the humiliation doesn't. She has made me look clumsy, ungraceful. The bitch. Throat tight with rage, I pull myself swiftly up the rope, recovering the creature's back even as it snaps at the other bull's neck. But Alicia is already wheeling her tyrannosaur away. I can hear her shrill laugh and then I hear your laughter, the laughter of all you millions and I scream in my fury. Unhooking from my beast I balance on its shoulder, ready to leap, spinning the hook on its rope in circles over my head to gain enough momentum and force. My aim is precise, my arm is powerful. The hook flashes in the air, in the colored lights, then slams into the other tyrannosaur's right eye. The creature flips its head back, that scream like metal. I have already leapt, I am already landing on its shoulder, sweeping my arm to catch Alicia's leg and throw her. She is fast, too; she is already flipping in the air over my head. I turn and meet her as she lands on the tyrannosaur's back, catching her swift kick on my arm and deflecting it. I jab my hand toward her face but she catches it in hers and twists, but I pivot, a foot aimed high toward her head; she dodges, and I wrench my hand free and we two are dancing, dancing on the tyrannosaur's back, kicks and sweeps almost too fast for the screens to catch, and you are roaring your approval and excitement and arousal, and I can hear your roar beating inside my body, the pump of my heart, the thrill of my blood. Alicia is old and I am faster and I am better and she knows it, and I can see it in her eyes. The egret flies above the gazelle. Always.

I get in a good kick to the back of her knee and her leg crumples and then she is falling back. Catching herself against the beast's shoulder, she tucks in her legs and flips in the air toward the other bull; she does it right, but she is too near the other tyrannosaur's head, the bull I hooked first. The creature must have caught sight of her in its peripheral because its head darts to the left and those overwhelming jaws snap shut over Alicia's legs and hips. It flips her from side to side, several times, her shriek piercing and high in my ears, then *throws her*.

She slams into the sand, a tyrannosaur's leap away. Her scream stops.

The bull's legs tense for the leap but before it springs, I have unhooked and leapt toward its back. I miss and slide down its leg and slam my hook in. Its head whips around toward me; it has forgotten Alicia and those teeth like desert knives and its fetid breath are all coming at me in a rush and I let go of the rope and drop. My feet hit the sand, jarring me; I hear the snap of its jaws above me but I am up and running, unwinding the rope about my right arm, readying my next hook. If I am not astride this creature in another second or two, I will be dead. I don't know why I have done this. It is stupid. Something about her scream; I acted before I could think. I might die for it, but I simply don't have time for fear, and the nanites are pumping so much adrenaline into me that I wouldn't feel the fear if I did. And you are all watching. I have to recover *now*, and not *just* recover, but recover in a way that will make you love me. The creature strikes at me again, and I leap right at its head. My hook slams into the side of its upper jaw, and I have my arms and legs about the jaw and it slams its teeth together but no part of me is inside, I am clinging to the top of its head. The goddess has blessed me, I am uninjured, it has nothing to grip, no way to flip

19

me about as it did Alicia. Its snort so near my ear is a sound like something heavy splashing into water, and its hot breath washes across my arm and back. I am shrieking with glee. You are all screaming my name again.

Panting, a little dazed but the nanites still at my organs, pumping hot chemicals into my blood, I get my limbs under me and half-spring, half-scurry over the bull's head, down the back of its neck. I cut open its flesh behind the shoulder, quickly, grimacing as I shove my hand in and grip the ragged edge of its hide. Holding on by its wound, I rip out the hook and sling it through the air, lashing its right flank, sending it lunging forward into a run, forgetful of Alicia, fleeing the sting of pain. Then I am on its back, on my feet, rocking my weight as it roars, lashing it on, while behind me Alicia lies in the sand, shattered, other bulls thundering past her, following mine, a few with other women on their backs.

Glancing over my shoulder, I catch Alicia's gaze for the briefest instant. Her eyes are glassy. She has a hand clutched to her hip, dark fluid pumping out between her fingers; the nanites might not be fast enough to repair her. Her face now is not proud but gentle and strangely sad.

I have seen her like that once before—on the night after our first training in the jungles of the conservatory world. I was fourteen and terrified, and I failed my first mount. I'd been trying to one-up Alicia, who had just thundered past on the back of a large albino bull, whooping and calling insults to us from its back as it careened by in a crash of foliage. So when the other bulls crashed out of the thicket following the one she'd caught, I took a risk. I moved too fast. I still remember a tyrannosaur crouching over me where I fell, its mouth gaping, the whole sky full of teeth, then the burning stench and the crackle of electricity against its tongue as Mai drove it back with a shock rod, her blue gown billowing about her. She stood over me, protecting her investment in grim silence, and I remember staring at her fabric, oddly fixated, in shock myself, seeing how fine the stitches were, how unstained by the forest around us. I realized it was real silk, rare as diamonds; there aren't many silkworms left, and they're supposed to be difficult to engineer. I remember Mai's hand, ice cold as always, grasping my fingers so tight it hurt, lifting me to my feet. I remember the sting of her slap across my face, and the burn she incited in my nerves in the airlock afterward, once we were all safe and awaiting our shuttle back to the training house above Europa's ice-covered saltwater sea. I screamed and twitched and jerked, and after the pain was gone I kept shaking on the metal floor.

Mai's words as she turned to face the other girls were as sharp and severe as her cheekbones, as the slant of her eyes. "This is not play. You don't giggle, you don't shriek, you don't show off unless the cameras are on, and you don't make stupid errors. You are expensive and the tyrannosaurs are expensive, and you will treat them with respect, or some of you will not be coming back through this airlock alive."

A dozen murmurs of "Yes, Mai," from the others. I just lay shuddering, pulling huge breaths from the air.

That night in my bunk, my hands *still* shook as I took sleep induction. Waiting for unconsciousness to come and replace a day of terror with a night of terror, I lay back naked on my bunk and sobbed. The first time I had cried since the early days. Great, heaving sobs that just about took me apart. I didn't hear the door open. Didn't hear the footsteps soft against the carpet. I just wanted it to be over, wanted everything to be over, the training, the nanites' work on my body, Mai's fire. The dreams.

"Shhh, shhh." A voice so soft in the dark. A small hand on my shoulder. Blinking away the blur, I glanced up into Alicia's face. Into sad eyes glinting with the dim light from the crack of the door. She sat with me a moment while I sniffled and hid most of my face in a pillow, knowing I must look ugly and swollen with tears, and not wanting to share this moment of absolute abandonment with anyone. Then she took her hand from my shoulder, gripped my fingers in hers—warm, not like Mai's—and pressed something small into my palm. She cast a glance to the door; I could see her fear then, in her posture, in the quickness of her movements. If caught out of her own room, she might be nerve-burned or worse. Mai could easily do worse.

"Shhh," she whispered again, without looking at me. Her fingers closed mine around the object. Then she stood in the dark, lithe and naked as I was, her braid hanging down her back. She flitted swiftly to the door. Our gaze met for an instant, then she was gone.

Blinking away more tears, I opened my hand. There was a small pebble of hard chocolate in my palm, something to be sucked on until it melted on the tongue. I stared at it for a long while, this alien object. My mother had used to give me chocolates like that. Long ago. With a final sniffle I slipped it between my lips and then lay back in my bunk, still trembling a little, waiting for sleep. The chocolate was warm and soothing. It had a rich, dark taste, like a little piece of some unimaginably good world.

Now, as she lies bleeding, Alicia shares another secret with me.

There is singing in the air around us, amplified like the voice of the goddess. The screens are showing you Alicia's face, wet with her blood, as the Patriot Choir sings for her, but I look away. I take the rope in my teeth so that my hands are empty, then cross my wrists over my breasts, bowing my head in the sign of Silence for the Fallen. You are intent on Alicia, I know, but you will see my gesture and remember, and this will make you love me even more. Beneath me, the tyrannosaur's breathing is labored. We are running them hard.

It must be a painful thing, to die faster than your nanites can heal you. Alicia deserves it. She was a hateful, proud, *old* girl who lorded it over us, made it clear to me and the other younger girls that we could never be her, never be half as good. Still, she must be in so much pain. She must be closing her eyes now, falling into the dark. I wonder if her mother read to her at night when she was small, if she is hearing that soft voice now. I wonder if her mother ever gave her chocolates.

.

6

THE STAMPEDE carries us far and fast, and I guide my tyrannosaur with skill and I am showy about it. Hooking its flanks again and again to bleed it, I drive the bull on, and soon mine is running ahead, far ahead of the others. But though your cheers are loud, they are distant noise; I am numb inside. I can't stop thinking about Alicia behind me, bleeding in the sand, waiting while hovercraft rush medics toward her. The run is nearly over, the garland is ahead of me, really I have won it already. I am the best, I am the fastest. The others are behind me. The only one who could compete with me may be dying.

The run is nearly over, until next year.

I blink back moisture and salt, and rappel down the tyrannosaur's back until I can slash open its flank again. It needs to be faster yet. It is not enough for me to be first. I must leave the others *far* behind. You all must scream for me. I will never lie in the sand, never. Because I am the best. Alicia wasn't, that's all. *I* knew that already; only you didn't.

So why am I crying?

7

WATCHING ME from above, from most of a kilometer away on the opposite interior surface of Liberty Cylinder, you must be intent on the screens: an aerial view of the tyrannosaurs in stampede, flecks of foam on their flanks, their eyes rolling now, muscles straining with exertion, most of them packed close together, thick tails streaming behind them for balance as they run, kicking up clouds of disturbed sand. My own out in front, me standing on its back, a rope wrapped about my arm. Close-ups of my face, and the others. Loud voices of announcers speaking fast, detailing what they see, what you see. Recorded tyrannosaur screams to add sound effects to a run that is now silent but for the pounding of massive three-toed feet and the pounding of my heart. That metal shriek is not the only sound tyrannosaurs make; I have heard the bulls hoot like owls on the conservatory world, mating hoots long and eerie in the thick forest. And I have heard a tyrannosaur dam croon like an oboe over her hatchlings. The screams you hear that make you think *tyrannosaur,*

25

those are the sounds they make when they are frightened or in pain.

Knowing I am ahead and you can see me, I raise my right hand high again, grasping the unseen, intangible torch that lights the sand road to freedom, guides ships into open harbor. You shout for me. I can hear the athletes behind me singing the Liberty Prayer. I do, too. I sing louder, though for the first time my heart isn't in it.

That death in the sand, Alicia's body bleeding out, seems to me the only real thing I have seen. I *know* why I have tears. It is because she is free. She will never again have to vomit up her food, or gaze at her reflection while the nanites reshape her breasts and thighs to some new standard, or feel her skin on fire at Mai's displeasure.

The garland is ahead and I can see the Liberty Shrine, the silhouette of Madame President against its golden lights and the flashing of the hovers above Liberty's crown, and in a few moments I will be there, there before all the rest—sand billows behind the tyrannosaur I ride—but Alicia has beaten me. I envy *her.*

An urge overtakes me, stronger than any I have ever felt, than any itch in my loins or hunger in my belly: an urge to stop running, to throw myself from the tyrannosaur and wait in the sand. I want to. I *want* to. To defy Mai and all of you. But what then? What will I have left? With all of you staring at me then in silence, or even *jeering* at me, none of you shouting in adoration *Egret, Egret, Egret!* If even that one solace, that one thing to live for, is taken from me? What then?

Oh, I want to.

I envy *you.*

Your freedom comes at no cost of being perfect. My freedom lasts one hour on the sand, yours lasts a life. I run, but you roar.

And yet, just as my own body, my desires and my dreams, are shaped for your entertainment, I suppose yours are shaped, too, for the entertainment and profit of others. Just less perfectly, less completely than mine. Maybe neither you nor I are free. Liberty's torch in my hand is unseen, unfelt: an imagination made out of empty air. Was it ever real? Was the goddess ever real? Is anything real but Alicia's blood darkening the sand?

8

BECAUSE I KNOW you expect it, I chop at the tyrannosaur's head with my hook, in whatever soft, vulnerable places I can find, forcing the creature to turn from the pain. The great bull skids to a halt, spraying sand, right before the marble steps of the Liberty Shrine, its breath huffing, fetid and rank, and the smell of sweat and musk nearly knocking me from its back. But I do this properly. I do this to impress. I slide down its shoulder and leap to the sand, landing in a crouch and rising quickly, my head lowered. Madame President and her attendants are descending the high steps toward me to fanfare, bursts of golden light from the stair at each of her footsteps. I know she carries a garland in her hand but I do not look up; my eyes are still hot with unshed tears. I cannot hear the other tyrannosaurs bearing the other athletes, over the blare of Liberty music, but I can feel the ground shake at their approach. I hope dully that none of them manage the dismount as well as I. Behind me, handlers with shock rods are already backing my tyrannosaur away. You all expect that I will keep my back turned, but in fact, it is all I can do not to flinch, knowing that the great bull I have danced and run is behind me, each of its teeth long as my hand. Yet I know that if I glanced over my shoulder, I would see it staggering as the handlers drive it back around the Shrine toward the waiting pens. The creature would be too exhausted, too docile now, to attack. As I, too, am exhausted.

The nanites have reached the limit of their ability to heighten my adrenaline. The reaction is coming, and it will be bad. I stagger a little, then catch myself, knowing I must look graceful for you, desirable to you. When you run the tyrannosaurs, grace is everything. Through blurred vision, I can see a hover zipping toward me over the sand, carrying my crew, to refresh me and pamper me and clean me swiftly for the cameras. My belly is snarling like a beast itself despite sudden nausea, but I know they will not allow me food.

I swallow back a little vomit, burning my throat; I am unsteady. That hovercraft is not approaching fast enough. If I throw up or pass out... I feel the soreness in my body now; I have never felt such fatigue, not even after hard training.

A different hover sweeps by, and I catch a glimpse of Alicia on the craft, wrapped in blankets, her face gray, her arms a forest of tubes, medics fussing over her. Bitch. But there is no venom in the word any more, only heaviness. And she was the only one, the only one almost as good as I was. Now no one is. Tomorrow there will be interviews and glamour vids and then more training, even fiercer training, because next year I will be old and the younger girls will be faster and they will look at me the way I have looked at Alicia, and I will have to be even better—my reflexes even quicker, my breasts even larger, my smile even more fetching. But there will be no one my own age to compete with. Just me. Last year's sensation.

I sway. The cylinder tilts, which shouldn't be possible. Then everything is sideways and I am looking at the sand and men are leaping down to it, boots running toward me, toward my face, except everything is in bright shades of yellow and green and then I am retching, my stomach hurling its way up my throat as if it intends to dance the beast, too. Lifting my head, the slime of my vomit on my chin, I can see, blurred, Madame President near the bottom of the stairs, her face stern and cold and pale in the floodlights, like Mai's. Maybe that is Mai. Maybe she is here to set fire to my skin, to rebuke me for this lapse of grace.

"I am sorry," I groan, or try to; when my mouth opens, more fluid comes out, then nothing but dry heaving. My mother held my hair once, when I was four, when I was puking my dinner into a glass bowl. Afterward, she pulled me close and rocked me and cried a little and said, "Poor baby, poor baby."

Firm hands grip my arms, pulling me to my feet. A damp cloth is scrubbed swiftly across my chin. The prick of a needle in my wrist and a rush of energy into my body. I breathe in quick gasps, the world becoming visible and steady again around me. I wonder what violence is being done inside my body to keep me standing. The faces of my crew, anxious. Fingers dabbing cosmetics on my face.

Then they are backing away, leaving me to the cameras and to Mai's displeasure, or the President's, or yours. Madame President reaches the bottom of the steps, ready to cross to me. Blue, red, and green lights sweep across the sand, and tyrannosaurs stand with athletes on their back a short distance down the road, surrounded now by handlers with quick, hard voices; I can see the snap and spark of their rods. The tyrannosaurs are silhouettes against the billowing red dust, mournful in their wheezing now that the run is over. I feel a pang of unease, knowing the great bulls will be butchered at the ceremony's end.

And up on the high walls, all of you in your seats, millions of seats curving up along the side of the cylinder and arcing over my head, enclosing me in an endless tunnel of your shouting faces. I hear my name. The cameras must have cut away from my retching; you have no idea. You are too far away. You only saw me stumble and then rise. I am not Alicia. I am not lying in the sand. I am yours, and all your voices claim me.

Though my heart is hollow, I lift my arm. Liberty's torch. You are losing your minds in a roar of praise and desire. Watch me. Love me. I am your sacrifice. I, Egret, stand on the red sand, and I am alone.

NYOTA'S TYRANNOSAUR

SOLASGNOSIS

From Latin solacium + Greek gnosis.
Noun. "Knowing home."
The realization that you are home, though you had thought
yourself marooned in a strange place, in exile. That strange
place has turned out unexpectedly to be more home than
anywhere you've ever been.

1

If you want to keep your ratings high, if you want to be the one the crowds roar for when you race the tyrannosaurs on Patriot Day, you need to not only be faster, stronger, better than the other girls; you need to be smarter. It is not enough just to react quickly so that you stay alive. You must react cleverly, too, so that you win. And gracefully, so that the cameras love you for it.

THE LESSONS OF MAI CHANGYING

IT IS DARK WHEN when I open my eyes.

I glimpse cedar branches and a night with no bulkhead above me. Liberty looms overhead, just out of reach, her graceful shape black against the green dark. My heart racing, I draw in a shuddering breath and lift my head. No pain, but glancing down I can see the shadows of bruises on my hip and belly and breasts. The nanites have knit me up again, repairing shattered ribs, perhaps sewing an organ or two shut, but they are still working on my skin. I run a hand over my body. Still no pain. But those bruises bring me alarm such as I've never felt before. I have been *damaged*. So damaged that I've been out cold, until there is no more day. I must have known I could be damaged like that, but honestly, the thought had never occurred to me before. Not really. Not in the way you think of something real, an actual threat.

I lie back naked against the roots and soil, gazing up past the branches at the distant mass that is the forest on the opposite side of the Conservatory World's interior. I try to think back to what happened. I had been leaping—the rush of my body through the air, the pounding of my heart. The tyrannosaur's jaws closed over me; I had misjudged the leap. Pain tore the world apart. Then I was here, opening my eyes, at night.

Afraid.

"Mai!" I call. My voice sounds hoarse to me. There is panic in it. "Mai!"

There is no reply—no human reply. A distant screech cracks open the night skin of the forest. That was no tyrannosaur. A raptor, maybe. I mustn't be caught here on the ground. My heart begins pumping fast, the nanites inside me already rushing to heighten my adrenaline, hyperoxydate my blood, prepare me for speed and survival.

And I probably shouldn't be yelling.

Breathing fast, I get to my feet. The nanites are still keeping the pain away, but my body is stiff and sore, as I haven't felt since my first year of training in Mai Changying's house above Europa's frozen sea.

A shiver though the night is hot, because I don't know where Mai Changying and the other trainees are. Given the dark, they must have left the Conservatory World hours ago, shuttling back across space. But why did they leave me here? The red ink in the jaguar tattoo above my right breast contains traces that would be easy to follow, *should* be easy to follow. Yet here I am, *alone*, facing a battle with onrushing atrociraptors without any competitor-sisters beside me and with no audience to cheer my name and love me.

I have to *think*.

Remember what Mai Changying said: I am sleek and lithe like a jaguar, but I am a thinking creature. I must be quick. Clever. Graceful.

Another screech in the distance.

Something kindles inside me, a chemical burn fueled and fed by the nanites. I stand and breathe deeply. I am Jaguar. I am fiercer, faster, smarter than these toothed birds will ever be. *I* hunt *them*, they do not hunt *me*.

Now there is no more screeching. The pack has gone silent, which means they are approaching—either me, or some other prey nearby. Silent as shadows under the trees. I must be ready; I probably have only a minute, if that. The bruises are already fading from my skin; soon the nanites will be freed to turn their attention to sharpening my eyesight. That would have already happened as soon as it became dark, if they weren't distracted by my wounds. It will happen soon. But for now, I can see little. Still, something lies near my right foot—I tug at it, but it is a root fastened deep in the ground. My fingers grope across the soil. Another root. A jagged rock. A scree of needles and fallen cones. Then a loose stick, a crooked branch, broken away perhaps in some wind of previous days. I lift it, finding the heft of it reassuring. It is too thick—I can barely close my hands around it at the middle—but it will have to do. No time to search for anything else. It is the right length at least, nearly two meters. I have trained in the use of the Japanese bo, which runners sometimes wield against consecrated atrociraptors, concavenators, and other fast species in the arena. I can use this.

Quickly, I strip twigs and smaller branches away from this staff, ripping them free of the green wood. I am breathing hard now, and there is sweat on my back. Holding the crooked bo as balanced as I can, I drop into a dancer's crouch, listening.

Everything is silent. No breeze. No bird calls. No rustle or tap of three-toed feet. I hold my anger near my heart, violent and hot. I am Jaguar. *I* am the one hunting. My hands are slick with sweat on the bo, and I realize my hold may slip. Cautiously, I crouch lower and drop one hand to the ground, rubbing it in the soil. Then the other hand. The grit on my palms makes my grip firmer. I force myself to keep breathing evenly. There are no cameras here to see me if I fall bleeding, but there are also no handlers with shock rods to hold the raptors back while my body repairs itself.

I hold tight to that core of anger. I need it.

A flicker at the edge of sight warns me. I spin on the balls of my feet, bringing the bo cracking hard against the head and neck of the raptor in mid-leap; a blur of feathers and fangs and a squawk and it crumples to one side. I complete the spin in time to see the second raptor leap, its claws scything the air. I crack the bo across its hip with the full force of my body, and it tumbles aside. The beast leaps to its feet again, backing away, small, dark eyes watching me in the night. Though the other is flapping brokenly on the ground, this one's regard is one of silent assessment.

Its head is no higher than my waist, but the hook-like tearing claw on each foot is the length of my palm. When it springs, the movement is so fast I am barely ready for it; dodging left, I bring the bo up and smack its legs, sending it tumbling again. A whistle in the air, and the bo cracks down on the bird's head.

The other is still convulsing in the dirt. I turn in quick, calm circles, though my heart is pounding. Were there only two of these? I am watching the dark, the bo balanced in my hands. I am grateful that the wood hasn't cracked; it's very green.

Another comes at me, wings spread, in a low glide. I drop, roll away, leap back up, narrowly avoiding attempted disembowelment from a fourth of the savage birds, flashing past me in the dark. My bo sings its song of wood and resin in the air; there are three raptors now besides the two I've dropped, and the three dance and dart about me, only the bo keeping shearing claws and teeth from my skin. A sheen of sweat on my body, the pounding of my heart, the rush and surge of nanites in my veins: I am alive, and I will *stay* alive. Pivoting on the balls of my feet. *Crack* goes the bo. Flipping into the air, spinning in the air, landing on my feet, all of my training and all the modifications inside my body, all of it serving now to keep me moving, unhurt, and unwinded. I slam one end of the bo into an atrociraptor's throat, hear the satisfying crack of bone. Panting, I spin back. One of the others leaps on its fallen sibling, ripping the dying raptor's belly open before ducking its head to feast; I crack it across the skull. The other flees soundlessly into the night, leaving me panting, on my feet, with four dead or dying creatures about me.

There are scratches and splinters on my palms from the unsanded wood of my improvised bo, but the nanites will take care of that; there is no other scratch on me. I did it. I survived. I toss my chin back, raise the bo in one hand high above my head, lift my face for the cameras—

—but there are none.

No screaming crowd. No worshippers waving pennants with the jaguar sigil. No resentful glances from my competitor-sisters standing near. Just the musty silence of centuries-old cedars, the faint gleam of Liberty high above the treetops, and the distant green shadow of the opposite interior curve of the Conservatory World, where other atrociraptors may be hunting in the dark, many kilometers above my head.

Just the forest. And me. Jaguar.

But none of you, my viewers, my watchers, none of you are here. This entire artificial world is managed by unseen machines, as my own body is.

Flushed, I lower the bo, glance at the ground torn by raptor feet and covered with a scattering of cedar needles and small cones. Though I am myself an ecosystem of microscopic, semisentient machines, I stand here alone. Truly alone. The thought seizes me with terror and a strange exhilaration. But I have no time to think about it; the battle catches up with me in a sudden wave of weakness.

My hands shake, and I drop the bo with a cry. In a moment, I collapse to the dirt, sick with reaction. The tiny machines that accelerate my metabolism for combat are harsh inhabitants. I need food. I need food *now*. I glance at the feathered dead, but my stomach revolts. Raw meat. I am a tyrannosaur-rider, not a tyrannosaur myself. Still. Forcing myself up, I lift one of the dead raptors—it is light, its bones hollow as if for flight—and sling it across my shoulders. I have to find Mai Changying and the other trainees—why haven't they come for me?—but I have to eat first. I have to eat. Despite the lightheadedness that always follows a hard metabolic burn, I run lightly into the trees, jaguar-fast, the machines within adapting me for speed. I dart downhill around thick, waterlogged cedars and pale alders luminous in the dark. Because downhill is how you find water. And I have seen berries by the water on this world. How many berries will it take to satisfy my nanites? I will eat an entire forest of berrybushes if I need to. If I am still ravenous, I can eat the atrociraptor. I can try.

2

Each act is sacred. Each step, each leap to a tyrannosaur's back, each sip of tea. Each moment demands elegance. Because each moment is this moment. There is only ever this moment.

THE LESSONS OF MAI CHANGYING

DAWN FINDS ME shaking in a cedar top, balancing on a high branch in a crouch with the bo across my knees, my belly full of foraged berries and bird flesh and my palms sticky with resin from my climb. I only found a few berry bushes. I tried to make a fire and failed, which might be for the best, as a fire would have brought dinosaurs. I tore the raptor's feathers out of the way, ripped meat out of its belly with my fingers, lifted handfuls to my mouth and ate as much as I could bear, though I vomited twice at the taste. The metabolic burn in my body permits no excuses, and my nanites work to make the food safe inside my body; I don't fear the bacteria in uncooked meat.

Now there is light. The remains of the raptor are far below me on the ground, and hunger still bites at my belly.

And I am naked and trembling—like the smallest infant just out of the womb. At least it is not cold here. The Conservatory World is hot, with heavy fog in many places among the alders and redwoods.

I should be clear about what kind of place this is. Egg-shaped, the Conservatory World is a vast asteroid, one of the largest, hollowed out a thousand years ago or more and set spinning in space so that its interior has gravity. Somewhere beneath my feet are stars and more stars and infinite cold. High above me beyond an ocean of air are the tops of trees, their roots grown down into ten centuries of humus on the asteroid's opposite interior hull. Funded by the diamond industry and owned by the Ministry of Religion, this asteroid is a terrarium and an incubator where the tyrannosaurs are grown, and all the species that populate orbital arenas and dinodromes across our system, and all the species that feed those. Mai Changying brings us here to ride the tyrannosaurs, to leap and dance on their backs, preparing ourselves for competition on the red sands.

This is only my fourth time here, and I was supposed to be on a shuttle headed back to the training station yesterday before nightfall. I would have been, this very moment, on a seat by a tiny ice-cold window, with one of my sisters beside me, others on seats in front of me and others behind, all of us quiet, all of us sitting with perfect poise, practicing "elegance." Mai Changying would be floating above us in the zero-g, her long fingers grasping one of the bars set in the ceiling for that purpose. She would be watching us, testing us. Lecturing us. Tiny camera-drones would be flapping like chrome butterflies from one headrest to the next, recording us, and all our postures would be on playback on screens floating in the air. Showing us our flaws and failures.

If she has left, Mai Changying must have taken that flock of camera-drones with her back to the shuttle. All night, the absence of cameras and monitoring eyes here in the treetops has shaken me. At several points during the night, I froze and didn't dare move, not knowing where to face or how to best present my body and my features to your gaze. I must *always* be conscious of where the cameras are. But this is the Conservatory World, not the shuttle or the training station or the arena. I have never before been here longer than a single day, and never alone. This world is blind and I am unseen where I cling to the creak and sway of this treetop.

The dawn is simulated; the microstar, a clear globe hovering at the exact center of this artificial and hollow world, flickers into life, then brightens for about twenty minutes to the shrieking and calling of birds and red howler monkeys. A flock of leather-winged yi qi, each barely larger than my hand, flick by in a rush of bright pigments just above my head, making me gasp. Then they're gone, chattering, into the high branches of a stand of redwood far to my left.

By the light of full day, I look out across an ocean of foliage. Nowhere do I see or hear any sign of the other athletes in training, or Mai our trainer and keeper, or the handlers with the hiss and snap and scorched-flesh reek of their shock rods. Where *are* they? Why hasn't anyone come back for me? I am a billion-credit investment, my body and my training, and I am consecrated to dance in the dinodromes and on the red sands of Liberty cylinder itself. Mai wouldn't just toss me aside into the brush, no matter how badly I performed yesterday. She wouldn't. Surely she wouldn't.

The treetops tossing beneath me and around me are an unexpected beauty. Like something breathing and alive, something that lives much slower and more rooted than tyrannosaurs or women. Like something seen in a dream, not quite real.

A stir of movement in the treetops far to my right catches my attention. The trees bend and crack, their tops moving in a bow wave. A pack of tyrannosaurs, or maybe the herd they are hunting. Staring at it, I marvel. I have often been on the earth staring up at a tyrannosaur charging at me, but seeing the very forest bend impresses on me their sheer size, as if I am encountering them for the first time.

I watch the forest move for a while, until my trembling stills.

If the others are not coming for me, I must go to them.

Besides the microstar, there is one stable point on this forest world I am certain I can find: there, Liberty's statue, towering one hundred meters above the trees maybe four kilometers away, to my left. For a moment my breath catches. She is beautiful, the goddess, shaped entirely out of the primeval rock of this hollowed asteroid, all but the torch she bears. The flames are made of glass, so that the artificial sun shatters on their edges and dazzles the forest around Liberty with a multitude of colors. Lifting my hand to shield my eyes against the blaze of that torch, I can tell Liberty is gazing toward my left. That tells me the airlock is to my right and slightly behind me.

There. I have a destination, a direction.

And I can run. I can run like no human before me ever has.

I hop down lightly from branch to branch, and drop the last fifteen feet to the ground, not winded – the nanites are keeping me oxygenated and agile. Their demands on my metabolism are fierce, and the hunger all but unbearable. If I can just get to the airlock. There might be a pod at the airlock, or a radio. I try to remember the radio delay between here and the station above Europa. Hours? Less? And the shuttle may not have the fuel; it may have to complete the flight to Europa, dock, refuel, and come back, which would take a month!

A flicker of fear in my breast—what if I'm not back to the training facility in time for another infusion of nanites? They are my torment and my necessity. I could starve after an energy burn like last night's, yet the nanites will keep me moving and alive, a tyrannosaur rider rather than tyrannosaur food. And they aren't self-replicating; we runners are dependent on Mai Changying for a fresh injection once every few months. Sooner, if I'm as active as I will need to be here. So she has taught us. The nanites will age and die and disintegrate in my bloodstream, leaving me weak as any young woman in the audience, or nearly. How could Mai Changying abandon me? Where *is* she?

* * *

The forest is eerily quiet but for the shriek and chatter of the animals that live in it. There are no human voices, no human eyes. I am running in the solar system's one blind place, the one location where there isn't supposed to be any human being breathing today. No one for the cameras to watch. And no one to help me find my way through that airlock, back to the world of close walls and quiet jostling in the mess and flashing numbers reporting my stats, the world I know, the world that owns me.

As I hurry, I daydream what I would do if there *were* someone watching. I could hook a tyrannosaur and ride it right to the airlock, dancing on its shoulders and lifting my arms in triumphant salute when the door irised open at last, revealing my rescue. Or I could make a drum, if I knew how, tanning a coelophysis hide and stretching it over some wooden frame—and I'd beat it with my hands, calling rescuers out of the ferns. After my rescue, the whole system would rave for weeks about Liberty's daughter drumming in the tyrannosaur forest. The vidcasters would make spintales about it. I grin; in that scenario, I'd walk out on the red sands on Patriot Day with *everyone* shouting "Jaguar!" Not just a few. They would *all* know me: the drummer in the dark under the trees, the girl who made the entire Conservatory World reverberate and rumble to the rhythm of her own heartbeat. How could they resist me?

* * *

Halfway to the airlock, I find a narrow creek. First the sound of it, the giggle of water over stones. Then the rank scent of the weeds that grow in the wet. Now that I hear water, my throat is sudden desert. I approach cautiously, slipping through the ferns that are thick on the bank. As I part the fronds before me, I imagine I might find the other athletes here, stopped a moment at the water to attend one of Mai Changying's lectures. But when I step through, there are no rescuers, no competitor athletes crouching to search the damp earth for my footprints, no Mai stern in her silk with a promise in her eyes of a penance unprecedented and vicious, due upon my return. No one is there. Just a few compsognathids with their necks craned down, their snouts half submerged in the stream.

Crouching low at the water's edge like a hunting cat, I dip my hands in and lift the cool river to my mouth without once lowering my eyes. I have to stay alert. The river ices my throat but I swallow anyway.

The ferns on the far bank stir and toss. Even as I duck back, a cedar bends a little to the side and a massive, elongated head rises from the greenery the way a whale rises from the sea. Startling me, the creature's feathers are entirely white, its eyes are a dull pink like unpolished rose quartz. The tyrannosaur dips its head, its shoulders emerging from the foliage too. Its tongue laps at the water, curling like a ladle to scoop up gallons of it. Yet its drinking is silent beneath the rush of the stream. It is a doe, I think, not a bull, and probably young; you can tell because the skin above its eyes is still wrinkled with youth. The creature is preternaturally still, only its tongue moving. It might be made of stone. I realize I am holding my breath. I have never seen an albino. This one is beautiful as the dawn, unique and perfect, as each one of us is unique and perfect, our bodies shaped for a single and public purpose, for a few holy moments on the sands. What moment was this tyrannosaur shaped for? This one? The air is sharp as crystal and I can hear so much—the skitter of small coelurosaurs in the ferns some meters to my left, the distant mating hoot of a bull somewhere back in the forest, the voice of the stream, my own breathing, the thunder of my blood in my ears. Strange. Not even training here have I felt so alive.

The tyrannosaur doe lifts its head and for the briefest beat of my heart, our gazes meet. It cocks its head to one side, a quick, sharp movement, then is still again, its gaze fixed on me, unblinking, like a bird. Though I could barely say why, I lift one hand tentatively and wiggle my fingers, like I'm greeting her. The doe's nostrils twitch; then she turns and is gone with a flicker of white into the trees, leaving behind only a momentary sway of branches.

It is day, and not time for hunting. Young tyrannosaurs are cautious during the day, if away from their nests.

Staring after her, I let out my breath slowly. Then rise to my feet, my still hands wet. I rub them on my thighs, grimacing, then shake them, hoping the air will dry them for me. My own nostrils twitch; I smell like shit. Back on station above the ice sea of Europa, there are—such *baths*. Nothing like that here. I'm not going to bathe in that river, exposed to any predator watching from the forest, or to leeches or eels or who knows what.

Imitating the tyrannosaur, I duck back into the trees. The baths. I need to get back to those baths, and the mess, and the training, and to my ratings before I fall too far behind. This is no time for gawking at a tyrannosaur like a seven-year-old at her first lesson. I have to find that airlock. Now.

* * *

Nothing that doesn't involve actual violence on the red sands deserves to be this difficult. Running in the deep fern, hiding as I hear hunting animals—by the time I believe I am anywhere near the airlock at all, I am sweating and panting and a mess. And that alarms me; shouldn't my nanites be handling the exertion better? Unless I have some internal injury that I can't feel, something keeping them busy. Unless I'm pushing myself harder than I think. Surely not. I'm Jaguar. I can do this. Though I would *really* like that bath.

The shadows under these cedars grow thick and dark. The microstar is dimming, because some scientist told the bioengineers who grew this place a millennium ago that tyrannosaurs are partially nocturnal and do their hunting only at night. So those who manufactured them had to manufacture night, too. Glancing up, I see through the branches the distant shade that is this same forest again, after it has curved up around the inner hull. A roof of tossing cedar boughs, too far away to hear.

At last, the trees part before me and there is a tumbled meadow of rock and wisps of old mist and the skeleton of a spiked tail—probably a kentrosaur's—rising out of the tall, tufted grass. And just beyond that thicket of spikes half-devoured in green, there stands a shining cube of black metal, maybe forty meters tall. My heart quickens. Embedded in one face of that cube is a door, round like an eye but closed. I've made it.

After a hurried glance to the left and the right, I break from cover and sprint across the open, tumbled, and stony ground. My nanites modify my feet. They sweep, invisible and intangible, into my ears to work on my balance, conspiring to keep me from a stumble or a shattered knee.

I slide into the door, catching up against it, my hands splayed on the metal. Breathing hard. My fingers find the palmscan, and I press my hand to it: *A human is here. Let me in.* But there is no tingle of warmth against my skin, no small vibration, no hiss of entering air as the lock cycles open. The door is still. I press my hand to the scan more firmly. Then again, swallowing. A tremor of fear. How can it not be opening? I'm here—doesn't Mai Changying hear me? Why won't anyone come for me? I slam my hand against the palmscan, then both my hands against the door's ungiving metal surface. "Hai!" I cry out. "Hai! Open up!"

Soon I am beating against the door, throwing my body against it, screaming. My own screams sound distant, lost in this vast place that is without other human beings. Lost in the roar of my blood. Hiding from panic in a flash of rage, I spin and kick the palmscan with my foot, cracking the glass. There is pain but then it is gone, blown out like a candle by the millions of machines who inhabit me. I stand panting, staring up at the silent door. At this wall of metal between me and my sisters and Mai. Just on the other side of that door, a ladder would drop me down into a vast subterranean chamber, the air still and silent and cool, small running lights barely lighting the titanium underbellies of behemoth shuttles. A place of metal and glass panels and quiescent engines. Not this place of cedar and fern and rotting fungi and the cries and cooing of tyrannosaurs waking at dusk.

"Let me *in*!" I scream my throat raw. "Let me *in*, you fuckers!"

But the cube is silent. And now it is night. I am standing here, panting. Alone. In the dark.

3

An alert girl keeps breathing. Sleep on your feet, and you die.

THE LESSONS OF MAI CHANGYING

THE FOREST THAT SURROUNDS this cube in its broken meadow is alive with roars and screeches and small, trilling things, with the hum of millions of insects, toiling inside their carapaces to murder silence. I imagine beetles the size of my hand, like the maidbugs that clean our quarters while we sleep. So much noise here. The sleek metal at my back is cold and not in the least reassuring, but at least the forest isn't at my back. It is before me; I am staring at it, staring into it, while the night gets thicker and hungrier.

There is no way out. No way back. I am trapped in here, as surely as the tyrannosaurs are—those magnificent beasts kept and fed, as I am, for a single purpose. Only, how am I to fulfill that purpose in here? I try to hold down panic, try to think of when the next training on this conservatory world is scheduled. How long will it be? Five weeks? Six? Tears of rage and hunger burn my eyes. More than a *month* of missed training! My ratings will plummet, I'll be so far behind the other girls that on Patriot Day I'll be useless, something for the crowds to laugh at rather than adore—if I make it there at all, if Mai Changying doesn't have me buried, still breathing, in a metal coffin beneath the red sands in a fit of pique at my clumsiness in becoming trapped here—at my clumsiness compared with Egret and Gazelle and the others when I finally get *out* of here. I rub at my eyes with the heels of my hands, furious. How could I let this happen? How could I have misjudged that leap so badly? Why was I *left* here? Why hasn't Mai come back for me? Why have they all left me? Why? *Why?*

Is it a test?

It has to be a test.

Could this be part of the training? Hope lights in my heart—but no, Egret and Anaconda are older than me, and they were never left behind. I am abandoned.

Throwing back my head, I scream. I let the forest have it. I scream myself hoarse. I am so *angry*, and while the nanites inside me can do many things—hyperoxygenate my blood, reshape my breasts to whatever will be most attractive on screen—they are designed to *increase* adrenaline and hormonal surges, not temper them.

I am good, one of the best. My ratings are high—how could they *leave* me?

Was my clumsiness, the clumsiness that injured me, *that* bad?

Won't all of you behind the cameras still love me?

Isn't…isn't anyone going to come back for me?

I don't have any screaming left and I am just breathing hard. The structure at my back is cold and absolute, severing me from my life, my ratings—my hopes of being first in the running of the tyrannosaurs—as completely as a bulkhead severs atmosphere from vacuum. I am alone here. Alone.

* * *

Time has passed—about an hour, I think. Difficult to tell. I still stand with my back to the airlock cube. By this time of night, I should be supine on my mattress, taking sleep induction, the dull metal walls of my cell close enough to touch. This place is open, so *open*. There is air over my head, and more air, and *more*. Far above me, I can see the other side of this forest. I imagine that there is another girl up there beneath those cedars, her back to another metal cube, as abandoned as I.

I start listing. This is what I am trained to do, each morning and each evening. Heart rate, fatigue level, resources available to me. I don't have my hooks or rope. I can *make* rope. Mai Changying taught us. But how does a girl make a metal hook out of vegetation, out of forest materials?

I bite down on my lip, letting the quick burn of pain still the rapid rise of panic. The nanites take away the pain almost immediately, and I taste only a single drop of blood before my lip is repaired. And that *is* a comfort. Right. I'm Jaguar. I have something like eight million microscopic machines working in my body to make me not only good but *better*—better than every other young woman in the entire universe. You bet I'll make a hook and rope. Then I can catch and ride a tyrannosaur anywhere I need to get to. For an instant I imagine riding the tyrannosaur right back to my cell on Europa station, never mind the millions of kilometers of empty space between here and there. And then I imagine riding the tyrannosaur on through this forest and just not stopping—just riding him around and around the interior of this conservatory world, forever, no one to watch me or rate me or send me back to the cell. The thought is dizzying, so much so that I shove it away hastily.

Breathe in. Breathe out.

What matters is that I am one of the best. I have been trained and honed and shaped. Whatever runs at me across the arena sands, I can overcome it.

I am Jaguar. I can do this. I have beaten every master at the bo save one, and at the isiquili and uboku, too. I can beat this.

I have water.

I have my bo.

But the snarling of my belly tells me I am going to need food.

Forcing myself to breathe slowly, evenly, I stand. Correcting my balance, I hold the bo lengthwise across my body. *The girl whose own mind outruns her can't hope to outrun a tyrannosaur.* Mai Changying taught me that. Should I forget it just because I'm afraid? This isn't early training. There aren't handlers here with shock rods to save me from my errors. Panic and die—or breathe calmly and live.

Counting down from fifty, I scan the surrounding trees. The same forest, the same shadowed earth beneath heavy branches, the same sheen of metal door behind me. Yet it feels less terrible now. I focus on my heartbeat, shift my left foot forward slightly, and to my surprise I find my lips have curved into a slight smile. The wood feels firm and familiar in my hands, something reliable. This bo and I: we'll get through this together. I spring forward in a kata, whipping the long shaft into motion, spinning it and moving through the forms almost faster than you could see me, if you were watching.

If any tyrannosaurs are watching, let them shiver to see me move. I am Liberty's daughter. I will ride them on the next Patriot Day. I will ride them right up to the feet of Liberty herself, because there is nothing under those trees in the dark that a woman, trained and honed, can't outrun, nothing she can't outdance. The air sings about my bo, and I laugh breathlessly with the exhilaration of physical exertion.

As I dance over the rocky ground, the trees ahead of me part and I gasp, halting in a crouch, but what lumbers out and then turns to move along the treeline to my left is no carnivore. It isn't small, either. It has a wide, flat bill and a long crest that runs out over its back as though the genetic engineers decided to take a katana, cover it in flesh, and stick it hilt-first into the back of the creature's head, just for kicks. It's a parasaurolophus. Has to be. I've never seen one, except in a sim in Mai Changying's library. It moves along at a surprising clip, barely pausing to duck its head and clip a few branches from the ferns at the forest's edge. After a few moments, it turns, its wide tail swinging in the air, strict and rigid, and I think it is about to dart back into the trees, but at that very instant, there is a blur of feathers, then another, and then the parasaurolophus gives a bellow of pain, and I can see the atrociraptors clinging to its back, two of them, their feathered arms and tails spread wide for balance, their shearing foreclaws sheathed in the herbivore's hide. Other raptors flash now from the trees, and their claws hamstring the larger animal, and suddenly it is crashing to its side in the dirt and I can feel the ground vibrate through my feet. One of the raptors springs to its throat; the other ducks low, slices open the parasaurolophus's belly, and ducks its head quickly into warm, steaming innards.

By that time I am running, though my belly doesn't feel right; I'm afraid I'll sick up. I didn't want to see that. I didn't need to see that. It happened so *fast*. So *easily*. I am suddenly anxious to put some meters between me and that pack. I'm running to the right, eyeing the trees, searching for a low-hanging branch and a cedar that will be quick to climb. Another raptor sprints from the trees, running directly at me. Fresh chemicals surge into my blood and I spin the bo in my hands and catch the creature's shoulder, a blow that knocks it down but not hard; in an instant it is on its feet again and that claw comes slashing toward me like a knife. The bo deflects it, but to my dismay, the bo cracks and I am left with a thing splintered and useless. Tossing it at the creature, I leap into the lower branches of the cedars and, spinning and flipping from branch to branch, my hands sweaty, my breathing short, I ascend into the top of the forest. The atrociraptor does not follow.

4

You do not give up. You leap on the tyrannosaur's back and you show the cameras what you can do. You make *them love you. You* make *them shout your name.*

THE LESSONS OF MAI CHANGYING

I FIND A SUITABLE TREE, or rather two grown together, with a nest-like space between where I can lie, but I do not find sleep. Years of Mai Changying's sedatives, and now my body has forgotten—entirely forgotten—how to rest when neither drugged nor wounded. No, not forgotten. Sleep has been *stolen* from me, by these nanites in their millions pumping energy into my body, hyperoxygenating my blood. It was the nanites those sedatives drugged, not me. Gazing up into the coniferous dark, I sob in my frustration. I realize how I must look now: bloodshot eyes, red-rimmed, maybe a stress line or two appearing as traitors on my cheeks, making me ugly for the cameras.

But there are no cameras to face, and no cheers thunderous in my ears. I can hear the roar of my blood, and I can feel—I imagine I can feel—the hum of the nanites at work, stirring everywhere inside me. Maybe they are cheering me. Yet here, in the silence above the forest floor, in the moist fog, there is a strange comfort in my invisibility, as though by speed and skill I have escaped not only the atrociraptors but all of you, too.

Up here, I may be crying, but none of you can see.

* * *

On the far side of the night, I lie in the crook of those conjoined cedars, still awake, holding myself and trembling. I have tried everything. I have closed my eyes and intoned the Liberty Prayer. I have tried staring up at the branches and counting shadows. Nothing works. Nothing makes me drowsy. Sometimes a shadow flits at the edge of my vision, and I startle, almost falling out of the tree. Part of me is near panic; part of me wants to leap up and scream at the empty night. Instead I whisper the goddess' name, over and over, *Liberty, Liberty, Liberty*, begging for her mercy, begging for rest. Maybe she hates me. I was to be her sacrifice, competing and running on the red sand, and now I am neither training for her nor dancing to entertain her millions. I can offer her no spectacle here; no one looks at me and praises her in their admiration at the curves of my body and the quickness of my movements. Maybe she thinks I have abandoned my training, abandoned her. I stare up at the far side of the hull, yearning for some pinprick of light that might be another airlock—if there is one—opening to spill Mai Changying and the other trainees out onto the inner skin of this world. To find me and rescue me. But there is no hairline crack in this eggshell station, and I remain, a restless hatchling who can't break free.

I slow my breathing, reciting under my breath, *I will be graceful, I will be graceful. Quick, clever, graceful. I will stun the cameras with my beauty.* The words, which I am used to reciting before bed, bring no comfort. The sky is so open beyond those branches, no bulkhead above me. In a moment of vertigo I am uncertain which direction is *up* and which *down*. I grab onto the branch, panting, fearful of falling into that green sky.

And yet, a part of me wants to.

What would be so terrible about falling into the sky? Without ceiling or wall to confine me, what if I spread my arms and they burst into feathers like a tyrannosaur's? What if I flew? I close my eyes, just breathing, just imagining that flight, and all the trees tossing in the wind beneath me. I imagine gazing down as though I am a camera-drone, seeing *every*thing, seeing the tyrannosaurs slide through the trees like lean jaguars themselves, the brachiosaurs lifting their heads above the foliage and lowing, the flocks of yi qi and microraptors, and underneath them all, the dozens of meters of moist soil. Beneath that, the hard rock skin of the world, and the vast cold outside that is so dark my pupils dilate as large as my eyes to catch the light, and somewhere out there, all of you in your apartments and cells and skyhomes on a dozen terraformed moons, all of you on the other side of the cameras, watching me watching you. All of you who were concealed from me until this moment, all of you who I have performed for, all of you whose eyes measure ceaselessly my body and my breaths. You are all like shadows, faint and barely substantial, billions of mapopobawa, none of your bodies as nourished or trained or active as mine. All of you in your tiny spaces, barely able to move, just watching your screens. Some of you, I can see your ribs. I can see some of you sweating just from the exertion of sitting up. I can see some of you weeping, though neither you nor I know why. But I see you. I can see you now.

Maybe I have slipped into a doze after all, because now I am back in the tree and Mai Changying is sitting with me on the branch and I am not startled to see her. She holds a small porcelain cup in her hands and steam rises from it. I can smell it—a red tea, a tea that smells like forest. I breathe deeply. It is not respectful to look right at Mai Changying's eyes, so I stare at her hands. At her fingers. At her nails, each two inches long and painted red today like the tea, but with delicate frost-patterns on them, as though each of her nails is a galaxy and I am watching stars frozen in time.

"Yes, Mai Changying?" I ask sleepily.

"Time for sleep." Her voice is quiet.

She extends her hands to me, holding out the tea. I fear to take it and I don't know why. I have accepted the tea from her hands every evening for years, until coming here. But tonight the sight of that steam rising above the porcelain horrifies me, so much that I almost want to leap from the branch to get away. I shake my head, risking her stern reprisal. Then there is a loud braying in the trees. At the sound, Mai Changying is gone like a wisp of smoke. With no woman to hold it, the cup of tea tumbles earthward, shattering against a branch below. I blink my eyes wetly. It is still dark, but only a little. I was dreaming.

That braying again, *loud*. Beneath me, a lone behemoth is rocking back and forth as it nudges its way between the trees. The shell covering its back is blood red. An ankylosaur. I catch my breath. The hunger is fiercer in my belly now, but I am a jaguar. I can hunt. But why leap from branch to branch like a gibbon in search of a meal, if I can ride a moving mountain through the forest? A wild urge seizes me, and millions of nanites inside me trigger a flare of adrenaline, hot as a sun in my breast. A jaguar doesn't need a *hook* or a *rope*; a jaguar leaps from *above*.

With nanite-enhanced muscles, I rip a long branch free from the cedar. Holding it clutched in my hand for a switch or a goad, I leap, yipping, to the beast's back as it passes beneath me, its feet shaking the earth. I land in a crouch on the shell. My body trembles with the shock of it, but the nanites are already at my joints. In a moment I am on my feet, legs spread, balancing on the rolling shell. Alder branches whip by in the dark, and I duck low, one hand splayed on the cool shell, the other holding my branch out for balance. Laughter peals from my throat. I am riding for the joy of it, because the speed is exhilarating. As is the roll and sway of the animal beneath my feet. As is the wind in my hair. I throw my head back and yip. The ankylosaur bleats and the shell lurches beneath me, but it can't dislodge me.

Laughing, I sway from my hips, keeping my balance. I lash the ankylosaur across the left side of its face with the branch. It barks—a low, coughing sound from deep in its throat—and banks sharply to the right. Look at me, all of you! Look at me, cameras! But the rush of fire and life I feel at being active at last, *doing* something at last, is doused swift as flames in rain as I remember that I am alone in the dark, alone on the back of this armored bull, and the night is full of the thud of her feet against the soil but no hum of hovercraft with their cameras and no cheers from ten thousand spectators. Just those clawed footsteps loud in the dark, then a sudden deep, resonant cooing from the trees ahead—*loud*. Like the largest bird there has ever been. My eyes widen as the treetops to my left bend and sway.

An immense animal lunges at us, its feathers white and nearly luminous in the forest dark. The albino tyrannosaur coos again through the hollow bones in its head. I cry out as the ankylosaur swivels, fast as a cat, bringing its tail swinging, the massive club on the end just missing the tyrannosaur doe's head and slamming into a cedar. The bole of the old tree shatters. The predator lurches back, nearly toppling in its haste.

I dance across the wide shell. The ankylosaur pivots again and I spring, landing on the thick scales of its neck. I cling there, the most stable point on the animal as it batters the surrounding trees with its tail. The albino tyrannosaur slips in and out of the cedars, cooing, its eyes bright and the color of my tongue. It lunges and the ankylosaur dodges, the carnivore's jaws snapping shut near my face. I can smell the reek of its breath. Entire civilizations of nanites surge and roar in my blood, and I am screaming, high yips of terror and exultation as I ride the dinosaur. The air about me is filled with splinters and wood-dust and scraps of bark spinning like derelict spacecraft.

Time to take a risk. Time to do what I've trained for, *be* what I've trained for. Maybe *this* is the test. Balancing a moment on my toes, I leap from the ankylosaur. A flip in the air—watch me!—and I collide, hands-first, with the tyrannosaur's shoulder. My fingers grip, grasping sleek feathers. I dig in quickly with my bare feet and scramble up onto the predator's back. Rather than ride low with its feathers in my face, I dance on the tyrannosaur's back, whooping, as though this is day in an orbital colosseum. I am *doing* it!

I feel more than see the swift lunges of the armored ankylosaur beside us. Its clubbed tail slams into a tree two meters from my head, and I am showered with bits of bark and scraps of moss and splinters of heartwood. The sting as splinters slice open my cheek. Nanites will repair me. I leap up onto the tyrannosaur's head, my feet planted on the feathered ridges over its eyes. I shout my defiance, all thought lost in the chemical surge triggered by the machines inside me. It takes me a moment to realize, again, that I hear no screaming cheers from all your throats in response.

For an instant I hesitate, teetering on the tyrannosaur's head.

Then its head drops, my stomach dropping with it, and as it tries to get a jaw-grip on the ankylosaur, the armored defender finally connects, its tail smacking the tyrannosaur across its jaw. The doe tumbles aside into a cedar, its great bulk crashing into the tree. I lose my footing and I am in the air, in the dark. The wet pain of a branch hitting my belly and the breath knocked out of me. I scrabble to catch hold of the branch but, stunned, I slip, and there's a lurching drop. I hit the ground *hard* and almost I black out, but the nanites inside me are quick and efficient and—oh gods!—my head and torso are hanging out over empty wet air, this is some kind of cliff. I scream as I go over.

Impact after jarring impact, I tumble down a long bank, then catch myself and slide in a scree of wet leaves and mud, then slam, back first, into a slap of cold water. The water rushes over me, covering my head, drowning my shriek in choking liquid. Forever and forever I thrash in the water, choking, but then my face breaks the water and I spew the pool from my mouth. My toes find the mud and I scramble up into the ferns. I am slick with mud and cold and shivering and I must look horrid, and that is *the second time* I have been thrown from a tyrannosaur's back. I am ugly and clumsy and ungraceful and no wonder Mai Changying doesn't want me. The sobs wrack me and I am furious at them but I can't stop crying.

Rolling onto my back, I see the ferns above my head, fronds darker than the night above them. Reaching up, still shivery with tears, I touch one; it showers droplets of water on my hand and arm and breast, and the water feels…clean. With a long, shuddering breath, I quench my sobs at last. Snapping the end of the fern, I use it to wipe the mud from my face. As I do, I find something bulbous and squishy against my cheek, and when I pry it loose there is the briefest sting of pain. Blood-fat in my hand, the leech squirms around to fasten itself to my palm. I crush it against the ground, then scramble away from it, panting, wide-eyed in the dark. I must be covered with them; this is *hideous*. How can this be happening to me— lost, and graceless, and alone in the dark, and cold, and soaked, and *leeches*—

At least no one can see.

It takes me a long time to find them all. I scrape the fern up and down my limbs and over my back, then search my body with my fingers, still shivering though I know the nanites are at work inside me, to warm me. There is a leech behind my ear and another stuck to the inside of my thigh, and three drinking from my right shoulder. Shuddering, I toss them all away into the dark, the patter of their small bodies falling into the ferns, and the quiet plish of one returning to the pool. I hop in place for a moment, shaking my arms, just wanting the slimy *feel* of them to be gone. Eugh, just *eugh*—leeches!

Glancing up, I can see the heavy shadows of old redwoods, immense and ancient in the night. Climbing up a long slope behind me, pale in the night and much smaller, are alders. White-barked and slender and numerous. None of them very tall or old; a fire must have burned out all the trees that weren't redwoods half a lifetime ago. Behind me, the still surface of the pool reflects a faint shimmer of light, almost too faint to see: maybe the first brightening of the daystar far above. Listening, I hear the plash of water, not far. I can see the wall of the cliff in the dark. Water tumbles down that cliff as I did, feeding the pool. Faintly, I hear the coo of the tyrannosaur and the bray of the ankylosaur and a distant crashing of trees, and I know those beasts have battled far on into the wood while I fought the pool and the leeches. Walking to one of the great redwoods, I press my cold back to its spongy, deep-fissured bark, limiting the opportunity for some night-hunting theropod to leap from the ferns and seize me from behind. My breathing slows, but an emptiness settles in my gut, as if the leeches drained more from me than just blood. I've never felt so achingly alone. I am shaking. What is the point of it all?

I lie against the tree, gazing up at a few cracks of sky in the canopy above. When I get to my feet again with a groan, leaving a smear of blood behind me on the bark, I step on something sharp. About my feet are brown shards; bending, I touch one. It is eggshell, I realize, running my fingers up the graceful curve of it. The original egg must have been larger than my head. I lift one shard in wonder. Squinting in the dark, I crouch and feel along the soft, damp earth. There are other egg shards here. And prints in the soil. Large prints, the size of my hand; not a hatchling, then. A step further, and my foot slips in something wet, and I realize the moss beneath me is dark with blood. It is torn, too, as if by tiny claws scrabbling for purchase. I lean close and touch my fingers to the green skin of the forest, still warm and wet from the blood. One of the hatchlings died here, snatched recently by something hungrier than I. Swallowing, I hold still and listen. Whatever hunted it, is not hungry now—I hope.

My nanites heighten my vision, as though triggered by my squinting, and my eyes dilate larger, darker than yours could. I can see the shards, the smear of blood, and the three-toed prints. Too large to be a raptor. And too many shards for a single egg. Maybe two.

Because I am crouching with my face low to the ground, peering at the prints, as I glance up I see what the predator missed. A few meters away, there is a fallen redwood thicker than I am tall, half rotted away, with hundreds of saplings growing from it, delicate and small: the tree's own clones, hatched upon its death to become lithe green cannibals. In places the dead tree has crumbled almost into wood dust. My nanite-enhanced eyes show me a smooth, pale surface nearly buried in the dust. Overtaken with strange excitement, hardly daring to breathe, I approach and gently brush away the flakes of dead bark to see the egg that had rolled into the refuge of this decomposing tree. This egg is whole.

It is the length of my arm from elbow to wrist. Lifting it in my hands, I find it surprisingly light, and warm to the touch—hotter than my skin. I turn it slowly. The mottled jaguar-spots, which I know would be violet in hue if it were day, can mean only one thing. I know whose egg I hold.

"Tyrannosaur," I whisper.

Is this the albino's egg, far from its nest?

Did it tumble down that cliff, too?

Did some predator seek it, only to lose it, clumsy as I was, down a scree of mud and old leaves? And now this egg is as lost as I: no one to see it, no one to come get it, no one to care. It—and the others—must have fallen recently, for the egg is still warm from its mother's feathers. Nervously, I glance about, but no vast carnivorous shape lurks in the trees, no eyes bright and resentful. But perhaps this lost egg—and the others, the eaten ones—are what had sent the tyrannosaur doe leaping from the trees to attack an armored, difficult prey: not hunger but rage at her violated nest.

"At least *your* mother is looking for you," I tell the egg. "Mine is halfway to Europa."

My own words stop me. For a moment, I imagine fashioning a quick pack or sack somehow to carry the egg safely, and scaling the high bank above the pool to track the tyrannosaur through the wood, and give her egg back. One of us at least could return home. I could do it, I know I could. I am Jaguar. The nanites would shape me for it.

But then the first of the hard shivers hit me, and I am shaking with adrenaline reaction, and weakness and hunger wash through me. The bank above me is high and the albino tyrannosaur could be many kilometers from here by now, or even fatally injured in its battle with the ankylosaur, and I don't know anything about *tracking*. And these waves of fatigue might actually knock me into true sleep at last. My whole body is trembling.

For a fleeting instant I consider cracking the egg open to eat whatever I find inside, devouring it raw as I did the atrociraptor the previous night, refueling my body. But something holds me back, some wonder at the warmth and smoothness of this egg in my hands, some kinship with the maternal tyrannosaur on whose back I danced. This egg will be a tyrannosaur like her: one of Liberty's sacrifices, a glorious bull or doe as yet unborn but that will one day grow vast enough to fill one of Liberty's shrines. I hold the egg close, fearful suddenly of dropping it. In training, we always encountered the dinosaurs as fully grown bulls and does, leviathans of tooth and feather and hide. But if something emerges from this egg, it will be small enough for me to hold.

The adrenaline reaction is hitting me harder; I had better find somewhere safe before it gets worse. And an impulse takes me suddenly to hide this egg somewhere, somewhere safer than this momentary pile of wood dust. I tuck the egg against my breasts with one arm and get to my feet. Stepping carefully, I slip through the trees near the pool, looking for darker shadows in the bark. I find what I need quickly, and I stretch out my hand to explore the edge of the shadow: a gap in the bark and in the wood, like a crack in the shell of an egg but wide enough for a woman to slip inside. Many of these older trees are hollow, or partly. I peer into the dark inside before entering. The nanites work at my ears, and in a few moments I can hear the near-silent squirming of the leeches in the pool and the snoring of a howler monkey in the high branches above, and the small footsteps of compsognathids in the forest above the bank. But I don't hear any breathing inside this tree. No animal is using it right now for a den.

None but me.

Inside, the air is cool and moist. Some past fire has burned out a vast cathedral room in here; I can feel the openness of it around me. My feet sink into thick leaves, blown in from the alders outside. I take a few steps into the hollow tree.

Lying down, I curl my body around the egg, holding it under my breasts against my belly. I wriggle deeper into the leaves with it, trying to trap my heat beneath these fragments of alders' forgotten lives. I am trembling with adrenaline reaction. "Shhh," I whisper to the egg, "shhhh," though I don't know why; my face is turned back toward the crack I crawled through. Though the leeches have left me marked with tiny wounds, my blood scent is probably covered by the musty rot of the leaves and the moist, ancient scent of the water-soaked redwood we shelter inside.

In this heavy, dark nest, I lie whispering to the tyrannosaur egg. Both of us orphans, both of us alone, both of us invisible in the dark night and in the whole universe.

As I lie shaking, a memory, an impression, surfaces in me and I have no idea where it's from. Just the sense of a strong hand caressing my hair and a low voice murmuring words above the sound of water. I murmur the words to the egg, not knowing their source, but the song warms me:

Lala mtoto lala,
mtoto lala, mtoto lala.
Mama anakuja, lala,
akupe maziwa, lala.

The singing makes me drowsy; perhaps my nanites are exhausted at last. Am I…am I about to sleep? Closing my eyes, I find the solidity of the egg in my arms reassuring, something that will still be there, unchanged, when I wake. When I wake. When I…w…

5

You worship what you crave. That which you would break a world to find and own—that becomes your god. So your two gods that they have taught you to bleed for, to lust for, to sacrifice even your daughters and sons for: they are the two you do not own, the two you have not found, the two you will break yourselves and your world to find: Liberty and Love.

THE GANYMEDE PROVERBS,
FROM THE FORBIDDEN BOOK
OF THE BATTLE-PRIESTS

MY EYES FLASH OPEN, and I gasp in the shock of emerging from a dream I can't remember but that my body knows was raw with fear. I am lying half-covered in rotted leaves, and the fissure in the side of the redwood is a wide door of daylight and full of the chirping of birds and yi qi and small lizards. Something is pressed warm and smooth to my belly: the egg. The shell is firm to the touch but also warm now. Is that my warmth, or warmth from whatever life is growing inside it? As I caress it with my hands, the events of the night come back to me and I flush with shame at my fall from the tyrannosaur's back.

But there is relief, too, like a breeze in my hair: I slept. Liberty and Love, I slept. Covering a yawn with my fingers—gracefully—I lie still, considering that. Not only did I sleep: I slept *late*. I have never slept like that—have I? In a flicker of memory like a bird's feathers brushing my cheek, just the briefest sensation before it is gone, I recall coarse threads under my back and hips, a home-woven blanket, and light unlike this light, through a window. Bunches of herbs tied with string and hung from the ceiling, swaying between me and the window. The slide of a knife opening a fish, the scent of it, and a man's low laugh.

Then it is gone.

What *was* that? When was that? Not on the station. Was that where I was, when I was small?

Sitting up, I breathe in scents of resin and moss. No whiff of herbs from that room I don't remember.

Lala mtoto lala,
mtoto lala, mtoto lala.

I catch myself singing under my breath and I stop. I start to tremble. There are memories inside me that I do not know. How can this be? I cast my mind back, but in the years that have been, I see only my training with Mai Changying, and her eyes cool above the rim of a porcelain cup, and the scent of tea, and ... and, somewhere further back, the sound of water and a man's hand stroking my hair.

I shake my head, and doing so, I find that my body is weak with hunger.

Mai Changying: *The nanites speed your metabolism, but your strength and velocity come at a cost.*

A cost, and my body is demanding payment.

After concealing the egg as thoroughly as I can beneath the leaves, I step out through the gap in the redwood's bark. The daylight is softer than it had seemed from the dark interior of the tree; it is diffused through the high branches of trees taller than spacecraft, green towers all about me. The soles of my feet harden at the command of microscopic machines as I walk slowly among the redwoods, careful to note over my shoulder where *my* tree stands.

There is the pool, wide and deep, and the fall of water trickling into it. The cliff is as high as it looked by night: twelve meters up, at least. Briefly I recall last night's fantasy of scaling it and finding the doe tyrannosaur. Her nest must be near, if this egg rolled from it or was thieved from it. But I glance back at my own nest in the hollow redwood where I've hidden that egg, and a sudden possessiveness closes around my heart. Last night, for the first time, I slept. For the first time, I felt—less alone. Warmth stole through me, even as I shook from adrenaline reaction, when I sang to the egg last night. The tyrannosaur can take care of her own eggs; this one is *mine*.

An urge nearly overwhelms me to run back to the tree and make sure the egg is still safe. But I know it's safe; I buried it beneath leaves warmed by my own body, and I would hear if any predator went rustling in them.

I turn back to the pool and its high bank. Yes, I could climb that cliff, but why do so? There is water here if I can avoid the leeches, and where there is water, there will be food to gather or catch. The nanites heighten my senses as they did last night, and I glance around me. Over there, a distant flicker of green movement in the ferns, that is a hypsilophodont. And I can hear compsognathids chirping—and skittering away unseen beneath the ferns as I approach, however softly I walk. My belly is loud, announcing me treacherously. *Catching* food won't be easy. Maybe I can find more berries, though. And if I can make a spear, maybe I can take that hypsilophodont, or another like it.

Leaning cautiously over the pool, I can see flashes of blue and silver in the water. Fish! I dart my hand into the pool, but the fish flicker away from my fingers, too swift to seize. The chill of the water bites at my arm and I withdraw it quickly, fearing the touch of the leeches more than I fear the cold. Nanites will keep me warm, but they can't do anything about leeches; those have to be plucked off to wriggle in your fingers, one by one. Shudder.

Nevertheless, I cup my hands in the water, scattering fish, and bring some of the pool to my mouth to drink. Stale water from the station's hydration tanks never tasted so clear and cold, never felt as clean on my skin. My body becomes more alert, more awake.

I keep my gaze on the ferns and the cedar-dotted slope behind me, but after filling my hands with the pool a few times, I glance down again, and catch my reflection among the ripples. It startles me, because the face—the face down there is familiar. Gingerly, I touch my cheeks. The bones are where they were a week ago. The breast bearing my jaguar tattoo is the same size and shape and curve as before. Gently, I lift that breast, then the other. They are unchanged. I can't remember the last time I looked at my reflection and saw a familiar face looking back, a familiar body mirroring mine. For years, the nanites have adapted me continually to keep me desirable to you behind the cameras—but what you find desirable changes so frequently, even by the week.

And now they've stopped.

They've *stopped*.

My reflection, gazing back at me, is someone I *know*. Not well: I've only known these cheekbones, these breasts, these particular curls of my hair, for a week or maybe two. But at least, that woman gazing back at me from the shimmer of water is not a *stranger*, not a version of me that I've met only now, this day. Everyone has abandoned me here, but this woman, ebon and young, this version of me, has stayed with me. Lifting my hand, I wiggle my fingers in a shy wave, and she wiggles hers back.

"Hi," I whisper.

Her lips part, though she cannot speak.

Which is all right. My mind is shouting loud enough for both of us. I stare at her, not understanding the pain inside me, the longing her face has awakened in my heart. I touch my lips, my ears. They haven't changed, either. Whatever the system's makers and arbiters of beauty are deciding this week, out there, across the void of space outside this orbital egg—I'm not keeping up. Not only are the nanites not altering my shape and my curves; I'm not even feeding myself right. That woman who wiggles her fingers back at me, in another week or two she will be ugly, inadequate when the cameras look at her, less than all her sisters, a sensation from the past, easily ignored and discarded. I have seen what happens to my older sisters above Europa when they are discarded, when they have grown too old for the cameras. I might *already* be ugly.

And yet: this longing. To know this face longer—to return later to this same pool and see this same woman looking back at me. A face I remember, a face to be worn for more than a day. I lift my hands to my cheeks. My heart is beating fast. The woman who gazes back at me out of the pool looks frightened, more like a prey animal than a jaguar after all. Slowly, she lowers her hands from her cheeks and takes a few steadying breaths.

I lift my gaze from hers and find that nothing has crept up on me while I watched her. A yi qi with folded wings sits on a branch high above, watching me, but it is far too small to eat me; if I were to catch it, I'd eat *it*. Swiftly, I snatch up a loose rock from the water's edge and hurl it, but the stone flashes just past the lizard's feathered head without striking. Startled from its branch, the yi qi takes flight, flits away between the redwoods. I hiss through my teeth. Almost.

I'm not going to catch a meal tossing *rocks*.

A spear.

I need a spear.

My belly's demands are violent now, and the weakness in my limbs scares me; the nanites might wreck me, keeping me going this way. But there was a hypsilophodont out there, and probably others, and I need to take one.

I begin searching for a suitable stick or branch. I wish I had my bo; I could sharpen the end of it. Something else will have to do. As I search, I gather up berries from a few viny bushes among the ferns, but these make only a brief difference in my belly; my metabolism burns away the berries like drops of water on hot sand.

It takes a while, but I find a stick green enough that it doesn't snap in my hands. I crack the end against a rock, until it is jagged and splintered and sharp. Humans lived in forested places like this once. Maybe some distant ancestor of mine hunted with whittled spears like this one. Or maybe she would see mine and fall over laughing, because it is really a pitiful thing, and probably she would have learned how to make a better one twice as quickly. Or her baba would have taught her. I blink back sudden moisture in my eyes, though I don't know where these tears are from.

Hefting the spear, I test its weight across my palms. My heart lifts. This spear is mine. I made it. My scornful ancestor can laugh all she wants. I bet she didn't have half the skills I do. I bet she was ugly, and probably beaten every night by some man, because men used to do that, though why women let them I have no idea. Mai Changying beats us, but I can't imagine anyone beating *Mai*. Bet my ancestor would trade her situation for mine in a heartbeat.

I try to hunt as the daystar brightens. Flushing compsognathids from the ferns, I try to spear them and miss badly, whether throwing or thrusting the stick. Twice I splinter the end beyond repair and have to waste time searching for yet another stick to use. Still my prey scampers away without wound or blood trail, leaving me staring after them.

I need to be better with this spear, but I have no trainer. I find myself wishing desperately that my imagined ancestor from the morning of time was here to teach me, and that I'd been less scornful of her. She might instruct me on how to read the spoor I find throughout the forest, or how to be quieter as I stalk through the trees, to not startle my food away. Mai Changying taught me to stand and breathe and run prettily, and to catch and ride a tyrannosaur, but what use is any of that here, where there are no cameras to perform *to* and no arena of red sand to perform *on?* Nothing she has taught me is of any use here at all. I haven't felt so helpless since early training.

A memory fills my mouth: the taste of ... fish. Succulent and sprinkled with herbs. I catch my breath, and as before, images fill my mind that I can't place: The flash of sun on metal as someone sitting beside me threads a fish hook. The sleepy rock and sway of the boat, the soft skin of the water parting around the blade of an oar. I gasp, and at the next pang in my stomach these fragments of an unremembered past crumble away, leaving me as frightened as I am dizzy with hunger.

I return to the redwood in search of comfort and sit a while in the warm interior with the egg in my lap. I caress the smooth shell and take delight in the deep, startling violet of its spots. For a little while I almost forget my hunger. A few times while failing to stab a meal, I had glimpsed the albino tyrannosaur again, moving massively between the alders in the distance, white as the wisps of fog. I had stopped and stared after her, awed by her beauty and wondering how *she* does it, how she has done it since she hatched: hunted and found food. No second thought came to me about returning this egg, this beautiful egg, to her. *My* egg.

Bending, I kiss the shell, finding it warm against my lips. Then I cover it again in the leaves. If Mai Changying and the others came for me now, right now, what would happen to this small egg? To the unborn tyrannosaur inside it? Could I take it onto the shuttle? Mai Changying would never allow that—the training station is small and tightly confined. My cell where I sleep is much smaller than the inside of this cedar. There would be no room for a tyrannosaur there, nor food for it as it grew to immensity.

Restless, I fidget and rock where I sit. I want to jump, to leap, to run, to slap the trees with my hands as I pass. The nanites inside me want me *moving*, want me hunting, spearing, eating. On this world I am free of Mai Changying and her beatings, but I remain *their* slave.

"You're safe here," I tell the tyrannosaur fetus, concealed under shell and pile of leafy detritus. "No one can see you. I won't be long."

Getting to my feet again, I slip from the tree, and now I do scale the cliff. The nanites toughen my fingertips and toes. Gripping rocks and roots, I scurry up the side and then pull myself over the brink. No need to lie panting a moment on the edge of the world; the nanites have me leaping to my feet, and I sprint to the nearest cedar and ascend into the treetops. Great leaps carry me from branch to branch high above the world, landing in bursts of needles, the scent of resin filling my nose. Laughter filling my heart. In motion, I am *alive*, like I have swallowed the sun, like I can do anything. I feel present in my body as I have not felt since I could remember. Maybe because I have been inside this particular version of my body for longer than a day, maybe because I think I will wake inside it again tomorrow. If only my sister athletes at Europa

Station could know what this is *like*. My body and my face are no longer temporary habitations. That makes it easier to glory in what my body can *do*.

Swift as a gibbon, I flit through the cedar-tops until I find the doe tyrannosaur. I see her from a distance, white as a ghost but massive, a popobawa swollen on all the lives it has eaten until it has grown larger than any of them. I follow her a while through the trees, disturbing her no more than the monkeys do. I don't try to drop down onto her back and ride her. I just want to know where she is going. I watch, hungrily, when she takes a hadrosaur by a creek, dragging it bleating into the crash and fume of water before snapping its neck with her powerful jaws. The creek surges about them. She hurls the body down and begins tearing flesh from its tender belly. The smell of meat, though raw, makes me dizzy with need, so that I clutch the branch I'm perched on, fearful suddenly that I might lose my grip and plummet into the water with them.

Sated, the tyrannosaur curls up like a ground cat—not like a jaguar in the trees—by the creek, her tail half in the water. I growl, frustrated, as the tyrannosaur dozes. I realize I'd hoped she would lead me to her nest. What kind of mother is she? Here she is *sleeping* when she has eggs to keep warm! I am angry with her; almost I want to rip a branch from this tree and throw it at her.

But maybe her nest doesn't exist anymore.

Maybe she lost them all.

Maybe I have the last of her eggs.

My exhilaration is gone. If earlier I swallowed the sun, now it has flickered out. I slip away downstream until I find a patch of berries and dare to drop earthward and gather them. I eat the berries and pluck a few leaves and chew on them, too, trying to cheat my stomach into thinking it's being fed. I can hear, faintly, the snores of the tyrannosaur further up the creek. I am sorry that I have followed her.

Anxiety for the egg drives me back. Yet, high in the cedars, I can see Liberty's statue, her head lifted above the upland trees, and navigating by her, I return first to the airlock in its open meadow. The kentrosaur's skeletal tail is still there, and the raptor-picked bones of the parasaurolophus. I drop out of the trees. Surrounded by the thunder of insects in the grass, I walk across to the cube and press my palm to it again. The metal is cold and gives no answer. If vast shuttles still sleep silent beneath my feet, no word or call of mine wakes them.

6

Your task, your one task, is to be better, each day. To make your audience scream in pleasure at the sight of you. Each of your cells has a mirror, and looking back at you from that mirror each week will be a girl that men and women will pay more to see.

THE LESSONS OF MAI CHANGYING

EVERY EVENING ON EUROPA STATION, while Jupiter filled the sky beneath us outside the Glory Window, I would stand in a line by the other girls while Mai Changying's servants measured our hips, our breasts, our waists. The numbers appeared on the opposite wall as fast as they were assessed—you could see each evening what the nanites had adjusted. It began early, because the goddess Liberty demands that her sacrifices develop beauty early. Beside the aesthetic measurements on the wall were others: heartrate, blood oxygenation, blood pressure, grace quotient, posture, agility, average poise, speed in meters per minute.

My memories of earlier years are of running, my legs pumping, with the other nine and ten-year-old girls up the long corridor that follows the inner curvature of the training station's hull, up the wall and around, so that we eventually arrived back where we started. That was how all my days started: before the morning meal, before even checking my stats against the other girls', before being even allowed to speak a single word, we had to complete our race. Once my breasts grew and I received the implant that stops my menstruation and once the nanites began to shape me, I started running at the second hour, after the smaller girls and after Mai.

For her own morning run, Mai Changying set aside the silk gowns we usually saw her in, choosing instead a form-fitting jumpsuit with slits all up and down the back to let her skin breathe. Her face had *such* wrinkles, and age had made her eyes gray as the hull, yet she ran *fast*. Maybe she has nanites too.

Afterward, she would stand toweling her neck and hair and would call us, the developed girls, out into the corridor and set us running, too. She timed us, and the slowest two would be beaten, but so would the two who ran least beautifully. "Grace is everything, girls," she told us, many times. "The only thing the tyrannosaurs respect. The only thing the cameras care about. Your grace is your dignity, the only dignity you will ever have. Speed without grace, and you might as well be hulking boys."

In my twelfth year I just struggled to keep up with the girls whose bodies were more grown than mine. I was beaten often, and it hurt. It *so* hurt.

In my thirteenth year, I tried to be first.

That didn't work, either.

In my fourteenth year—last year—I began watching Mai Changying. I watched how *she* ran, effortlessly, her eyes always turned inward, watching herself, watching her own breath, perhaps the systole and diastole of her own heart. And I realized she ran faster and *better* than any of us.

Our trainer was the subject of awe and speculation at the fourteen-year table at mess. Vividly I remember a fight at midday meal between Anaconda, with her serpent tattoo coiling around her arms and across her shoulders, and blonde Egret, with her sigil-bird's tattooed wings cupping her breasts, a ploy to capture the cameras in the arena. I sat eating beside them but listening rather than speaking, as I usually did. Let the other girls squabble; I saved my energy for outperforming them.

"Mai Changying has been training victors forever," Egret said.

"She might be four hundred years old, and she's still faster than me," Anaconda scowled.

"She is *not* four hundred years old—"

"She could be."

"—but she *is* faster than you."

That started it. Anaconda slapped Egret's face, and Egret threw Anaconda on the table, screaming and scratching. I slipped away. Their fight, not mine.

For some reason, I couldn't bear to be there with them another moment. I slipped out the round door and down the hall toward our quarters, leaving their shrieks behind me.

As I paced up the curve of the hull, I passed Mai Changying's quarters and stopped, startled. Her door was open. I could see her, sitting on a stool, facing her mirror with her back to me, with her gown lowered about her waist. I glimpsed her in the mirror, wolves tattooed leaping across her breasts, and her face—Her eyes shone with tears, but none were on her cheeks, and her shoulders were still. I stood struck. To see Mai Changying vulnerable, to see her unaware of her door, unthinking—Mai Changying who did everything so deliberately. To see that shine in her eyes. To think that *Mai* wept, as we did.

"Get back to the mess, Jaguar," she said, without turning and without any tremble in her voice.

My heart pounding, I turned and ran, and didn't stop until I was back at my table. The food had all been swept to the floor, and Egret and Anaconda were still rolling by the far wall, scratching at each other, Egret with a fistful of Anaconda's hair. I didn't watch them. I just sat, my blood hot in my face, unable to forget what I'd seen. Mai. Mai Changying weeping.

Was she four hundred? How old *was* she?

How long had she lived here training young women like me?

How long had she grieved at that mirror?

And if even she—the quickest, the best, the most graceful, the woman who trained victors for the running of the tyrannosaurs on Patriot Day—if even *she* wasn't happy here, how could I ever be?

* * *

Now, in my sleep, as I dream inside a redwood tree, Mai Changying sits beside me, with that same shine of unshed tears in her eyes. She passes me the cup of evening tea. The cup is cold, though I know the tea inside is hot. Her fingers tremble, and almost I glance up at her face, but I don't dare. I don't want to be beaten.

"I am training you, Nyota Madaki," she whispers, "the only way I know how, to live in the only world you have. Only your pride, only your grace will make it possible for you to survive the arena. And that is what we do here, that is what we do first—we *survive*. You think the danger is being consumed by tyrannosaurs on the red sands. No. The danger is being consumed by the crowds. By your worshippers. By those who will swallow you and vomit out your bones. As an owl with mice, so are they with us. Drink."

"My name…" My own fingers tremble. "You said my name. How had I forgotten my name?"

She presses the cup firmly into my hands, then covers my fingers with her own, warm and paper-dry. "Drink, little Jaguar." She lifts the cup toward my face. I smell the tea and I am frightened. I look down into the cup, and it doesn't seem like a bowl of porcelain anymore, but like a whole ocean that will drown me. Behind me there is a crash of waves and a man's voice calling, and a woman singing—*Lala mtoto lala*—and I yearn to turn and run to them, but Mai Changying's hands have become strong. She holds my fingers pinned to the cup as she raises it. My lips part in a scream and the tea fills my mouth, and it is too hot, scalding my tongue.

I burst awake with a gasp. The dark musty scent inside the redwood, the hot sweat of the forest, and the warmth of the tyrannosaur egg pressed to my belly. Panting, I wrap my arms around the egg. Soft sobs. The terror of that scented sea and the burn of it in my mouth is still sharp in my heart. "It is all right," I whisper soothingly to the tyrannosaur inside the egg, as if in calming that unborn bird I might calm myself. "It is all right. No one will hurt us."

I keep whispering that: "No one will hurt us. We're safe. We're safe."

Once, I had a name.

Not Jaguar. Another name.

In that dream, I had a name, and when dream-Mai spoke it, it rang in my heart and it rang in my blood and it burned me hotter than the tea, as if at the voicing of it, all my nanites that inhabit me and shape me and enslave me had caught fire and burned away, leaving only flakes of ash behind, tiny motes dissolving within my my hungry cells. Burning away everything that wasn't me.

I had a name.

Awake, I am forgetting it. Almost, I can form the sound of it in my mouth—almost.

I blink back tears.

What was my name?

"It's all right," I whisper to the egg. "It's all right."

* * *

I slip down to the pool for a drink. The air is moist and warm as ever, but there is a softness to the edge of the dark that I have learned means the microstar will soon flicker back to life. My spear is with me, and I am glad of it as I approach the water, because several hypsilophodonts lift their heads, eyes alert and wary. Stopping, I hold as still as a pillar of rock. Then lower myself slowly, so slowly, into the long grasses, out of sight. I grip the spear tightly, my palms slick with sweat. I am nerving myself for a throw, before my belly can growl and startle the animals away.

I creep closer, watching the animals through the last veil of grass, the green blades dew-wet against my cheeks and arms and thighs. The hypsilophodonts lower their heads again, drinking in great swallows. A leaf falls to the water beside them, and that makes me glance up at the alders, pale on the water's edge. The alders! I stifle a gasp; almost, I want to jump from the grass and dance in my excitement. The nanites surge in my blood. The alders: that is how I will do it. *That is how.*

A jaguar leaps from above. I saw a vid of a jaguar hunting the night I chose my sigil, the sigil tattooed across my body. I remember the grace, the lithe, unstoppable power of that feline hunter as it flowed out of the tree like water to land on a gazelle's back, and its swiftness as it seized the gazelle's throat in crushing jaws. That's what I have been doing wrong! Lost in this wood, I've forgotten that I am *Jaguar.*

The hypsilophodonts flicker away through the trees. Others will come; I don't waste the spear throw. I go to the pool first, to touch my reflection's fingers—that name rising suddenly from my dream like a fish from the deep, a ghost's whisper in my mind: *Nyota, Nyota*—so that I and my reflection tremble together. Then I go to the alders, embracing one and climbing its bole as easily as I climbed the bank last night.

In the branches above the water, lithe and silent as a jaguar, I wait. Twice I drop from above onto my prey. The first time I miss entirely. The second, I land on the hypsilophodont's back, tightening my hand on a gripful of feathers as my weight knocks it off its feet. It rolls onto me, crushing, kicking. I stab at it with my spear, holding the stick near the point as though I am wielding a dagger and not a length of wood. I hear the spear snap as we struggle on the bank. Growling, I cling to the animal. Getting its powerful hind legs under it, it springs into the water, pulling me in with it. The cold is sharp against my eyes and skin. Submerged, we roll. I lose my grip and come up sputtering. Coughing, I try to chase the creature, but in a moment my meal has splashed bleating up onto the far bank and is bounding away, leaving behind a bedraggled and infuriated jaguar.

Standing in the pool to my hips, I heave for air. Realizing I still have a broken piece of stick in my hand, I cast it from me, disgusted; the disturbed, rippling water spins it lazily away. I stand burning in fury. Some jaguar. If I don't get *out* of here, I'm going to end up dying. Goddess, that would be *embarrassing*. Scrubbing the tears from my eyes with my hands, I try to think, but thinking clearly is for girls with full bellies.

I climb out of the water, checking the trees for predators larger than I before taking the time to pluck the leeches painfully away. For an instant, holding one fat with blood in my hand, I consider—no. No, that is *not* a meal. Disgust wriggles inside me. I throw it away into the water. I take care to check the insides of my thighs and other places warm with blood for any more of the ugly things before I scramble back into the foliage and seek material for a new spear.

* * *

The bark scratches my arms and thighs as I climb, a new spear clutched in one hand, but I don't care. The nanites will repair me, and I will clamber out on this branch and wait, and try again. For one thing, I am *really* hungry. For another, I am Jaguar. I am among the fastest and best of the fifteen-year girls, among the fastest and most highly trained organisms in our entire solar system. I am fierce. I do not give up.

Here, I need no chanting of my name, no adoration of shouting crowds behind the cold stare of the cameras. I just need a meal. I wriggle out on the branch and peer down at the water below, which has grown still again. Tiny insects skim the surface. I could catch them, but they would be less filling even than the berries. I need a hypsilophodont. One grazing-fat and bred to provide a meal for tyrannosaurs. Something I can cook, something that will fill me. I settle in to wait.

Slowly the grazing animals come back, a few of them, to bend and sip the water, but none near enough yet to my tree. I wait … I wait. Then my stomach snarls its discontent, betraying me. The hypsilophodonts turn and flash away into the ferns, leaving behind a few green feathers that drift down to rest, light as dreams, on the pool's surface. Without opening my mouth I scream in my throat, exasperated. I could go back to my nest tree, curl up around that smooth egg, and wait until hunger makes me too weak to move, but I am Jaguar. If anyone anywhere in this asteroid is catching a meal today, it is going to be *me*.

Mid-thought, I stop, caught by the sense that someone is watching me, someone who is hungry, someone who sees *me* as a meal. I glance up and suck in my breath. There, on the cliff above, staring down at me, is the albino tyrannosaur. Her eye, crimson amid headfeathers white as fog over cold water, is very still. She is gazing *right at me*. I gaze back, and her eye is deep as time and ravenous as the cold between the stars, and I can't look away. I can't even move. I just breathe, my heart racing.

Not ten meters above me, her jaws part. I can see the pink of her tongue and the red of her maw, and those teeth, curved knives long as my hand, sharp as grief. A few broken off on her right lower jaw. Teeth made for tearing flesh. Powerful hind limbs flexing as she leans over the brink of the cliff, her clawed feet digging into the damp soil. My sister athletes and I are not the only sacrifices that race the sands on Patriot Day; the tyrannosaurs, too, are sacrifices to Liberty goddess, more elegant and powerful than we, though we ride them. Gazing up at her, I whisper, "You are beautiful."

The cliff's edge under her right foot crumbles then, and she topples, her great bulk carving a scrape in the side of the cliff; an avalanche of white feathered tyrannosaur plummets almost into my tree, so that I shrink back with a cry. That cry is lost in the screech of the tyrannosaur as she crashes, a rending-metal scream that tears open the forest. Water fountains up, drenching me.

Dripping water from my skin and hair, shaking, I crawl forward along the branch until it bends beneath me. I peer down. The tyrannosaur's head lifts from the water, the pool pouring from her jaws. She lets out that shriek again. I clap my hands over my ears and almost fall into the pool with her. I wrap my limbs quickly around the swaying branch, dropping my spear. My heart pounds. A small whimper escapes my throat; I do *not* want to fall in. She thrashes beneath me and her tail strikes the bole of the cedar. My branch shudders, and I jump up and run back along it. Nanite-fueled, I leap and spin in the air, catching another branch with my feet and leaping again. I hit the ferns and roll through a crash of green and a shock of bruising pain in my body.

Then I get shakily to my feet, standing above the ferns to look back at the pool, at the tyrannosaur. There was no cushion of ferns for her to land in, as I did, and as her egg did; she is too massive. Her hindquarters are on the bank, but one leg is bent beneath her. Broken. She is trying to roll onto her feet, but each time, I see her fall back. Each time she tilts back her head, her screams hurt my ears. Her clawed foot and the squirming of her immense, feathered body is churning the bank into mud. Her claws dig into the soil, bringing more of the cliffside down on her in a shower of dark earth.

Her pale red eyes roll in terror.

My own bruising is fading already. I must have broken legs and ribs in the fall that first left me here on this world, alone. But I wasn't alone. I have millions of nanites living inside me. Repairing me. Strengthening me.

Watching the tyrannosaur wallow half in, half out of the water, hearing her cries through my palms, I doubt she has any nanites to repair her. She will die here. Standing helpless with my hands over my ears, I can only watch, my breast heavy with sorrow. The dying tyrannosaur is muscled and immense and determined, and her tail slams into the cedar again, snapping it in two, so that I have to run quickly to the other side of the pool to avoid its fall.

I crouch at the edge of the water as it is lashed white by the tyrannosaur's struggles. I stare across at her. Her eye turns toward me but she doesn't seem to see me, too lost in her own anguish. She screeches and then her head slams back into the water, sending a wave of it over me. She struggles again to get her good leg under her and push up. In awe, I watch her fight to stand. Her head rises and for a moment she towers over the pool, over me. I can see the sleek white down of her belly, and the small forelegs held against her breast. But her shattered leg won't hold her and she comes down like a mountain breaking; I duck back a few meters into the ferns, and I can feel her fall in the soles of my feet. An alder to my left crashes earthward with her.

But a thought is rushing through me now like a wind. I don't have my spear—it is probably under her—so I run to the fallen alder and tear away a branch and hold the splintered end up before my eyes to check that it is sharp. I can't let her suffer like this. She is old and strong and beautiful as the dawn. Her death should have been elegant, as she is—the flash of a sacrificial blade and the spray of bright blood at the end of a forty-kilometer run, or a last deep breath released from sleep, a giant majestic in her nest. She shouldn't suffer like this.

My heart pounds as I wade in, forgetting leeches, needing to get near enough to her. She lifts her head. Her jaws open, and the rush of her breath is warm against my body and her scream makes my bones ring, and my head—I have the broken branch in my hands and I can't cover my ears. I splash around to the side of her head. Before she can slam her head into me to knock me away, I spear at her eye with the jagged end of the branch. The nanites give me strength and velocity. The branch shears through her eye to the softness underneath that is her mind and her memory and her living self. Her body convulses, ripping the branch from my grip and tossing me aside onto the bank.

I hit hard. I need to get up, dart away, avoid being crushed: but I am winded, body and heart both. Above me, across an expanse of empty sky, a far green forest tosses in winds I can't feel. Somewhere to my right, a redwood and an egg hidden in dead leaves. To my left, the water-crash of the dying behemoth, the kicking of powerful legs, the last violent suck of air. Then an immense carcass settling, a sudden-silent mountain of dead flesh. I breathe in quick gasps. "I'm sorry," I whisper. "I'm sorry."

7

You see my daughter. She helps me mend the nets. She sings in the boat when I row back home before dawn. This Empire takes our daughters. It will take her one day soon. So you look at her now. You look at her laughing. See how happy she is, today. You look now, and never forget. She is why we resist. She is why we must fight.

SHAKA MADAKI OF TITAN

FRESHLY ROASTED, the tyrannosaur meat is heavy and has a tang to it. The fire—I did it, this time I did it, I *made* a fire—crackles in its pit near my feet, the sound of it pleasant in my ears. I sit with my back to the fallen carnivore, where her head lies lifeless on the bank. It's dusk but few animals have dared approach the pool yet—except for a growing host of midges and some feathered beast that growls at me from the deep grass, wanting the carcass. I shake my spear at it and shout, and my competitor stays hidden.

That's right: Stay back, little coelurosaur, or whatever you are. I am Jaguar. I am fierce, unstoppable. I killed the tyrannosaur.

Mostly by accident—except the finishing blow. And

now she is only meat that will rot and waste unless I and others feed.

I will not let myself think of her nest and its eggs, nor even *my* egg concealed in my redwood tree. I wanted meat, the nanites cruel inside me wanted meat, and I have it. The fire crackles and hisses. I have lain sticks across the flames with globs of tyrannosaur skewered on them, the meat blackening and spitting fat in the heat.

Leaning back against the albino's head, I lick the grease of her from my fingertips. Berries and bits of leaves had given my body just enough energy to keep moving, but her meat fills my belly and wakes up something in my body, makes me strong. I feel that I could run the entire interior circumference of this hollow world.

And something else is waking, too.

When I close my eyes and breathe in the scent of the cooked meat, I can hear low voices. I can smell … bass, that's bass frying, and … and spray from the sea.

The fishing-boat scent of my father, my *father.*

The gristle of his beard against my cheek, the scratch of his old jacket.

An oxygen-flood of sensory memories. All of them had been hidden inside some station-cabin in my mind, and the hull is breached. Or hidden in an egg, memories waiting to be born. And the scent of the tyrannosaur meat—this meal that I, not Mai Changying, have prepared—has cracked the shell. All the memories are tumbling out. As though, with the meat, I have taken into myself also the tyrannosaur's vitality, its continuity, its clarity of purpose. Its sensory connection with a genetic past stretching back sixty-five million years. I recall smells, sounds, textures from days forgotten, so many of them, overwhelming me, all at once. The low rumble of a man's voice, singing at the oar. The kiss of water against the side of the boat. The salt scent of our sea. Saturn rising until she fills the whole sky, turning the night into soft twilight, her rings and her roundness vast and graceful and perfectly reflected on the dark water. *Look at her rising. Rising beautiful, and the fish love her deeply. They'll be here and hungry in a moment.* That voice. Deep and roughened by nights spent breathing in the cold salt breeze. My *father*'s voice. His arms about me as I sit in his lap in our shelter at the brink of the sea. Other men and women pressing close, their eyes glinting in the pale light from the solar cells. The vibration of my father's voice in his body, under my cheek. "She's why we're fighting. She's why we resist tyranny," he says. "That's what you must unforget." His chin against my hair.

Then he is gone, and there is an aging woman's voice. *Drink, girl, drink.*

Porcelain cool against my palms, the smallest cup of tea in my cupped hands, tea smelling of mint. Tea green as Mai Changying's irises as she watches me lift the cup to my lips. Watches me sip, watches me swallow. The tea is too hot and it scorches my tongue, but though I wince I keep drinking, fearing her displeasure.

My eyes watering, I lower the emptied cup. Through my sheen of tears I glimpse the slightest creasing around her eyes. Not enough to call a frown. "I do grieve for you," she says. "I grieve to repeat an ill that was done to me. Rather I would cut out my eyes." Her tone is even. "But it is necessary."

When I open my eyes here, at the coals my fire has left, smelling resin and roasted tyrannosaur and woodsmoke and not mint, my hands are shaking. It's a while before I can still them.

There is no chill in the air to tell me the night is aging, to warn me that more scavengers may come for this carcass. It is always warm here and humid. Still, I get shakily to my feet and smother the embers. I walk alertly through the grasses, into the forest to my nest tree. Inside the warm safety of its interior, I uncover the egg, resting my hand on its shell to make sure it still feels warm. It does, so I cover it again.

My body quivers with a strange anticipation as new emotions riot within me. As though the woman I was this morning and the woman I am tonight are not the same. My nanites are a turmoil inside me. Almost I can feel the jolts of chemicals, little bursts inside my body—but they are conflicting, as though the thousands of civilizations of microscopic machines that each hour are born and thrive and die inside my blood cells are no more certain what to do with this night, with these feelings, than I am. Some are trying to calm my body, others to waken it. Some want me to sleep, others want me to sprint. Shaking, I walk to the outside of the redwood and lean into it, gripping its spongy bark in my hands. The nanites harden my fingers and palms, toughening my grip. Then the soles of my feet and the bottoms of my toes. I begin scaling the trunk, climbing toward the branches I can see high above, each branch thick enough to set a table on. I ascend into the resin-scented, moist air, leaving the pool and the grasses and the tyrannosaur's silent body below, a great gash in her left leg where I tore meat out of her to roast.

Closer to the sky, I crouch on one of the high boughs, alert and tensed like a jaguar prepared to leap, my hands resting between my knees, my fingers sticky with sap and tyrannosaur grease. I stare out at the motionless forest. No breeze, no stir of air. Above me, the microstar flickers briefly, a faint wink of light like a flash of memory, like a secret, but then is dark. I stare up at the distant shadow that is the other side of the forest, the far side of the world. My own blood is a thunder in my ears. I wish I could see stars. I wish—I wish I could see Saturn rising above the waves like half the sky.

I remember so much.

I am shaking.

I *remember.*

Remember standing on my father's balcony when I was a child. Remember standing in his boat, laughing in the quiet before dawn. Remember the phosphorescence on the seas of Titan. Remember the plash of the waves and the stars like a billion fires lit in the night after curfew doused the lights of New Ulundi on shore far behind us. The sea wind and the spray against my cheeks as I gazed back at the dark houses receding. Baba's breathing as he heaved at the oars. The boat could hover over the waves in an emergency—I remember, I *remember* the flash of the sea and the song of the air propeller and the speed humming in every timber of the boat as I lay injured once and we rushed back to shore. But that was for emergencies. Usually Baba liked to row with his own calloused hands, as our ancestors did during the years when Earth was silent.

I touch my hair, remembering the wind in it. I used to have locks, beautiful locks. My hair is growing out again now. It was always trimmed short on the training station above Europa. But now I have more than two inches on my head, curly and thick beneath my fingers. I touch it in wonder, knowing soon I will have more.

Once New Ulundi slept behind us and before Saturn rose, Molalatladi—that arm of our galaxy that holds up the night—would fill the sky so full it hurt my eyes. Gazing up through our manufactured atmosphere, I would see all those stars flicker and wink as though I were looking at them through smoke. My father and I would stare up at them and whisper their names, quietly so as not to startle the fish. Tracing constellations on our fingertips, smiling to see a moon hurtle by, while the nets filled beneath us.

My heart aches to see the stars again, like that.

Now I know why I have always made sure to fight for a window seat on the shuttle from Europa station to this training world. I wanted to look through the porthole and see my father's stars. My heart wanted to find them again, even when I could no longer remember my father, or his boat, or Molalatladi burning in the sky. I would press my face to the bioglass, feel the faintest hint of the lethal cold of space sharp against my forehead and nose, but they weren't the same stars. Out there in the empty, between the worlds, the stars never flicker. They never waver. Their light is dead and merciless, like holes punched in dark paper, as though out here the universe has been pierced and pinned in place. As all of us are pinned in our places too, pinned to the seats of the shuttle, pinned by Mai Changying's sharp gaze, pinned where she wants us, pinned by the sharp glare of camera lights, pinned where we must squirm and leap and perform as all of you wish.

Now, with my head tilted back and the reverse interior of the world above, its millions of cedars growing down toward me, I can't see the stars of my childhood, the stars above the foam on the sea. But I can't see the brutal stars of my womanhood, either. Just an empty, rustling, vegetal dark. I close my eyes; I listen to my own breath. My breathing comes easier. Even my nanites have calmed. It is a relief to be alone in the night, to hear no human sounds around me, to feel no one's gaze on me. I am naked, but no one is here to admire me or to claim me with their cries of appreciation or desire. My nakedness is my own. Something like a bubble is rising in my chest, not painfully, something that might reach my mouth and burst out in a song or a shout or a moan. Something like joy.

Something like *me*.

That tea.

I touch my lips, recalling the heat of it. The scent of it. I used to drink it each evening, taking the cup from Mai Changying's hands.

I understand now.

She *took* my memory from me, took it with her drugged tea.

She took it away, with the burn and the bitterness on my lips and tongue, with the mint that didn't quite hide the bitter taste, with the steam rising from the cup to my nostrils and entering my body. Night after night, she took my memory from me and made me a slave, my mind emptied for her to write in, even as she filled my body with nanites, tiny machines to rewrite the rest of me. Sip after sip of nanites from that cup. I, who danced for Liberty goddess, have been a slave, and I didn't know it. How had I not known it?

I had thought myself Liberty's daughter, strong and swift and graceful for the cameras, as beautiful as I was unthinkingly miserable, but I had been no one's daughter, anymore. Exiled from my surviving parent across hundreds of millions of kilometers of empty cold. The dancer on the red sands, the holy sacrifice, the goddess's daughter: in reality I had been a property—not Mai Changying's, but a property of those who owned *her*. A billion-credit investment.

But now they have lost me. I have been misplaced.

I did not place myself here—any more than *they* intended to.

But tonight, here on this branch, with a tyrannosaur carcass and an unhatched egg below, this *is* my place.

Joy, fear, anger, grief, all of it together, the nanites rushing down a thousand blood rivers inside me. I can't stop shaking. Tea scent took my memories from me and tyrannosaur scent has given them back.

I crouch in this tree, naked and free as an infant, free as an Earthsent standing solitary and liberated on the shores of Titan before the moon was warmed and its oceans thawed. Like her—like that first Earthsent, a thousand years gone—no one owns me. Not anymore.

For the first time since I was small and had no nanites, I can smell the fishing-scent of my father when I close my eyes. I can feel the roughness of his jacket against my cheek. And I can feel his arms, strong around me. Can remember being held. Being *home*. I am full of tears.

All this ocean of memory overwhelms me, leaves me giddy, and I have to grab at the branch to keep from falling.

* * *

I have not remembered this in years. When I was eleven, I stole into one of the shuttles after curfew. I bribed the sentinel, a wiry teen, but not one of my sister athletes, with a chocolate I'd thieved from the mess. Once I was in the shuttle, I left all the lights off but powered up the radio. It didn't take me long to figure it out; the controls were simple and at that time, I could still remember the frequency that would reach home.

The time delay to our terraformed moon made me nervous; I didn't want to be discovered here—Mai Changying does not believe in *light* punishments—and I didn't want the sentinel guarding the shuttles to demand anything more. I didn't have any more chocolates.

But at last I heard my father's voice crackle from the unit, and the timbre of his quiet "Yes? Who is this?" made my breath catch.

We talked for a while, each of us saying what we could and then awaiting the delay while the radio message arrived and was heard. Behind all my words was what I didn't actually say: that I hated it here, that I missed home and the stars and the sea, our balcony above the water, and our hovercar with its torn and patched seats. That I missed *him*.

"I want to come home," I whispered, glancing at the shuttle windows, wondering how near morning it might be, how close I was cutting this.

There was the long delay—too long, this time—and when his voice came back, it was deep and sure, yet quivering with emotion. "I miss you too, Nyota, my little star," he said, as though he'd heard everything I'd left unspoken.

My cheeks were wet now.

"I have missed you every day for five years," Baba told me. "And if I could, I would come out there and get you and bring you home, this very day. But I can't. I ... I would never make it back here with you. We should not be talking like this. It is very dangerous for you. But I promise you, when the Patriot Days are done and we are free, I will be there to take you in my arms and bring you home at last. And you ... you promise me something, Nyota. Promise me that no matter what they tell you, and what they do to you, and what they teach you, that you will not forget home. You will not forget your mother and your grandmother dead, or me, or ... "

I was sobbing now without sound, not as a child cries but as a young woman does.

"Every night, little Nyota," he said, "every night, I go out in my boat and once the nets are down, I lift a little telescope and I look for you. I look up at Saturn's rings and past, to Jupiter and its moons, I see Europa and I know I am looking at you. I think of how far away you are but also how brave, how strong, my little Nyota who used to shout at the sea at dawn. You are all I have. I have no other children. No other sons or daughters. And with your mother gone ... You are our family. You are our future. You remember, always. Bring honor to your family. *Never* forget who you are."

I sent back only two words: "I'm afraid."

"I am too," he said after the delay. "Very afraid. I will tell you a story, little Nyota, the one best story I have. It begins with your great grandfather. He was one of the first in our family to come here, soon after they made the air breathable. He survived the Silent Years when no supplies came from Earth. He lived here with his husband and his children and made a tiny boat from the guts of the colony ship. He had no hovercar. He had no Inlibrary access. Those things did not exist here then. He knew a few other people on the shore, but so few. You understand, this was long ago. It was difficult. He died when I was so young. Your grandfather, he raised me, and took me out in his father's boat, and I looked at all the lights on the shore and all the satellites above our heads, and he told me how new those were. And when I was just a little older than you are now, they built Titan University across that sea, and I wanted to go there. To go to a far place, a school, as you have done, my daughter—but by my own choice, not by force. I had an Inlibrary book, it was very expensive. And I had in my hand a ticket for one of the first aircars that would cross that water with me seated aboard. And my grandfather, the day I was to leave, he sat down by me. I can still see his face, how weathered, how burned by Titan's winds. He gripped my shoulder, and pointed to the door of our house, where a great oar and an electric spear were propped up against the jamb. He said to me, 'When I was your age, my father gave me that oar and that whalespear.' My grandfather, he pointed at the oar. 'And he said, with this oar you will go out on the sea and hunt and fish and bring food in for your family, your spouse and children. And with that spear, you will defend your family when the soarwhales leap over your boat.' And then my grandfather tapped the ticket I held. 'This is your oar,' he said. He tapped my Inlibrary book. 'This is your harpoon. Feed and defend your family.' And so I have tried to do. Nyota, I do not know what your oar and your spear are, up there. Maybe a tyrannosaur and a coil of rope. I cannot even imagine. But I know that you are my daughter, always, and you are our family's future. And I know you are carrying your oar and your whalespear, as I carried mine and my grandfather his. Hear me. I am so proud of you, Nyota. I am *so* proud."

"I will never forget you, Baba," I whispered back over the radio. "Never, never."

8

My vow is to ensure that you survive and thrive on the red sands. The only way that can occur is if every affinity is sheared away—yes, even the affinity you might share with the other athletes, so that one only remains, one kinship: the connection between you and the tyrannosaur. When only one connection is possible, it will burn hot as a sun, a bright and blazing thread, a line to grip and follow over the red sands, right up to victory, right up onto the steps of Liberty's shrine.

THE LESSONS OF MAI CHANGYING

THE MICROSTAR BLAZES, and across an ocean of cedar boughs, Liberty's torch kindles, fire made of glass. I drop down from branch to branch until my feet hit the mossy soil. I crouch a moment, my hands aching with tension. My nanites surge in my blood, millions of tiny boats on my current. My face is hot with anger. So many times I gazed dumbly into an empty cup, the tea washing away my memories as water washes away sand. Mai Changying. How could she do that to me. Take *that* from me. Take from me the warmth of Baba's arms and the sound of his voice and even the scent of his sea. But I remember now. I *remember.*

And I will make sure no one ever takes this from me again.

I check the egg first. I draw it into my lap and wrap my arms around it and warm it a while with my body, before burying it deep in leaves again.

Then to the pool, snatching a stick on the way that might serve for a spear. Ahead, a dozen chirping coelurosaurs, none of them taller than my waist, perch on the tyrannosaur corpse. They peck at it with their jaws, stripping its ribs of flesh, bite by tearing bite.

I don't bother them. Instead I move quickly along the forest floor, listening, watching the trails, my stick ready. I am learning this forest now, in ways I never did while training. I know now when something is watching me. I know when something is fleeing me. I know when something is hunting me. And I know now how to find things.

The ferns are cool and wet against my fingers as I brush them aside to get at a small, struggling berry bush. The earth is almost hot against my hands when I dig deep into a creek bank with the broken end of the stick, digging out a handful of dirt red as copper wire. Deeper in the forest, I find a compsognathid nest between the roots of a spruce, and I steal three eggs. That should be enough. Half an hour later and further in, the frantic, piercing chirps of grown compsognathids hurt my ears as the little, feathered creatures scatter at my charge, abandoning the half-gnawed ribs of some dead mammal that must have weighed a hundred kilos at least, but that no longer has a face or any way for me to identify what it was. But that is all right; I'm not interested in its identity, only its utility. I snap off the end of a rib and take it with me.

In the silence of my nest tree with that rib across my thigh and the egg quiet under its leaves near me, I devote an hour to whittling and honing the slender bone. I use a sharp flake of nickel that I found near the cliff, a chipped-off piece of the inner shell of this hollow world that encloses me like an egg.

When I am finished, I have in my hand a slender needle of bone and a bowl that I've improvised from a curved strip of bark. I use the bowl to mix red soil and egg yolk from the raided compsognathid nest, and juice from crushed berries. Red like copper. Red like my insides. The bowl and the needle: my oar and my whalespear. I lift the bone needle and it glints in the crack of dim light through the door of my tree. After a whispered prayer to the twin goddesses Liberty and Love, I begin piercing my skin. I clench my teeth against the sharp jabs of pain.

All my life aboard Europa Station, others' desires have been written on and into my body. Week by week, the nanites have shaped me for you, rewriting the genetic record that tells my body how to breathe, how to run, how to grow breasts. For years they have adapted my body to new perfection for the cameras—though what 'perfection' means is always changing, so that my breasts and belly and butt and thighs and the line of my jaw and the shape of my eyelids are always changing, too. They have worked inside me when I sleep and when I wake. I was their slave; they were yours. But you behind your thousand cameras, though you are made monstrous by your thousands of glass eyes, you cannot see me here. My breasts haven't shifted size or shape since I came here. Nor my thighs. Nor my lips. Except when threatened, except when running for my life, my body requiring a sudden metabolic inferno of hemoglobin and adrenaline, except for that, I change now almost as slowly as any of you do.

Now, with ink, with tattoo, *I* rewrite myself. Beginning this time at the *outside* of my body while the nanites do their work *inside*. My skin is the part of me I can reach. Just as the shuttle brought me inside this forest world through the asteroid's outer skin, so this bone needle enters through my skin. Giving me access to myself.

It takes a long time to make this new tattoo on the soft underside of my right arm. But I don't stop, even when throbbing fire spreads up and down my arm and my breath is hissing between my teeth. I trust my nanites to deal with any risk of infection and I use a few moist leaves to dab away the blood. Last night I didn't dare sleep, for fear of forgetting, for fear that Mai Changying would find me in my dreams and wrap my mind again in the cold weight of whatever spell she'd cast. I must never forget. I am not very literate—none of the athletes are—because we are for looking beautiful and running gracefully and inspiring the lust and worship of millions. We are not for going to Titan University. We are not for sitting by our father's bed when he is ill and reading him a story. That is not the life we have.

But that was the life I had once, the life I forgot. The life stolen from me. When I was six and in Baba's arms, he was teaching me to read a little primer; I read a few sentences from it to him, again and again during our last winter together, when he had the fishing-wind fever. And now, I tattoo the first two sentences he taught me to read—the only two I can remember clearly—into my skin.

Though making them hurts, these letters I ink into my right arm – *I am Nyota Madaki* – are more important than the jaguar tattoo on my breast. The letters I ink into my left arm – *Baba loves me* – are more important than my stats, my measurements, my ratings.

I may never get back to Europa Station. It has been days and days. Maybe Mai Changying will refuel the shuttle and turn it around to come get me—but if she means to do so, why did she leave me here in the first place? Maybe she is never coming back. I hope she is never coming back. Let Egret and Anaconda drink her tea. I don't want to ever taste it again.

That thought stops me with a sudden pang of guilt— and loss. Maybe the other girls are like me, with homes and fathers and memories stolen from them. I swallow against the tightness in my throat and work on inking the last letter into my arm. I can't worry about *them*. They have to find their own escapes. I dig the needle in deep, wincing. Blood wells up, then the nanites seal the wound.

I must never forget Baba again. I must never forget Titan and his boat on the sea. I must never again become Mai Changying's trained animal, prancing for her amusement, or for yours. I *am* Jaguar—I have become Jaguar over years of training and fierce competition—but I am not *only* Jaguar.

I am Nyota.

And whoever Nyota is going to be, *I* will decide that. Here. In this forest. Where there is no one else to watch me, no one to pressure me or shape me. I am alone here, and I am *me*. Finished, I snap the bone needle angrily in two and cast its shards to the ground. I pat the tyrannosaur egg once, then rise and stand at the entrance to our redwood, gazing out at all the pillars of the wood and the dim, green-filtered daylight and the far alders by the broken pool and the shadow of the dead tyrannosaur glimpsed through a break in the trees. I grip the bark near my head, the edge of the crack that permits entry into my tree, to steady my balance. I am breathing hard. It is evening now, I think, and my belly grumbles again. I can hear the wind stir a thousand branches high above us.

And now the aloneness hits me in a different way, and I choke back a sob. I think about the starlight on the seas of Titan, and the way the waves moved. The alien wind is audible but too far above me to touch my face, and the still forest air I breathe smells thickly of tyrannosaur musk and rot and cedar resin, but the sound of boughs tossing in the evening above is like the waves of that green and familiar sea. One small connection with home. It gives me comfort. I think, *That is the breath of my father's voice, my father's prayer. His prayer that I will be safe and free and fight for my future.*

A sound behind startles me. I turn and peer into the tree. Still breathing heavily, as though I've run and *run*. And so I have.

What was that sound?

A tap, so quiet I am not sure if I heard it or imagined it. I glance at the egg. My heart beats fast. Bending low, I press my ear to its surface. It is silent as a stone, and the shell is smooth and cool against my ear. Too cool. With a tickle of worry, I wrap myself around the egg, ignoring the soreness and fire in my arms. Sharing my warmth. After a moment, I draw leaves and moss over it, over us. I press my ear to it again, listening for another tap.

But nothing.

My heartbeat is loud.

"Are you in there?" I whisper.

The tiniest vibration in the egg. Am I really feeling it? Is it really there? A stirring like the universe has rolled over in its sleep, the little universe sleeping inside my egg. Did I imagine it?

My eyes are still moist. I caress the egg with my hands, wondering if the small life sleeping inside can feel that touch, the way I think I can feel its stirring. Wondering if some message can pass through that eggshell. Though I can pass no message through the shell of this hollow asteroid world to my father outside, maybe I can pass some message inside, into this little egg, and it can pass messages out to me, too.

"I've lost my Baba, and you've lost your Mama," I whisper to the egg. "I am sorry I couldn't help her. But I guess she is still here, too. I suppose she is inside me now, your Mama, like the nanites are. You have me, and both of us in me. You aren't lost. You aren't lost. I have you."

I talk softly to that hidden life for a while longer. The egg's smoothness against my belly and breasts as it warms is oddly calming. I rest my cheek against it, and before long I am napping.

* * *

When I wake the egg is as warm as I am, though still silent. I lay there with my cheek against its surface for a while, until the growl of my belly reminds me that if I do not eat, the nanites will exact a harsh penalty. My arms hurt, too, but lifting one and gazing at the letters, I smile. Those letters are good, and they are mine. The pain is mine, too, and I don't regret it.

Rising, I cover the egg carefully in soil and dead leaves and torn-up moss to prevent it from cooling too much. Then I stare at that pile where it is buried, aware of how small it is, how fragile. The thought strikes me, strange and sudden, that the egg of the Conservatory World around us is small too, and fragile, a pebble adrift in aeons of empty night. That frightens me, so I shove the thought back and hurry from my nest tree and find an alder with low-hanging boughs. I ascend, swift and agile as a howler monkey, into the high branches.

I spend most of this day and the next foraging, hunting, and exploring, leaping from treetop to treetop—the nanites toughening the soles of my feet and augmenting my balance as I land on each heavy bough—until I spot a patch of wild blackberries or a swollen moonburst of mushrooms beside a still pool. Then I slip quietly earthward, branch to branch, and drop lightly to the ground. I gather the food quickly, ears straining for any footstep or rustle of a body against ferns. Then back toward the sky. It is safer in the trees.

And from the trees, I can hunt. I finally catch a yi qi, leaping down on its nest from above. The tiny dinosaur has a rich, tangy taste when cooked that night.

From these boughs, I can watch, concealed, as the organisms that inhabit the Conservatory World pass between the thick boles below. On the second night, I see an ankylosaur, lumbering and heavy, its club of a tail lifted above the ground for balance, and following it, a small flock of juvenile ankylosaurs, smaller than me. Once, as I climb high after foraging berries, I see a pack of atrociraptors catch a snorting tapir at the foot of the very tree I am hiding in. They cut the mammal apart, their curved claws spilling its entrails wetly onto the moss. Even as the tapir still kicks and squeals, they bend over it, feeding. Their jaws red. With a chill in my blood, I climb as high as I can, until I fear the small branches will snap beneath my toes, just to be further away. A red howler monkey owns this treetop and it roars at me, but I swing the bo at it, striking it across the shoulder, hard. The animal spits at me and leaps to another tree, leaving me shaking with adrenaline and clinging to the slender top of this one.

After the raptors have moved on—I can hear them trilling contentedly to each other as they disappear into the deep fern—I descend to the middle of the cedar and feast on my handful of berries, until the juice runs down my chin and stains my hands and neck purple. It is near dusk, and I sit my back to the bole and rest, careful to keep my eyes open. It would be a long fall. Doubtless the nanites would repair me, but that would be a stupid risk. I don't need sleep now, anyway. I just need a few moments to breathe. In the dim light, I make out the letters I've tattooed on my arms. *I am Nyota Madaki. Baba loves me.* I breathe full and deep. This world may be fragile, a grain of sediment in an ocean of space, but it is beautiful too. And I may be fragile, but I am beautiful. My heart pumps blood throughout my body and I hear the roar of it. I sit just feeling my body *alive* and hot, and then I retreat swiftly through the branches toward my nest inside the redwood. The moist dark within is comforting, like being inside the womb. I spent some of the day gathering fresher, drier leaves, and now there are heaps of them inside the nest to keep me and the egg warm. I burrow into them, feeling their gentle brushes across my skin. I find the egg where I left it and draw it to me, cradling it in my arms beneath the leaves. It is warm now, softly warm, as though emitting its own heat, and I marvel at it. "Did you grow in there, while I was away?" I whisper. "Is that *your* heat, little one?"

In answer comes the quietest sound—a tap like a drop of water on a distant leaf. Except not distant. Quiet, so quiet—but right here.

I gasp.

9

Everything in the world wishes either to eat you or feed you. Standing naked under the violent gaze of the cameras, you can either be consumed or worshipped as a goddess. What will you choose? I am training you to appear edible—a delight and delicacy to millions—but I am not training you to be eaten.

THE LESSONS OF MAI CHANGYING

THIS TIME, I am certain I heard it.

A tap from *inside* the egg.

My heartbeat starts a tyrannosaur run. I crouch down by the egg, palms pressed to our bed of leaves and torn-up moss, my face near the shell. I listen. And listen.

"Are you hatching?" I whisper.

A second tap makes me jump, losing my balance, nearly falling over. There is a bubble high inside my breast, expanding, so that on the next inhale I might float right off the ground.

"You *are*," I breathe. "You're being *born*."

I sit back and make a space between my legs, and I pull the egg, larger than my head, into my lap, holding it between my two hands. A third tap. This time, I feel the vibration of it against my palms. I even *see* the egg quiver. I think. It is slight, but no, I am *sure* I saw it. I am alive with glee and I can't look away. The damp, interior walls of the redwood around us feel close and safe. I am breathless with the sense of sharing a secret. Here is something no other sister athlete has ever witnessed. Maybe something even Mai Changying has never seen with her own eyes.

In training, we always encountered the dinosaurs as fully grown bulls and does, monsters of tooth and feather and hide. But whatever comes out of this egg, feathered and soft, will be small enough for me to hold. I have sheltered this egg for so many nights, protected it, kept it warm with my own body, as though I am a doe tyrannosaur myself. As I listen to the tapping, tapping, tapping—quick now and unstopping—I quiver with the egg, trembling with a hot, possessive joy.

"That's right," I call to the baby bird through its shell. "That's it. Come out. Come on. Break the shell. Be born. I'm right here. Come see me. Come see me, little one. Come on. You can do it."

No lullabies for the dinosaur now. Instead I am urging it, calling to it, insisting it keep going, keep attacking the hard enclosure that keeps it from me. "Come on—come out."

And it does.

Snout first. A crack in the side of the egg, then a flake of the shell falls away and I can see its nostrils and its teeth, already sharp, already a tyrannosaur's. Cracks spiderweb across the rest of the egg, and I get my own nose right next to it and whisper, "I'm here, I'm here.

Come on. Come on!" My palms are sweating and my eyes must be shining. I feel like *I* am bursting out of an egg! "Come on!"

Then the egg falls apart, and the little tyrannosaur tumbles free of its curled-up confinement into my arms, with a faint musty smell. Its eyelids flicker back and its eyes are the palest blood hue. It lifts his head and screeches, a wet sound. It coughs up the fluid, then screeches again, clearer. And I want to clap my palms together for sheer joy but I don't dare move *because I am holding a tyrannosaur*. A tyrannosaur *far* smaller than any I have ever tried to ride. From nose to rump it is the length of my arm from elbow to fingertips, and it has a long tail held lifted behind it, giving it enough balance not to fall over. It gets its hind legs beneath it and shakes itself like an animal emerging from a swim. All its feathers tuft out, white as the doe's I killed. It is the most wondrous thing I have ever seen. Judging from what I can see between his legs, he is a little bull.

He blinks at me, screeches again. His head is absurdly large for his body, though maybe he'll grow to fit it. I wonder if human babies are like that too: all head and tiny body. I can't remember if I have ever seen a human baby. I must have as a child, sometime, right? *This* baby is standing already, though he wobbles. He cocks his head to the side like a bird to look at me, and I giggle. He makes a low cooing sound back, like a dove. I touch my lips, lost in wonder.

Suddenly the infant lunges at my face, startling a cry from me as I scramble back, heart pounding. Startled as well, he trips over his own toes and lands in a pile of leaves. He lies there half-curled, half-fetal, his eyes wide, his mouth opening and closing soundlessly, red inside and festooned with teeth larger than my fingernails.

"Shhh," I whisper. "Shhh."

Gently, I reach for the small tyrannosaur again, and his jaws snap near my fingers. I jerk my hand back. Getting his feet under him, he stands, steadier this time. He growls. Frustrated, I crouch back on my heels and consider him. If I had any meat here in the nest tree, or any of the berries left, I could maybe coax him toward me. Or maybe not the berries: this baby tyrannosaur probably needs something that smells of hot blood. Sucking in my breath at a sudden idea, I glance about quickly, find a jagged twig. Taking it up, I snap it in two. The break leaves me with a strong, sharp splinter of wood the length of my hand. The tyrannosaur flinches back at the snap, then watches me warily. I watch *him* warily, too. Clenching my teeth, I drive the stick into my arm, puncturing the skin, piercing myself. Blood wells up, warm and sticky on my skin, and after it, pain, but only for a moment. The nanites are quick.

I let the stick drink me for a moment, then remove it, extending it toward the small animal. "Come," I coo. "Come. Smell it. It's good."

His jaw opens. A small roar, deep and long. This little one has *breath*.

As the nanites close my wound, I take a crouching step closer. I reach the bloody end of the stick toward his jaws. The tyrannosaur doesn't retreat. His eye, watching me, is so wide and pale and—beautiful. And deep with memories not his own, genetic memories bequeathed him by his species, memories of hunting in the dark, of the bones of small mammals cracking in his jaws, of baths beneath a young moon that has never been seen in the sky of this world. That eye is moist, and not like a camera's eye. Suddenly, I want to be seen by *this* eye, seen as kind and gentle and good. I have never felt such a longing before.

Swallowing, I move the stick in slow, slow circles. "Come on," I whisper.

His nostrils flare. He stands very steadily now, every muscle taut, as alive as a quivering wire. I hold my breath. Then his small tongue licks at the end of the stick. "Ohh," I breathe. "My good tyrannosaur. Yes, eat. Eat."

When the stick is dry of blood, I stab myself with it again, wincing. And again. And a fourth time. Entranced by the sight of the tyrannosaur taking in his first meal. He licks the blood off with his tongue, faster. Then he bites the end of the stick, breaking it off with a sharp crack that makes me jump, then laugh. He closes his eyes and totters on his feet. For a moment I fear I've poisoned him somehow—is wood poisonous to tyrannosaurs?—but as I spring forward and catch him in my arms, I feel his small sides moving as he breathes and I realize the infant has simply fallen asleep.

I hold him, overcome with warmth and wonder. He is so small, yet so hot under his feathers, and those feathers are soft as one of Mai Changying's silk gowns. I used to sneak into her wardrobe in the tiny gap of time between mess and evening prayer, when I knew her outer quarters would be both unlocked and untended. I'd slip in and just run my hands over the fabric, because it was the softest thing I had ever touched. Like part of a world infinitely better than the one I knew, the one made of metal and cool, recycled air. For just a few heartbeats I could touch that better world. Then I'd have hurry out so I wouldn't be late to assemble with the others on the glass floor of the Glory Window to gaze down at Europa's frozen sea and sing our praises to Liberty and Love.

Now I touch that world again. I hold it in my arms. That world that is softer than the one where we compete and bleed and scream for the cameras. Swallowing, I pull the infant close and hold him against my breasts. He stirs, one of his tiny forepaws twitching, little claws grabbing at the air.

I can hardly breathe, he is so beautiful.

I tell him that, though he is asleep. His heartbeat is small and swift against my arm. The fragility of that heartbeat stirs me. Bending my head, I nuzzle my cheek into his feathers, and I start laughing, almost silently, but it just bubbles up in me. "My little tyrannosaur," I whisper. "My little tyrannosaur."

A memory comes to me of my grandmother singing me to sleep, Bibi's eyes green like a forest that goes on forever, her voice old and creaking and calm, a voice like trees and things made from trees, like the creaking limbs of the wooden dolls I had. I hum her tune now to the baby tyrannosaur, over and over again, until the infant is purring softly. I hold him close in my arms and after a while I dig up a few of Bibi's words again out of my memory, out of memories that are older than Mai Changying and older than Europa, memories that feel warmer now in my breast than all the cold days on the training station:

Lala mtoto lala,
mtoto lala, mtoto lala.

Mama anakuja, lala,
akupe maziwa, lala.

There may have been more words. I don't know. Since that is all I can recall, I just sing them softly to the tyrannosaur, until my voice is hoarse and the infant is still in my arms, his breathing as slow as a planet's. Each beat of his tiny heart against my breast.

Holding him, I feel as warm as the sun.

The dark is less heavy; dawn is flickering to life inside the microstar, far above us. Then a huff of breath warns me. Something is outside our tree, its feathered hide brushing the sodden bark.

I set the tyrannosaur down in the leaves beside me; he stirs but doesn't wake. Beneath my thrill of fear, a sudden determination to keep this small creature safe seizes me, hot and tight in my chest, fiercer than anything I have felt before, more driving than hate for the other girls or the need to win. I snatch up my most recent makeshift spear, my eyes wide in the dark, my ears straining for other hints of our visitor.

"Come on," I whisper. "Come and try it."

Another huff of breath, so quiet I don't think you or another human would hear it. But my nanite-enhanced ears do. From that small sound, I try to guess at the size of the creature. Little larger than I am, I think. Too big and too alone to be an atrociraptor. It might not even be a carnivore; it could be some juvenile hadrosaur separated from its herd and nosing its way around the tree in search of a place to hide. If so, there's no room for it here. I place myself between the crack in the tree and the softly wheezing, slumbering infant. In a battle crouch, I hold the spear ready.

Slowly, a darker shadow against the dark, a snout noses its way past the crack in my tree. Then the rest of the head, and I know this is no hadrosaur. A frill of feathers of no color I can see in the dark. And a three-clawed hand, each claw long as my entire arm, longer than its own head, curling like hooks around the edge of the entrance to my nest. I catch the glint of its eye. I don't know if it can see me, but it freezes, and I watch its eye move in the dark. Its nostrils flare; it *smells* us.

It's a therizinosaur, young, not fully grown, drawn perhaps by the smell of birth—or by the soft murmur of my lullaby. This species, like many, has been genetically altered for battle in the arena, adapted with heightened aggression, longer teeth, and an omnivorous rather than herbivorous diet, its long claws that were evolved for digging up deep roots changed now into war scythes. Three curved blades on each forepaw. My throat goes dry. If it tries to get in here, it might slice me into three sections faster than thought. In answer, the nanites set me on fire with adrenaline. I lift the spear. This is *my* nest and *my* tyrannosaur, and nothing is getting in here. With a cry to confuse the beast, I lunge, and the whittled end of spear stabs through feathers and flesh, shearing into its paw, pinning it to the bark.

At my cry, the infant tyrannosaur wakes, lurching unsteadily to his feet. The therizinosaur screeches like a wounded falcon, but so loud and piercing that my ears ring with pain, and my tyrannosaur screeches back, a high wail of terror and fury. My heart swells with pride in the little tyrannosaur bull, *my* bull. I wrench my spear free before the therizinosaur can rip it from my hands. The tyrannosaur stumbles at a run past my feet—he means to *attack* the therizinosaur!—and I bend and scoop him up in my arm. The monster's claws scythe past, above my head. Gripping the edge of my tree with its other paw—hear the wood strain and crack!—it thrusts its head, tufted with feathers and gleaming with teeth, into the tree. I dart beneath, clutching my infant to me. Out of the nest and into the open! But even as I duck beneath the therizinosaur's belly, it rips its head out from within the tree and one of its powerful hind legs comes up and catches me by the hip, flipping me onto my back on the ground. Releasing the tyrannosaur I shout, "Run, little one! Run!"

Then the therizinosaur bears down on me with the weight and strength of its leg, and its hind-claws dig into my hip, scoring flesh and muscle, and the pain is searing fire. The therizinosaur brings its head whipping about on its long neck to bite at me, but the nanites are a thunder of millions in my blood and I am screaming; dropping my spear, I grasp its foot with both hands and with the surge of strength my constituent machines give me, I break the bones of its foot. The beast rears back, and its weight is off me and I try to crawl free through the inferno of pain; my hip has been bruised or crushed—I can't get to my feet. The therizinosaur and I are both screaming.

A flash of white in the predawn dark, and my tyrannosaur *has leapt onto the beast's back*! A few hours ago he was a wobbling hatchling, but now, with my blood in his belly sustaining him, look at him *spring*! He growls as he bites down, getting a mouthful of feathers and a mouthful of hip, his jaws a trap that no living thing can break. The therizinosaur cranes its neck back, trying to bite at my baby, but my tyrannosaur clings to its rump like a bur and can neither be shaken off nor reached by the snapping, toothed beak. My heart beats with terror for the little thing. But I am swift, I am Jaguar. An instant's scrabbling of my fingers across the ground at my side, then I snatch up my spear and thrust upward. Screaming, the therizinosaur strikes at me, and the long blades of its foreclaws slice away the top half of my spear, the claw points whooshing through the air before my face. With a roar that echoes the battle-roar in my blood, I force myself to one knee and stab with the half of the spear I still hold, driving its sharp end up into the beast's face, into the soft vulnerability of its cheek. Blood runs down the wooden shaft like rain.

This is too much for our assailant. With a gurgling, anguished shriek, the creature staggers back, then turns and is gone in a thunder of paws against soil. The tyrannosaur lets go and tumbles from the therizinosaur's back, then runs, wobbling, back toward me, as I watch the therizinosaur disappear like a shadow of death between the giant trees. Wincing and clenching my teeth against the agony in my hip, I sweep the tyrannosaur into my arms and fall back on the earth, sobbing in shallow little gasps. The nanites are in my hip repairing bone and sinew, knitting me up like a torn coat, but it hurts, it *hurts*. "Block it," I whimper through clenched teeth, begging them. "Block the pain." That is what they do. That's what they're for. Block the pain, repair the wound.

The tyrannosaur snuggles in between my breasts and presses his boxy head up against the underside of my jaw.

His tiny paws dig into my skin and he coos, his head vibrating with the sound. I cling to him and he clings to me. When the pain finally dulls and I lay panting, I gasp, "Thank you, little tyrannosaur. Thank you." Shaking, I cry as he coos beneath my chin.

10

You can wound my body, and it is only blood and bone. But wound my home, and you have wounded my heart.

Shaka Madaki of Titan

THE BRUISE AT MY HIP darkens, then fades in a few hours, while the world brightens around us. I am sore, but I can walk again. Entire civilizations of nanites inside my cells are committed to knitting me up, strengthening me.

At first I feel such fatigue. Carrying the tyrannosaur in my arms, I limp back to the nest tree thinking again, I might die here. But then I find defiance in my heart, whether lit there by my nanites or by some flame that is my own. I *might* die, but I am Nyota Madaki, I am Jaguar, and I and a baby tyrannosaur just fended off one of the most vicious and well-armed predators this world can throw at us. I won't just *live* here. I will *thrive* here. This is *my* world, where I have found my memories and my name and a friend and ally, the first I have known since I was a child. Unlike my sisters back at Europa Station, the little tyrannosaur is not a competitor. Nor is he only a worshipper, like those of you behind your cameras. He is something else altogether. His eyes, gazing up at me as I carry him into our tree, are soft and liquid.

I set him down amid the leaves. He chirps a question at me, and I rub the top of his head with my fingers until I find a spot under his soft skin that makes him close his eyes and nearly purr with comfort. Then I inspect his body for injury, but he at least has passed through our combat unscathed. In the daylight streaming through the crack in our tree, I take a good look at my own hip. The bruise is gone, my skin as smooth as though I have never been so much as scratched. Yet I am sore, stiff, and I still clench my teeth when I move. I wince, but I press my palm to the place on my hip where the soreness is worst. "Thank you, nanites," I whisper.

Next I inspect the damage to our tree. There are great claw marks across bark and wood, and in two places the claws tore entirely through, letting in additional chinks of green daylight. I run my fingers over the injury to my redwood. Rage hot in my heart. This was my *home*. Ideas flash through me of barriers I might raise, a perimeter around the tree, a low wall or a line of objects that clatter when a predator tries to approach through them. Gourds, maybe, if there is a fruit tree somewhere in this forest. Or maybe shells? If I can find some small shelled creature. Or perhaps I can build a mesh of sticks and leaves across the door to our redwood, a gate woven too tight for a beast to thrust its head through, but with gaps just large enough for me to send a spear thrusting through at *it*. A fierce joy lights in my heart at that thought. Yes, you *try* to enter our home again, therizinosaur. It's a woman who lives here, not a maiasaur or a microceratus. I am smarter than you. You just try.

The little tyrannosaur hops about, practicing on its new legs, following me as I exit the tree and inspect the torn bark on the exterior. Pausing, I give him a look. "You're going to be hungry again soon, aren't you?"

He gazes back at me. And chirps.

"All right. Stay here. I'll catch you a hypsilophodont."

We fought together, without cameras but with victory. We *survived* together. Of course I'll hunt for him.

* * *

And I do—though at first it is difficult to persuade the tyrannosaur to wait for me in the nest tree. Perhaps, after the therizinosaur's attack, like me, he begins to fear that the redwood is not as safe as we had believed it. But I will *make* it safe. I will build that mesh to screen our door. Or maybe the little tyrannosaur simply doesn't want to be alone. He will need to learn how to be alone. I have had to learn that all my life. Even though before coming here I was watched at all hours—by Mai Changying, by my sister competitors, by you millions behind the eyes of the cameras—I have been *alone*.

Yet the look in his eyes each time he comes hopping after me melts something in my heart. I shoo him back, but he follows me again. At last, I set to making a short screen of brush across the door, anchoring it with sticks and binding it in place with the stiff, sap-filled fronds of the ferns around our tree. Then I lift my spear and flicker into the treetops above the pool, above the tall grasses filled with prey, above the compsognathid-gnawed hulk of the dead tyrannosaur, the doe picked nearly clean. Her ribs might make a fence later around our nest tree. Though maybe—maybe my little tyrannosaur would not like that.

I hear him now, trapped within the nest tree, keening for me, his high calls desperate and trilling. "I'm not leaving you," I whisper as I stretch myself out along a wide branch over the water, a jaguar ready. "You know I'm not."

But he doesn't. He's too far away to hear my whispers. Too young and too animal to understand if he did. He only knows that he's alone. Did I cry like that, when the master of revels and the armed girl gatherers who serve Liberty Goddess took me from my father's house? Did I cry like that, the first nights I lay in my bed in my cell on Europa station? Sudden yearning for Baba's voice, for the crackle of a radio, takes me the way a wave takes sand, washing away all control and poise, and ungracefully as a child, I weep where I lie on the branch.

"I am sorry, little tyrannosaur. I am sorry."

* * *

Once I stop shaking, I manage to catch something—not a juicy hypsilophodont, but a juvenile lambeosaur approaching the pool with several adults. I drop from above and take it through the neck with my spear; then I screech, as loudly as I can, to send the others stampeding away. The juvenile bleeding out at the edge of the water is small with a gorgeous scarlet crest above its head, but it is still too large to carry. I spend over an hour dragging it by its tail through the ferns, shouting at any compsognathids who hop close to try and steal a bite.

Near the nest tree, but not too near, I light a fire and cook some of the meat. My little tyrannosaur is hoarse from calling for me, yet I dare not go to see him until I have the meat kebab'd neatly on sticks, because I dare not leave such a tender catch untended. Once I have enough for a meal, *then* I leave it. That will be my tactic until I get defenses made for our tree: leave the remains of dinner out for the predators and scavengers, out just far enough that they will go feast on it and ignore us. Why shove your snout into a dark tree when there's juicy, fresh meat just sitting on the ground?

I smother the fire with damp ferns, then walk the last twenty meters to our tree, carrying the sticks of warm meat in my arms on a mat of several plucked fronds, cool green foliage to keep the meat from burning my skin. Clearing the brush out of the way, I duck inside, lay the meat on the carpet of dead leaves, and scoop the little tyrannosaur into my arms. He coos, shaking a little. "I am sorry," I tell him again, nuzzling the top of his head with my cheek. "But look, I brought food."

I lift one of the kebabs to his jaws. He's hungry enough; his powerful jaws snap off both meat and the end of the stick with it. I laugh and wait for him to swallow, then lift another for him. I cut a *lot* of chunks out of that lambeosaur, and we have more than enough for a good meal, even though he shocks me with how much of it he devours. And I thought *I* had the rapid metabolism.

After the meal, he sleeps so deeply that at first I fear he might stop breathing. But he is warm and soft in my arms. I stroke his white feathers with my fingers. He is beautiful. "Nyota loves you," I whisper. "Baba loves me." Reluctantly, I lay him down in the leaves and get up to replace the low screen of sticks and ferns across the door of our tree. Then I return and take him into my arms again and try to doze with him, for the exhaustion of the previous night is catching up with me, no matter how many nanites surge and swarm in my blood. Yet picking him up might have been a mistake. His eye opens and he yawns so wide it is like his face might crack in half. He coos, then bellows—a tiny little roar but deep, so that this close, it rumbles and reverberates in my bones. He runs and hops. He digs at the leaves with his hind feet and noses them about with his head, as though he is hunting a beetle. His foreclaws are small and he doesn't use them. I glance at my own toned arms and wonder what it would be like to hop about on just my feet. I tuck my hands in close to my body and wiggle my fingers in the air the way I see him doing when he is excited, and I imagine holding the spear in my teeth instead of my hands, and that sets me giggling. He looks at me in alarm, and I giggle harder. It feels good to giggle. Then I draw him near and rub the feathers above his eyes to make up for it. He likes that, makes a little rumbling noise in his throat when I do it.

The therizinosaur doesn't return tonight, though I hear, not too far off, smaller predators—raptors perhaps— screeching and clawing each other in their haste to devour the lambeosaur I left for them. This night and the nights that follow, my greatest concern is getting sleep. The tyrannosaur learns quickly to be quiet during the dark hours—or maybe that is instinct, not to attract anything hungry—but my little bull is restless, scratching at the leaves, moving about, waking me often. Sometimes while I doze, he butts his head against my belly playfully. At least, *he* thinks he is being playful. It is a good thing that my nanites heal bruises swiftly.

Sleepily, I tuck him in warmly against my body when he does this. I scratch his feathers. "Go to sleep, little tyrannosaur," I tell him. "Go to *sleep*. You can be nocturnal later."

11

When you gaze into the tyrannosaur's eye, you gaze in a mirror. What you see is instinct. What you see is intensity. The tyrannosaur mirrors that which is inside you that you have already tamed. That is your gift to the tyrannosaur: your grace, your elegance. The tyrannosaur's gift to you is its strength and speed. Together, you are like water through the dam: power perfectly channeled. That is how you delight the cameras and the crowd. That is how you delight Liberty goddess.

The Lessons of Mai Changying

THERE IS A RHYTHM to our lives now and it is a rhythm we have made together. No one has imposed it from outside. In the mornings, we sleep in our nest tree, recovering from our night's hunting. In my sleep, more memories come—snatches of conversations I had as a small girl with Mai Changying that the tea later tore from my mind. And earlier memories: the water lapping against the boat as I sang for my father. Many of my mornings now are spent gazing up, with my eyes closed, at Saturn filling our sky, its rings radiant above us. And there are memories of lying on my mattress in the loft, listening while Baba argued with other men and women who stood inside our house in damp fishing-coats, as if ready to leave at any moment. Yet they would argue half the night—or it seemed that way when I was little. Baba's voice in my memories is loud and powerful, and when he speaks, the others listen. My sleep is filled with his booming voice. And when I wake, I hear the rumbling my tyrannosaur makes in his chest, which is deep like Baba's voice. I press my ear and my hand to his feathered side and listen, and it comforts me.

Well before noon, I rise and open the heavy curtain of sticks and ferns I have made across our door, and I step out into the open space near our nest tree. That is a patch of earth about five meters by six with no trees growing in it except one lone sapling, a green shoot no higher than my hip. It's my training ground. I have cleared that ground of ferns and sorrel and needles, leaving just a square of soft earth and that sapling. Here I exercise each morning. Stretches. Then katas. Then the dance of the uboku and the isiquili, two sticks I have sharpened for use in the battle katas, one for defense and one for attack. Then the bo—I have made another of those, too. Mai Changying isn't here to assess my stats, and none of you can see me. But I do this each morning because my body feels good doing it, and because I must be skilled and strong and graceful and swift to survive, to hunt and to feed myself and my tyrannosaur. He lifts his head and hops, ungainly, from the nest to watch. He is the only spectator I need.

After my katas are done, I go to the pool and to the trickling fall down the cliff face, to drink. My tyrannosaur stays at my side and drinks also, dipping his snout deep into the water. I lift water in my cupped hands, always watchful. The ribs of the tyrannosaur doe stand in colossal ruin by the brink of the pool, but they do not trouble my young tyrannosaur, who doesn't know what they are. Nor do they trouble me; the tyrannosaur doe fed me. I have thought of using her bones for a fence, but I don't. And I have thought of burying her, but her ribs are strangely beautiful against their backdrop of green forest, and they look *right*.

Once, as we flick back through the grasses and ferns, we see two kentrosaurs canter to the pool's edge and duck their narrow snouts into the water. The tyrannosaur and I both stop and gaze through the brush at them in wonder. Their tails are a forest of blades, each spike longer than my arm, and another spike curves outward from the shoulder on each forelimb, blades longer than a meter and a half. Only a redwood forest would be great enough to contain these animals, which look bred for plains, not trees; here, the branches are too high to tangle the kentrosaurs' blades. I watch them drink, wondering if they are wives or sisters, wondering if I should hunt them. But the tyrannosaur and I have already fed well on heterodonts that we found splashing in the pool last night, and instead of leaping toward the kentrosaurs with my spear, I stand in the tall grasses with my hand on the tyrannosaur's feathered head, just watching. The kentrosaurs are lovely, and when they lift their snouts and trill, their voices are full of melody. When they leave to run through the trees, their tails rigid for balance, I remember how the sight of the graceful leviathans of this hollow world made me feel lonely, those first days and nights of my stay here. I do not feel lonely now. It has been long weeks since I have seen another human face, but I was lonely when I was surrounded by human faces. I press the tyrannosaur's head to my hip and tell him that I love him.

Each trip to that pool, I take a few pebbles from the water. At first, I keep these in a pile by the tree, just admiring their beauty. Before dawn, I pluck a fern frond and wet the stones with dew, bringing back for a few moments their color and wonder. One morning, an idea takes me and I start pressing the pebbles into the soil at the edge of my exercise glade, one at a time. I arrange them in patterns of Kartic script, making from memory the first hymn to Liberty. And when I have that done, after many days, I start pressing in the pebbles to make the script for the first hymn to Love, Liberty's sister. I haven't been taught to read, beyond the little in Baba's house, but these two hymns are emblazoned on the walls of each sleep cell in the training station and on the ceiling of every shuttle, and I know the shapes of these letters by heart.

Sometimes the little tyrannosaur sits by me and coos while I press the pebbles into the earth. I like that. I find his soft gaze makes me feel calmer. The eyes of the cameras and the eyes of my sister athletes never made me feel calm the way his eyes do.

* * *

The hours immediately preceding the late day-heat are for foraging, because though roots and tubers do not *fill* me—and the little tyrannosaur can't subsist on them at all—my body needs them still. The tyrannosaur usually naps in the tree while I search, trusting me to return now. There isn't much, except when Liberty and Love favor me and I find a bank of edible, moist mushrooms or a stand of wild raspberries. Once, as I'm gathering them up inside a bowl I've made from a gnarled tree root, something tickles the edge of my mind, just below hearing, and I glance up. Gasping, I duck low beneath the thorned bushes. A massive shape is passing through the trees, silent as a shadow.

A shadow with uncannily long foreclaws and a wedge-shaped head.

The therizinosaur. Larger now, grown fat on easier prey than us. Or else another therizinosaur like it, although they are territorial and vicious and I doubt there is another such hunter for many kilometers.

At first I fear it is heading toward our tree, but no, that is the opposite direction. Its head turns toward me but I don't think it sees or smells me, and after a few silent steps, its head turns away. I flush with shame. My tyrannosaur is braver than I; he, less than a day hatched, leaped onto that beast's back to tear at it with teeth the size of my fingertips. Yet the memory of that thing's hindclaws scoring and crushing my hip and of its foreclaws slicing my spear in two overtakes me, and I sit trembling like a rodent in a burrow, hardly daring to breathe or even *think*, until I am sure the therizinosaur is far away.

* * *

The hot hours are for sitting in the shade of the nest tree while my tyrannosaur sleeps, and making things. And then dusk—Dusk is for hunting. That is when larger beasts come to the pool to drink and smaller animals slip between the trees to catch tiny rodents or insects or to duck into egg nests abandoned by thirsty does. I have taught myself silence at last; I no longer send everything fleeing at a footstep.

At first, I intended to leave the little tyrannosaur behind at dark. But he is not an awkward hatchling any more, and he can travel in the night as silently as I. More silently. As quietly as that therizinosaur, quiet and alert as an animal whose ancestors have not forgotten how to hunt, not for sixty-five million years. The stillness that comes over him the moment before he pounces is eerie— as though he has turned to stone. He doesn't even breathe. Only his eyes flicker with movement and life. I thought he would be awful at hunting, and doubly awful because with no feathered mother, he would have only me to teach him. And a few short weeks ago, I was falling off a hypsilophodont's back into the pool, to be left soaked, hungry, and covered in leeches. Some trainer I'd be. It would be like Egret trying to teach *me* to mount and ride. I am not Mai Changying; I have never *trained* anyone.

Yet I needn't have feared. The first time my tyrannosaur saw herbivores at the pool, that alien stillness took him, as though something ancient inside him had wakened and told him these were food, as though he needed no parent, feathered or otherwise, not with millions of years of tyrannosaur secrets concealed in his DNA, waiting to be unlocked by the scent of prey.

Twice already he has flushed prey from the ferns, sending them hopping toward the sharp jab of my spear.

Once, recently, he even came padding toward me out of the dark with a tiny ceratopsian clutched in his jaws, its neck broken, a rabbit-sized thing I could have held cupped in my hands. We have enough to eat now, and in the early hours of night I make small fires, watching the darkness warily as I cook.

No, I needn't have feared. The tyrannosaur is teaching *me*. And he is stronger and more enduring than I have ever known a tyrannosaur could be, as if some drug courses hot through his system, driving him to running speeds and to powerful leaps that might astonish the adults of his kind.

Seeing what devastation he wreaks with his curved, tearing teeth, I return to the carcass of the tyrannosaur doe one night after the hunt. As my tyrannosaur watches curiously, I break one of the teeth out of the doe's jaws—which have now been picked clean of all flesh—and with tough, dried grasses I bind the tooth, as long as my hand, to the end of my spear. Better than whittled wood: a bone grown for just this kind of work, just this kind of hungry killing.

It does well enough.

Take that, unnamed, spear-making ancestor, jaguar-woman, cave-woman from time's dawn—whose laughter I earned crashing into the pool. Take that.

If I am very quiet, I can slip near enough to spear a meal, pouncing from out of the grasses rather than waiting in the branches above. With feathers plucked from a coelophysis, I decorate our hollow and even make a few skirts for myself: simple things but beautiful because they're mine: I made them.

I have so many memories now, in this world of sweat and heat and no poisoned tea. Each night, as the fire dies to coals, I wait a while before smothering the embers in soil. Sitting with my back to the fire and the forest an eternity of green dark before me, I listen to my tyrannosaur breathe in his sleep and I think about the memories.

Baba was important—*is* important—on Titan, I think, as Mai Changying is important on our spinning steel station. Not because people fear him, but because he and his family have fished there on Titan's sea since fish were put there. I remember other fishermen in their heavy coats and gloves, and spacers, men and women in mesh suits, coming to talk with my father. They'd sit at the table as he cleaned and gutted the fish we'd caught, and I'd watch through the cracks in the floor of my loft, peeking over the edge of my bed. Sometimes those visitors' eyes would darken with anger, sometimes not. But always they nodded, and I knew they meant to do as my father had said. Not from terror of nerve pain—like us girls who obey Mai Changying—but because they *respected* him. It shakes me, thinking of this. My tyrannosaur follows my voice and my lead, too, not because he fears me but because he trusts me. As I him. It is so strange—and so good.

I wonder if all the other girls, my competitors on the training station, had parents like that. Important fathers or mothers, ones other people trusted. Did that have anything to do with us being here? With why we, and no others, were selected and taken from our worlds to train and be honed and be beautiful and run the tyrannosaurs? Anger burns in me each time I remember my father's words from that furtive transmission in the shuttle, his fear for me—*I*

*would never make it back here with you—Nyota, never forget who
you are—*

I was *taken* from him, as he was taken from me.

After smothering the fire, I set my isiquili and my
uboku close at hand, within easy reach if anything assails
us in the night, and I curl in close to my tyrannosaur, who
is now nearly as big as I. My memories are mine again but
because the seas of Titan are far away across an ocean of
cold space, there is little comfort in them. So I seek
comfort from my tyrannosaur's warmth and his gentle,
slow breathing.

12

For the people downwell in Jupiter orbit, in all their gleaming, starlit cities, Liberty is just a word. A goddess not because she is holy but because she is far away and abstract and her name sounds pretty. For me, liberty would be a belly filled with smoked salmon and moonsea soup, and an afternoon laughing with my family before going out to fish. Liberty would be rowing out to sea while Saturn rises, without fear. Without worrying that my house may be rifled when I return, and my stores empty. Without fearing that the authorities will be there waiting to take my child. Liberty would be not sweating when the patrol stops my boat, not having to wonder if this is the night they will leave me bleeding out on the planks. Liberty would be going to sleep without a projectile weapon concealed in my bedding. These are liberties I want, which I can never have.

SHAKA MADAKI OF TITAN

I CAN'T BELIEVE HOW FAST he is growing. What seems only a few days ago, I could hold him in my arms. Now he is as heavy as I am, and his shoulder is high as my hip. The little cooing sounds he makes are more resonant, and now he also makes this long call like an elephant's, but as if underwater. The call burbles out for a minute or two, as though the little creature has no need of breath. There are notes in it, up and down the scale, and not all of Liberty's anthems ever sounded so sweet in my ears. His little throat swells out when he makes the call, and he tilts his head back, and at those moments he is especially beautiful.

We hunt together at dusk when animals come down to the water. He is so fast; I have started calling him Mkimbiaji, "runner." He is like me. Both of us thrill in the strength of our bodies; both of us push ourselves to go faster, leap farther. This evening, we take down a hypsilophodont together; my spear pierces it in the hip. As it tumbles, Mkimbiaji springs and seizes its throat in his powerful young jaws and breaks its neck.

I cook the meat afterward, though it is difficult to keep my tyrannosaur from devouring it before I can build a fire. After plucking the feathers, I try to tan the hide as best I can, remembering the deep-seal hides on my father's wall. I sleep in the hide for a few nights so that it will absorb oils from my skin. It is hot and uncomfortable, though soft. If I do this right, I can use the hide as a blanket or a cover for the door in our tree. But the reek from the hide worries me. I may need to try a few times.

How strange it is to think that inside my own body are the greatest feats of the Republic's nanotechnology, that I have been shaped, enhanced, honed as a tool by our most advanced science; yet here I live naked but for the grass-and-feather skirts I weave for myself, with a spear made from a stick, without cameras, without journalists, without the cry of the crowd; there is just the hunt, and singing before sleep, and the breathing of the small tyrannosaur curled against me, his head nestled between my breasts where it is warm. Almost I might think we are in another

universe altogether, one that has never known cities or
flyers or anything but young, proud animals hunting
together.

Mkimbiaji loves to bathe, splashing and rolling in the
pool like a crocodile, and I have put away my fear of the
water here to bathe with him. If there's no danger to my
tyrannosaur, hopefully there is none to me, though
afterward I must sit somewhere with a lot of light and
pluck off the fat leeches, which makes me shiver. Yet the
water is worth it: so clear and so cold, and swimming in it
with powerful strokes of my limbs I feel *clean* again. I miss
my perfumes, less for the scent than for the insect
repellent, but just being clean of dirt and grime and muck,
that is a beautiful thing itself. One of the best things. I
never knew how much I might value that. That is strange,
too: the thousand things I thought I'd never be without,
things I never valued before. And the two or three big
things that I never thought I'd have, that I didn't *know* to
value. The freedom to eat and sleep as I please, the
freedom to speak of whatever I wish, in low tones to my
tyrannosaur in the morning, without any fear of nerve pain
or other punishment.

Mai Changying, if she were here, would crave these
freedoms I have found. She would yearn to dry her own
tears against a tyrannosaur's feathers. But she would be
afraid, I think. She would call these freedoms frivolous,
would speak coldly of a life lived without purpose. I do
not feel like I am living a life without purpose. I roll my
shoulders back and breathe more deeply than I have ever
breathed before. No walls around me, no walls nearer than
the hull beneath my feet and the green sky kilometers

above. This hollow world is shaped like an egg; when I sleep tonight, I will rest deep in its warm yolk, I and my tyrannosaur with me. The void outside must be cold, but we don't know it. In here it's warm.

I breathe, I sing, I hunt, I and my tyrannosaur keep each other company, and maybe that is enough. I have been so surrounded with people for so long that now, bereft of others like myself, I do not feel lonely or lacking. It is a relief. I don't have to compete; I can just be. Though there is no one to see it. Maybe this is purpose enough.

I have lived someone else's purpose.

Possibly no purpose at all is better than living someone else's.

When Mkimbiaji is larger I will ride him, and I will need no hooks, no ropes. He will crouch low so that I can leap on his back. I will not fear his teeth or his hunger. And we will break through the trees of this conservatory world in furious thunder and we will make its stone hull shake as we run.

* * *

Night comes. Our bellies are both full from the fat ptarmigans he herded toward me. I speared them and roasted them, watched their flesh crack and ooze juices. I licked my fingers when I was done, and let Mkimbiaji lick mine, too. He was gentle, his breath washing warm across my hands: clean and good. Now his head is resting in my lap and I am stroking the feathers on his neck. For a while

I watch the branches of high cedars toss above us against a sky without stars. Sleepily, I listen to his breath lift and fall. His body is powerful, as mine is, though there are no nanites at work in him. Or are there? Is that the secret of this place? That there are nanites in the forests, in the animals, in the very skin and hull of this world, keeping everything strong and vital? Mkimbiaji's feathers shine with his health; they are lush and full and soft under my hand.

My fire is just coals now. I doubt it will draw anything to us. If other tyrannosaurs come we will run, as we have before, but nothing smaller will tangle with my Mkimbiaji. Look at him, warm and content, his belly full of bird. I touch my own belly, laughing silently to myself. Mai Changying would never have let me eat like this. Slender and toned for the cameras, for the eyes of millions, I needed to be. Now all I need to be is healthy, and happy. Resting my cheek against the top of his head, I watch the coals glow for a while. I *am* happy. I am home.

SOLASTALGIA

From Latin solacium + Greek stalgia.
Noun. "Yearning for home."
Distinct from nostalgia (yearning for the home you've left),
solastalgia involves yearning for the home that has left you. It is
your longing when you have not left your home but are still in
it; your home has been torn from you, destroyed around you, as
in ecological disaster. You see the devastation but cannot stop
it.

13

Long time ago, they killed a world. Mars had been made blue and beautiful, and they killed its seas and they killed its farms and they killed its people, so completely that Mars remains quarantined even now. And we have never forgotten, and we have rolled over on our backs like dogs and have never stood up again. Whatever they want, it is theirs. Our stores, our service, our children. We do not want any more dead worlds. But my friends, I wonder what our lives would be like if those with power were not the only ones to hold that weapon in their hands. I wonder what it would be like if they, too, could taste the copper of fear on their tongues.

SHAKA MADAKI OF TITAN

I SEE IT IN THE TREES first, the white rot. The bark cracks, and the pale fur creeps out from inside and begins to cover and choke the tree, as though I am gazing at a rotting fruit and not a cedar. I stare at it quite a while, unsettled. Nothing as majestic as a cedar should die that way.

After that I notice it in the small amphibians in the creek in the forest, in newts and salamanders long as my arm, their legs splitting open even as the trees are doing. A lacework of what looks like white hair covers their limbs, reaching tendrils up across the back. And later in the fish. I crouch for hours on a tree that has fallen across the creek, while Mkimbiaji bathes and cavorts downstream. I watch the fish, my unease growing, then sharpening into panic when I realize the log beneath me has split, too. I scramble away from the white fuzz. Leaping to my feet, I run nimbly down the long bole to the bank, whistling for Mkimbiaji, wanting him out of the water, away from whatever it is that is marring and killing all these other organisms.

He charges from the creek, water streaming from his feathers; the creek is still raining about his feet as he rushes up along the bank. He has grown fast, these past months; his shoulder now is higher than the top of my head. He charges toward me in that loping gait of his, and as I've done many times, I dance to the side, grasp the short, tough feathers at his neck, and spring to his back as he passes. His body is warm between my legs, his feathers soft against my arms and cheek, and I ride him back to our cliff, to a spot where a gentle slope of scree, held in place by a few powerful roots from trees at the brink, allows Mkimbiaji to carry me in a sliding run down to the lower land below.

We have lived many months in our hollow redwood, and my nanites have not faded; I can still run fast and far without collapsing to pant for air. I can still leap and spring, branch to branch, across kilometers of forest without exhaustion, though the metabolic toll requires a meal afterward that takes even Mkimbiaji aback. Mai Changying lied to me. My body is not as dependent on the resources of Europa station as I was told. Either the nanites *do* self-propagate, or else they are as long-lived as infinitesimal planets inside their cardiovascular galaxy.

What must it be like, to be a nanite? To live out a mechanical immortality in complete darkness, amending and mending and shaping the biological universe of which you are a part—but your microscopic toil is unseen by any camera, uncheered by any crowd. And your name and your numbers, your measurements, if you have any: no one knows them.

Or maybe the other nanites do.

Maybe there are entire cities inside me, entire worlds, earnest miniscule machines loving and warring and building without end, in societies known only to themselves. Maybe my liver, my stomach, my heart are worlds as self-contained as this conservatory world Mkimbiaji and I inhabit. I press a hand to my breast, trying to imagine the nearly infinite lives inside my finite body. And maybe somewhere inside me a solitary nanite has become separated from the rest, in some back vein that has little to do with enhancements to my strength or speed or allure, where no other nanites think to look for it. Maybe that lone nanite has discovered a mute companion in some red corpuscle or white cell, as I have in Mkimbiaji.

At an impulse, I dig my knees in and send Mkimbiaji loping past our tree to charge in a thunder of flesh and feathers though the redwoods, wisps of fog wet against my legs as we run. Unsettled by the rot in the trees, I don't want to get down from his back for a while.

* * *

After hunting each night, we hear the hooting of adult tyrannosaurs—the does. And sometimes the deep bay of a bull. Mkimbiaji is large enough now to fill the entire hollow within the cedar when he curls up to rest. I nestle into his feathers, dreading the day when he is too large for it. I suppose when that day comes, he'll claw out a scrape near the tree. Nothing you could call a burrow, but a nest scooped out of the earth.

And I'll help him.

His chest rises and falls beneath me as he sleeps, and the rocking motion of it brings me dreams of the sea, and a boat, and a father's hands both calloused and gentle.

14

I have heard it said: What you love is what you cannot bear to live without. That is a proverb of Empire, and so it is part true and mostly false. This is true: What you love is what you cannot bear to see hurt.

SHAKA MADAKI OF TITAN

THE ROT IS SPREADING. It has devoured the lichens that covered the stones by our pool; the rocks appear to have grown white fur instead. And it has begun to sprout from cracks in the roots and stones in the cliff, so that the waterfall trickles and spits through tufts of pale mold before feeding the pool. That is why we've taken to climbing the scree and returning through the forest to the creek where I first glimpsed Mkimbiaji's mother drinking. We go to the creek once in the morning, then run and play in the forest. Another drink at noon, then back to the tree to sleep before the evening search for meat. There are two sleeps, one in the afternoon and one in the late night after we've fed.

But tonight, at dusk, as the light empties from the forest like blood from a wound, I can't stir Mkimbiaji. His eyelids flick open, but he looks dazed, and he won't rise to his feet. I tell him sharply to get up. It's time to catch food. It's time to eat.

He doesn't rise.

I sit by him a while, watching him.

His breathing is normal. His feathers just as soft to the touch. He watches me but won't stand.

"Are you unwell? Or just lazy?" I scratch behind both his eyes, digging in with my fingers. He closes his eyes and rests his head heavily in the leaves.

"What's wrong?" I ask gently, trying to lift his head with my hands. He remains listless.

"All right." I swallow against a sudden tightness in my throat. "Fine, I'll go alone, then. Maybe I can find something too fast for a mere tyrannosaur to catch," I tease him.

He huffs out a breath.

Uneasy, I get to my feet and go to collect my hunting spear and my isiquili and uboku.

* * *

When I get back, I have a kulindadromeus slung over one shoulder, and I am sweating a little from carrying its weight. It is a small creature, but I've had to walk far. Now, as I flit through the trees and catch a glimpse of our redwood ahead, my pulse quickens and I know, somehow I know something is wrong. More wrong than before.

"Mkimbiaji?" I call.

Approaching, I hear him breathing within the tree, that slow breath that means sleep. Yet my heart beats quickly; the nanites send my pulse surging toward battle. I delay a moment at the entrance to our nest tree; glancing inside, I can see the rise and fall of Mkimbiaji's chest where he lies curled like a cat. I don't want to wake him. Also, I am afraid. And more afraid of discovering why.

I sling the kulindadromeus down to the leaves at the entrance, relieving myself of the burden, and I begin to circle our tree, slowly, looking at it, trying to understand what's bothering me, what the nanites are doing to me, sending such a cold flood of fear through my blood. I check the earth around our tree for pawprints. My nostrils flare, breathing in moldering leaves and soaked redwood bark and slow-rotting wood and the musk of my smell and Mkimbiaji's, sweat and skin and feathers. The memory of the therizinosaur's attack sends my blood pumping even faster, but other animals tend to avoid our nest tree now, because it is so heavy with the scent of tyrannosaur. Only a few bugs invade at times, confident they are too small for Mkimbiaji to catch.

There has been no predator here. There is no spoor.

So what is it?

What do I fear?

Straightening, I glance at the trees around us, shadow towers in the deepening dark. Tilting my head back, I can see little pieces of dark sky caught in the branches high above. The scents of the forest thicken at night, and I find them comforting. For a moment I lean against our redwood, resting my brow against the water-heavy bark, feeling the damp roughness of it against my skin. I don't close my eyes, but I rest, forcing my breathing to slow. "Quiet down, nanites," I whisper. "Quiet down. Let me think."

Under my breath, I recite from memory my measurements and the stats of my competitor sisters on Europa Station, from the last time our stats were thrown up on a wall in stark comparison. Liberty and Love alone know what my stats are now, but it doesn't matter. The act of reciting the numbers forces my mind into a patterned, calmer, routine place. I take a deep breath and lift my gaze.

And gasp.

There, inches from my cheek, in a deep canyon in the bark, is white fur, gleaming faintly in the dark.

A fuzz, a fungus, eating away at the tree, at *our* tree. Erupting from the bark like pus or some more malignant growth, with a faint reek of decay.

I lurch back, tripping and falling on my rear. I gaze up the long bole of the redwood in horror, as far up as I can see before the dark swallows the tree entirely. There are other bursts of white rot up there, more than a dozen pale infections

"No," I gasp. "No, no-no-no." Leaping to my feet, I approach the infected bark, where I had so nearly pressed my face moments before. I am cold all through my body, as though I have swallowed a river of ice. With a shiver, I reach for the white rot…and stop, my fingers almost but not quite touching the white fur on the bark. I tremble. It's here. At home. At our nest tree. It's here.

"Mkimbiaji!" My voice is pitched high and wavery.

I hear him stir within our nest, perhaps lifting his head. He snorts out a breath. I hurry to the entrance, feeling nanite-induced waves of adrenaline crash through me. I peer in. He is a heavy, male shadow inside the deeper shadow of our hollow. His eyes glint in the dark.

"Mkimbiaji?"

He gazes at me where I must be silhouetted against the night. I can hear him wheezing. He is *wheezing*.

Then his head falls, as though he can't hold it up, and the low whimper he makes tears a hole in my heart.

"You're ill." My voice quivers. "Oh gods, you're ill."

I step inside, forgetting the kulindadromeus, and join him, kneeling by his massive bulk that fills the tree. My hands can't stop shaking, yet I reach for him. Wiggling nearer, I lift his head and rest it in my lap. The heat of his breath on my arm. But now that I hold him, I can *feel* his labored breathing.

"Don't be sick." My heart is loud with panic. "Don't be sick, Mkimbiaji. Please."

Bending, I kiss the feathers above his eye.

"Please," I whisper.

He shifts his head to nuzzle my chest a moment, then wheezes and lies still, as though breathing is all he has strength for, and barely enough for that.

"Oh gods," I whisper, holding him and kissing the feathers on his head again, and again, and again. "Oh gods, oh gods, oh gods. What am I to do? What am I going to *do*?"

15

If we are to do this, we must master the heat and the fire and the sea-surge of our own bodies. We will be angry. We will be terrified. But we will stand outside our anger. We will stand outside our fear. These things will not master us.

SHAKA MADAKI OF TITAN

FERNS SLAP ACROSS MY thighs as I search, frantic, through the undergrowth. Mkimbiaji sleeps in the nest tree, and I *must* find something, anything that will help him. Herbs, I need herbs—like the ones my father knew, the ones that grew in the hills above our sea, bursting from seeds brought there a thousand years past by the first Earthsent. Herbs my father always called by name.

There are many herbs here in this night forest: small ones like needles; tiny tubers with green heads poking out of the dirt and hair of white petals; stones carpeted with miniscule violet leaves softer than Mkimbiaji's feathers. But I don't know what these are, which are poison, which are medicine, which are nothing at all. My heart leaps into panic and my nanites answer with surge after surge of adrenaline, until my feet are pounding the dirt and the cedars are a blur to either side, until I slip and fall crashing into moss and mud and slide screaming down a steep bank. The dirt cold against my skin. I slide into a dirty pool and lie half in the water. Yelling in rage, I beat the mud with the palms of my hands, screaming because my body is tossing in an arena-rush of adrenal fire and there is nothing else I can do.

Some time later, my voice hoarse and raw, I fall silent. I lie panting with my legs in the water, a prey to leeches, my insides a prey to my nanites. But the chemical fire has been slowing since I stopped moving. I am wet and cold with mud; one side of my face is caked with it. Mai Changying would be livid, if she were here. I can hear her voice in my mind: *Never let the cameras see you ungraceful. Never let them see you fall. Never let them see you less than beautiful.*

But there are no cameras here.

Lightheaded, I glance up at a blur of cedar boughs and green, distant, pre-dawn sky. Green. An entire green world. Not a bulkhead or a sheet of bioglass anywhere. Just plants, all those plants, and I know hardly any of them but *moss* and *blackberries* and *alder* and *redwood,* and alder and redwood would only be *tree* if I hadn't heard Mai Changying name them. This is my world and I don't know any of its names. I know how to run and I know how to ride and I know how to be beautiful. But none of that will save Mkimbiaji.

I lift my hands, seeing how they shake. Turning them, I can just glimpse, so faintly in the dark, the veins in my palms. In each of those veins, an invisible turbulence, a galaxy of silver motes. The nanites are rewriting my body, rendering me a creature of panic and adrenaline. I glance down my arms. The tattoos reassure me, dousing the panic, and now I am breathing again.

I am Nyota Madaki, the tattoo on my right arm reads.

I have written my name into my body.

Those nanites: I am not their slave. Not anymore. They are *mine*.

"Mkimbiaji needs me on my feet." I take a breath. "*I* need me on my feet. Get me on my feet, nanites."

Then I am standing.

Panting. A bit dizzy.

But my tears and my rage and my terror all are spent and past. In their place, a hot surge of exhilaration into my body, so that I want to shout.

These nanites are *mine*; I am not *theirs*.

I didn't know that until this instant. They are *mine*.

I am standing. I should be exhausted, my heart still pounding in terror, but I am standing.

And now that I am silent I can hear it, what I couldn't hear before. Now that my blood no longer thunders in my ears. The sound is distant but growing louder. A cracking, a breaking: like bones, hundreds of bones snapping, faster than any nanites could possibly repair. Hundreds of bodies shattering. Loud now, and louder, so loud and so near, a sound that, once started, must go on and *on*, breaking upon breaking, a sound nothing can stop, not ever.

"Let's climb," I whisper to a million machines that have no ears. Taking hold of the nearest cedar, I shimmy up the trunk, catch a low branch, and swing myself up. My climb is swift, my head steadying as I go, the nanites correcting the giddiness, soothing the adrenaline reaction. I will pay a steep price later for my fear and adrenal shock, and for a brief moment I burn with anger. "*I* will decide when to panic," I tell the colonies inside me. "I am not Mkimbiaji; I am not new-hatched. I am taking care of him, and of you, and of me, and *I* will decide when to panic."

Nearing the treetop, I edge out on a bough that bends beneath me but does not break. I am higher than the cliff, by far. And higher than many smaller trees. Gazing through a green haze of a few branches, I can see far over the forest. Out there, cedar tops toss and sway without any wind. A wide band of the forest, on our side of the cliff, is—withering.

Withering, and *writhing*. Like corpses dead two weeks, hollowed out by maggots that now swarm and squirm beneath veils of skin. The conifers out there are like that: as though what is left of their bark is pulsing and rippling from the expansion of the white rot inside. Dead— devoured entirely—yet still in motion, animated by living horrors within. Some simply sway like kelp in the sea, twisting and undulating as their bark flakes away. Others burst with sharp reports, cracking like dry kindling in a fire. White flecks—like spores, or like sparks above a furnace— dance and spin in the air over the dying trees. The nearest of the infected redwoods are little more than an hour's walk from where I watch.

Queasy, I hurry back to the ground, my mind awed, dropping the last few meters to land in a crouch. For a few steps, I walk. Then I break into a run. "Mkimbiaji," I gasp. "Mkimbiaji!"

* * *

He is weaker. I cook the kulindadromeus in a small firepit I carve in the ground not far from our tree. Not far, because I want to *hear* him breathe. Close, because I want the smell of sizzling meat to rouse him. The snapping of trees like brittle fingers echoes through the forest, the cracking sounds eerie in the dark. I find myself jumping at each report. Yet I keep stern control over my nanites. I don't need to panic while cooking meat.

Afterward, I carry bits of kulindadromeus, dripping with melted fat, to Mkimbiaji on the end of a stick, as I did when he was an infant. But he refuses to open his mouth, even when I prod his lips and nostrils with the meat. With a growl of frustration and fear, I set the stick down and try to pry his jaws open with my hands, but to no avail. He just lies there, his eye half open and glazed with pain, the blood hue of his irises paler than I remember.

"Eat," I beg him. "*Eat.*"

Another sharp crack in the forest.

"Don't you hear that?" I plead. "It's getting closer. We have to get you strong. We might have to get you *out* of here. I'm strong, but I can't carry you. You aren't a hatchling any more, Mkimbiaji." Tears sting my eyes. "You've gotten so damn big. Please eat."

But he just gazes up at me. I imagine there is love in his eyes. There is a yearning for comfort, too, for a release from pain and fatigue. I bite my lip to hold back whimpers, and I keep trying. He *has* to eat. I even lift the morsel to my own mouth and chew it until it is pulpy and then try pressing it between his lips. He takes one bite after much insistence, but I can't be sure if he has swallowed it or if he is holding it in his mouth, a lump of dead flesh cooling on his tongue. An image rises from the dark waters of memory like a mwezi from the deep, having been submerged not by Mai Changying's tea but by the pressure of passing time. My grandmother in bed, her fingers plucking listlessly at her blanket. And me, a tiny child carrying a small bowl of soup to her, one step at a time, taking such care not to spill any of it. The heat of the bowl against my fingers—enough for discomfort, not enough to scald. The panic as I lift the bowl to her lips and she still won't open her mouth. "Eat, Bibi, you have to eat. Eat, Bibi."

My eyes burn. "Please eat," I beg Mkimbiaji, bending low to kiss the feathers on the top of his head, and his leathery eyelid. "*Please* eat. You have to eat, Mkimbiaji. You have to."

* * *

The cracking is louder at dawn. I step outside, gaze up the bole of our redwood, and shiver when I see the bark, starting at two meters above the ground, nearly covered in white rot. Half in rage and half in nanite-adrenal surge, I take up my spear and hack at the bark above my head, trying to scrape away the rot, but though a few flakes of that white fungus feather down around me like snow, in the end all I achieve is snapping the end off my spear. I throw it aside in fury and stand there with clenched fists, gazing up at this horror that has infested our home, this thing that is killing Mkimbiaji, this thing that has no name.

Maybe it does have a name. Dim in the back of my mind, in those rooms once locked up by a drug in the tea,

I hear my father arguing with elders of New Ulundi in our house, while I listened from my bed.

"They wouldn't use that again," the mayor of New Ulundi, a woman with white hair, told my father. "They wouldn't dare."

"People who are afraid will dare anything." Baba mended a net while he talked. His hands were always busy, my father. "And these people, they are afraid at all times. They drink in fear with their water, they breathe in their fear, they excrete it when they take a shit. It is in their blood, that fear. They seize our children. They poison our seas. They unleash monsters from past ages to silence our voices under the thunder of their feet in orbital arenas. They *are* afraid, and that fear makes their actions extravagant. Who can say what they will or will not do?"

"But *jūn lèi*—" the woman protested.

Her half-whisper of those words, *jūn lèi*, made me shiver, as though she were naming a monster that devoured children, a monster so evil my father had never dared even mention it in my bedtime stories.

I asked him about it after the others went home, when he realized I was still awake and had been listening. Haltingly, he told me stories, tales that return to me this morning as I listen to the forest breaking. For a spacefaring civilization like ours, he said, living on scattered, terraformed habitats and worlds, a bioweapon that can unwrite entire ecosystems is cataclysmic: centuries of growth, of cultivation, of atmosphere management and hydration, wiped out with one injection of engineered, lethal fungi.

This rot in the green of my world. Is it *jūn lèi*? Is it the thing Baba spoke of when I was a little girl? How did it come here?

I suppose it doesn't matter what it is or why it's here. If Mkimbiaji were well, I'd flee with him, but he is too weak to stand. And where could we flee, if this white rot is already inside the trees? That withering in the forest is coming for us. Maybe it is already all around us, ready to close in like wildfire.

But I can't leave him.

Ducking back into our nest, I sit with him and hold his head in my lap, listening to him wheeze, and I want to scream my frustration at the forest, the earth, the daystar above, at Liberty and Love and Mai Changying and everyone out there, all of you in your shuttles and your space stations and your space colonies, all of you that don't know that we're here, that he's here, that he's—that he may be dying. All of you who don't even care.

* * *

"Don't die," I whisper after dusk, "don't die."

His breathing is faint, as shallow as Bibi's was when she lay dying in her bed, as Baba stood over her with a face grown hard and as I tried to spoon soup into her mouth.

All day I have stayed by Mkimbiaji, terrified to leave. Chunks of kulindadromeus lie in the leaves beside us, spoiling. Hunting is pointless. Searching for herbs I don't even know…is pointless. Everything is pointless.

I listen to him breathe, while I can.

Fury and futility wrestle in my heart like atrociraptors clawing each other over a meal, and the meal is me. Hours pass, and my heart doesn't recognize them or count them. My heart doesn't know how old the night is growing. Only that Mkimbiaji's breathing is barely even audible. That each shallow lift of his breast might be the last. His eye is so pale it is nearly white. His head is still warm in my hands, and I kiss his feathers sometimes, dreading that I might later feel his head cooling on my lap. That will break me. I sing him lullabies or whisper to him stories of my father. I tell him how Molalatladi used to burn in the sky above my father's boat. How Saturn rose with rings of ice. I tell him about the vast animals that swam in that sea. I tell him about my abduction and the years of fierce training on Europa Station. I tell him about Mai Changying's tea. "And if you die," I whisper, "all this is nothing. I might as well have stayed on Europa Station forever and forever, drinking tea and competing without name or memory. Being here, taking care of you, seeing you grow big, hunting in the redwoods—that's all I want to do. That's all I want to do, Mkimbiaji. I love you.

"Why won't you eat?" I cry.

A thought takes me, a memory of another time he hungered. My breath catches but hesitate only a moment. Gripping my spearhead, I gash open the back of my arm just below the elbow—slicing shallow but enough that it will bleed profusely. The pain fades quickly. Casting the spear aside, I bend low over Mkimbiaji's head, one hand under his jaw, tilting him until his jaw falls open. "Drink, Mkimbiaji," I whisper through my tears. "Drink. Please drink."

The blood comes hot from my wound, not lukewarm like the chunks of meat I've been bringing him. His nostrils flare, and the stab of hope in my heart is so sharp I can't breathe, and no nanites can do anything against the pain of it. I press my arm to his jaw, letting my life flow into his mouth. When I see him swallow at last, the quick movement of his throat, I gasp and tears of relief blur the world.

I cut myself a few more times during the night, as much as I dare, until I weaken almost to passing out. When he sleeps and his breathing is easier, I lie against his belly listening to it gurgle, my head cushioned in the soft feathers at his shoulder, and I watch the daystar brighten. Lifting my arms, I can see white, faded scars, already mostly healed. And turning my arms to see their undersides I can see the Kartic letters I tattooed there: *I am Nyota Madaki* and *Baba loves me*. I am Mkimbiaji's Baba, his Mama, his world. And he is mine. If he stopped breathing, I would too. What would I have to breathe *for?* The thought of being alone again sends fear lashing through me.

I move my head so that I can press my ear to him between his two small foreclaws, and I listen to him breathe. Slow, deep breathing, like ocean waves approaching and receding, the ebb and flow of air. I cry again for a while, then dry my face, rubbing it across his feathers.

Once, he was small and I held him in my hands against my heart. Now he is large, a warm hill, his feathers a blanket against my cheek, but he is just as fragile as he was then. Pressing my hand to my breast, the pumping of my own heart quick against my palm, I whisper: "Work quickly, nanites. Make more blood. Mkimbiaji will need more."

The thought of leaving him here to hunt chills me, though I know that I must eat if the nanites are to do what I have asked. Still, I clutch Mkimbiaji's long white feathers in my small hands and cling to him until the morning is old.

16

What is Empire? Empire cannot be tasted or touched. You cannot smell it or breathe it or fuck it. It is not a fleet or a capital or a person. It is a story that is only real as long as people keep telling it. So we are not attacking a fleet or a capital or people. We are attacking the story. We are attacking the symbols that roar and screech at the heart of that story. That is how we will uproot and destroy Empire.

SHAKA MADAKI OF TITAN

MKIMBIAJI REGAINS STRENGTH quickly, though while he's awake his breathing is often erratic. At last he hops to his feet in the evenings, wanting to hunt with me, but I refuse. "Stay," I beg him, "stay. Get strong." The look he gives me pulls at my heart.

I never go far, and so I bring back little. But it is enough. The first long nights, he will drink only from me, and so I hunt for myself, to keep from weakening as I carve ever more deeply and frequently into my body. The night that he eats a fresh-killed compsognathid from my hand, I give two quick sobs of relief and exhaustion, though now I am dry of tears. I hug him around his neck and whisper in his ear that tomorrow night I will find him *two* compsognathids. "You are so good," I whisper to him, "and I am so proud of you, Mkimbiaji."

Watching him bolt down the last mouthful of flesh, I marvel at the speed with which his young tyrannosaur body has leapt and lunged out of death back into life. I think of his hot blood pulsing somewhere under all those feathers, and his fast little heart. Heart like my heart, blood like my blood.

Like my…

I gasp.

* * *

Hour after hour sinks into the warm earth under my naked feet. Mkimbiaji sleeps beside me. Still a wheeze in his nostrils, but not as frail, not as *scary* as it was before.

All this time I've stared at my arms, at the faint lines where I opened myself for him. Where I fed him my blood.

Where I fed him my nanites.

As I think I must have done once before, when he first hatched. And a few hours after that, he showed such speed and ferocity and strength—leaping onto a therizinosaur's back, tearing into its hide with its teeth. And I marveled at him, the baby whose vitality matched his infant bravery. Now I know—when he leaped that night, an ecosystem of infinitesimal, semisentient enhancement devices leaped with him, carried inside the cells in his blood. Rendering him capable of feats that might break another creature, though at terrible metabolic cost.

And I wondered—naively, foolishly—at how ravenously he ate in the days that followed!

My poor tyrannosaur. What have I done to you?

"I saved him," I tell myself.

"I changed him," I weep.

"He and I are the same," I whisper.

He doesn't stir beside me, though a million microscopic machines toil inside him. I press my hand to his feathered belly, wondering if I will feel the rush and surge of them, or sense the tiny vibration of their labor. But I feel only the lift and fall of his breath.

* * *

The shattering of cedars cracks me from sleep. The microstar is just flickering to life outside and above. That snapping and breaking of boles is close. *Close.* My heart races as I leap to my feet. Mkimbiaji's eyes shine in the dark. His breathing is easier, deeper, and I almost moan in relief.

"Wait here," I tell him.

Swift as a jaguar, I climb up the side of our nest tree. Doing my best to avoid those fissures in the bark that are festering with white mold, I find handholds where I can until I reach the first branches. Soon I am high in the foliage, above the tops of other trees, and I gaze out over this morning world. The cracking of forest sounds closer now. And in a moment I see it. Along the bottom of the cliff, between our nest tree and the distant shadow of Liberty's statue, treetops are swaying and tossing without a wind. A green fog clings to those treetops, made up not of water droplets, I realize, but of debris: cedar needles and bits of bark and chippings of wood. I stare in horror as whatever unseen thing is chewing up the trees approaches, one cedar after another bursting in a thunder of wooden death, each one closer to our own nest. Closer to home. Coming *right at us*.

Shimmying back down our tree takes too long, with that sound of cracking and dying always in my ears, always in my heart, and I curse my nanites. I wish I could tell my body that I don't *want* it to burn with adrenaline and run and slide down riverbanks and break my bones and heal them after; I just want to be able to stop and think and *focus*. But I need them now as I never have: I need to move fast.

Dropping to the ground, I call Mkimbiaji from our undertree hollow. His steps are slow and the fever glaze is still in his eyes, but he is moving.

"Come on!" I cry. "We have to get away from here. We have to *go*."

I take hold of the long feathers at his shoulders and break into a slow run with him loping beside me, his breathing heavy. To resist the fresh adrenaline the nanites are giving me, I recite aloud the measurements of the other athletes, Egret and Hummingbird and Gazelle and all of them: breasts, waists, thighs, and all their scores from training. Numbers that defined the boundaries and constraints of my world for years. I start adding them, averaging them, running tables in my head as I used to do before each competition on the training station. The numbers steady me a little. The cracking behind us is nearer now. I am frightened to glance back, for fear I will see our own nest tree shatter in an explosion of wood and bark and white rot.

Beside me, Mkimbiaji begins coughing hoarsely in great explosions of white breath. But he keeps running, and I with him. "Faster," I gasp, tables flashing through my mind, "faster, Mkimbiaji, faster, please, run, run, I love you, I love you, run!"

He puts on speed, his powerful legs pumping, and his eyes clear a little. "I love you, run!" I keep panting, "I love you, run!" because he is following my voice, he is listening, he is not giving up because *I don't want him to.*

And the cracking, the terrible cracking, is so loud behind us and maybe it is all around us now—I can't tell— maybe the white violence and the withering will take us in another instant, but I am one of the ten or twelve finest athletes in the universe and he is a tyrannosaur, the most powerful running land animal that has ever, ever lived, and he and I, we can outrun anything. Now the adrenaline is overwhelming every number in my head but I have his feathers in my hand and I am not letting go, not ever, and I am running, *I am running*, the cedars a blur again, and he is running with me, he is charging. He is faster, even faster than I, though the nanites burn and crisp and die inside me to give me speed. I grip his feathers in my other hand too and spring to his back. Then I am on him, blood pulsing through my heart, pounding in my ears, and we are charging so fast! A glance to my left shows trees twisting and writhing and shriveling before my eyes; a glance to the right shows the same. The taint, the illness, is even in the ground beneath us, for I can see the mosses blackening beneath Mkimbiaji's feet. "Run, damn you, run! I love you, run!" I scream in his ear, and he is bearing me through the forest as though he is a battleship of flesh and sinew.

A scream like metal tearing itself apart. An answering shriek. Two other tyrannosaurs burst from the wood just ahead of us and to the right, and then we are beside them and we are all tearing through the forest in stampede. They are larger than Mkimbiaji, two massive does. They swerve to avoid larger trees, smash through smaller ones, and I duck low over Mkimbiaji's neck as one of the trees they wreck crashes to the ground beside us. Birds white and black screech overhead, fleeing with us. We leap over the crumpled, moaning bulk of a fallen eustreptospondylus, its feathers violet as the sea at dusk, but with white rot spilling—*blooming*—from a gash in its thigh. The whole world is coming apart, the air thick-scented with wood-dust and rot. Ten meters to our left, a herd of deer bound over fallen trunks; then the trees around them twist and the deer fall, mid-leap, to the ground. Their bodies twist and writhe and kick in terrible silence.

"Run," I pant, so over-drugged on adrenaline now that as I turn my head I seem to be moving dream-slow; only Mkimbiaji and the other tyrannosaurs and the cedars flashing by are fast. "*Run, Mkimbiaji!*"

Dizzied, I grip the thick feathers at his shoulders tightly. I will *not* faint, I will *not* fall. Fuck you, nanites. I duck again as one of the tyrannosaur does swerves and its tail swings above my head, tree-thick. Mkimbiaji screeches angrily and at a fresh sprint he overtakes the doe, who dwarfs him as a lion does a cat. He nips at the doe's hip as he passes. She doesn't bite back; her eyes are rolling in fear. Tuojiangosaurs trample bellowing out of the cedars behind us and to our right, their spiked tails whisking through the ferns. But we are soon far ahead of them and amid the cracking of the world I can hear their screams of terror, then nothing but the slaughter of the redwoods and the pumping, pumping of my heart. More deer burst from the trees before us and we run them down, the tyrannosaur doe to our right colliding with a yearling stag and crushing him beneath her clawed feet without slowing. Then they are behind us, food for whatever evil is eating the forest—and though trees sway and crack, we are still running. We are the wind, we are the wind. Trees are popping to the left and the right now and wood chips fly in the air. I am riding my tyrannosaur through fire that is without flame or heat, not under the eyes of cameras but under the eyes of thirty thousand women on thirty thousand days who will be my future selves, looking back at this moment in their memory. I don't care if I look graceful for them, and they don't care either; they don't care if I am sleek or reeking with sweat, all they care is that my tyrannosaur and I live, that our hearts go on beating from this day to the next. We are not here for their entertainment but for their survival. *Run*, they are crying with me now, *run, Nyota! Run, Mkimbiaji! Run! Run! Run!* That word, over and over, *run, run, run*, like a drum beating. Trees cracking and the doe we've passed collapsing suddenly on a snapped leg, a hoarse and almost silent screech, then convulsions in silence. I watch her over my shoulder, her dying and the whole forest thrashing like threshed wheat behind her, trees hundreds of meters tall bending like willows and rippling like water and then falling in explosions of sound that thicken the air with splinters and white dust.—I stare forward again, and everything in my body and mind has collapsed into the singularity of that one word, that one cry from my lips: "*Run!*"

And we do.

We pass the other doe, her jaw flecked with foam. Birds crash to the earth about us, owls and yi qi, missiles from the sky. One smacks the ground right beside us, another hits my shoulders, startling a cry from me, nearly knocking me off Mkimbiaji's back. It *hurts*, but my nanites rush to work, wiping the pain from bone and tissue.

"We are not going to die," I whisper in Mkimbiaji's ear, hearing him wheeze. But the nanites in *him* are at work too, and he is piling on speed as no genetically engineered tyrannosaur ever has. We run alone now, all other animals, predators and prey alike, fallen behind, eaten out of wood and world. Fungal growths, round like mushrooms but unfurling like the sprouts of trees, burst from the ground all around us and ahead of us, growing meters tall in mere instants, until we stampede through a forest of fungal spires. With unbearable noise and fury, a redwood crashes into the earth across our path, its leprous wood dissolving in white flakes. And I *scream* because we are about to slam into it!

Mkimbiaji doesn't even slow. He *crashes* into the side of the fallen giant and it is like diving through dry leaves, and then we are through, trailing decaying flakes of the dying tree. Mushroom towers rise, pale and quivering, from the crumbling ruin behind us. I am shaking.

"Don't you stop!" I gasp to my tyrannosaur, who is groaning with effort. "Don't you stop! Run, Mkimbiaji! You run! You RUN!"

He lowers his head as though to wedge his way through the infected air. I press my face to Mkimbiaji's feathers and stop my breath because the air is filled with white spores and I can feel the dry brush of them on my hair, on my arms and back. Madly I cling to Mkimbiaji and trust him and feel the roll and surge of him beneath my hips and then the lurch in my belly as he leaps some crack or crevice or river creek, and then we are *out*— He is thundering up a hard slope as though he finds it easier to run uphill than down, and the air is clear and my eyes fly open and I suck in oxygen like I am bursting from Titan's sea.

We are out of the redwoods and the brush here is thicker, and the trees are pine and spruce. We run upslope, racing that devouring fungus-evil toward the sky. A glance behind and I gasp, for the redwood forest is *gone*, a few last cracks and sharp reports beneath a smothering fog that is not moisture. The nest tree, if it still exists, is far behind. All of it is far behind. The patterns of stone I pressed into the soil, the mesh door and the extra skirts I made, the moist redwood in whose warmth we slept two hundred times, until its insides smelled thickly, pleasantly of Nyota and Mkimbiaji—gone.

All of it, dissolved in an ocean of white mold. Like memories in tea.

I press my face to Mkimbiaji's soft feathers. My hands clutch him more tightly, so that my sobs will not shake me from his back as he runs.

17

I breathe in the scent of the sea and I gaze on beauty, and I am glad to be alive. Tomorrow, we will decolonize our world. Tonight, I am decolonizing my heart.

SHAKA MADAKI OF TITAN

WHEN THE GROUND levels out at last, we find ourselves on a plateau covered in shoulder-high ferns and empty of trees. I ride Mkimbiaji the last few hundred meters to the plateau's abrupt edge, leaning down to tell him in his ear at every step that he is strong and good and that I am so, so proud of him. Flakes of *jūn lèi* that have clung to my hair and to Mkimbiaji's feathers fall away behind us like ash. My nanites roar inside me, and I hope his roar inside Mkimbiaji too; I hope they are doing whatever is necessary to keep our insides safe from the devouring rot.

From the edge of the world, I can see far out over the forest and up the green curvature toward the arch of the sky. But so little of it is green anymore. Our artificial planet does not look as it did before. Only Liberty, distant now but regal where she stands carved from the rock face of the asteroid itself, remains unchanged and solid, like an

irrevocable promise that the world will persist. Yet
everything beside her is ill. The white rot has devoured
entire kilometers of forest, expanses of cedar converted
into roiling billows of mold. I strain and search, and then I
know I am looking for the nest tree. But if anything but
fungus is intact in the fields of *jūn lèi*, I cannot see it. Days
ago, pressing my hand to the bark of my tree, I *feared*—but
I could not have dreamed of this: a forest where the trees
are replaced by the white growths that ate them, the
ghostly imitations of thousand-year-old conifers, a forest
of mapopobawa, in restless, constant movement as flakes
of death stir on the air.

Elsewhere, nearer Liberty statue, stands of true forest
remain, but with broad avenues of withered death running
through them. The white rot is beginning to bloom there,
too, the only thing still growing, as though the forest is the
world's skin and it has gone dry and has everywhere
cracked and bled out that lethal whiteness. My beautiful
forest. I feel its pain in my own body, like I am the one
cracking. I wonder what cosmetic could moisten this skin,
what nanites could ever heal this wound.

Movement catches my eye. A lone pterosaur soars just
above the waves of decay as though skimming the sea for
fish, and I watch the graceful swoop of its flight. It is far
away but I can make out, barely, the stripes and bands of
its pycnofiber plumage, white and black, a zebra of the sky
with its radiant pelt rippling in the wind. A creature that
feels no need to hide, a creature that wants the entire
world to see its glory. It's a quetzalcoatl, then. A preying
bird with a ten-meter wingspan and a beak longer than I
am tall. It glides above the desecration. Cedar-shaped

pillars of white dust crumble and dissolve at the passage of its wings. It flies high and fast as hope, and it alone is alive down there. I can hardly breathe for wonder.

Then the quetzalcoatl tilts to one side, veering brokenly. I gasp. For an instant it appears to right itself, like a boat surging up after a crushing wave. I stare intently, hardly daring to breathe. Then it crumples and topples from the sky. I cry out, and Mkimbiaji's head jerks up in alarm.

"No!"

The quetzalcoatl drops into the white rot like a stone into snow, vanishing from sight, a hope killed from the heart as completely as if it had never been there at all.

I sink back against Mkimbiaji's side and he warbles near my ear, but I can't answer. I am breathing in quick gasps, blinking quickly. I will *not* cry. Not yet. I must be steady, must *feel* steady, so the nanites don't think it is time to send me into another panic-rage. My face burns with humiliation at the memory of the last. This body belongs to me, not to a million microscopic machines; I must retain what control of it I can—if I am to keep Mkimbiaji safe. The nanites want me to win the race, to kiss Madame President and take the laurel and lift my breasts for the cameras, though I die of adrenaline shock and exhaustion the moment the cameras are gone. But that is not what *I* want: I want to live, and protect my tyrannosaur, and I want my *home*. I want my home to be green and safe and beautiful, and it isn't, it is dying, and there's nothing I can do.

I tap the side of my tyrannosaur's jaw gently, to turn him. "Come on, Mkimbiaji." I force the words past the tightening in my throat. "Let's go hunt up something to eat."

* * *

There isn't much, up here. No hypsilophodonts nosing their way through the ferns. No compsognathids chittering in the brush. Not even deer. Echoing over the high slope I do hear an eerie but familiar call, and I know the therizinosaur—or one like it—has survived the devouring rot, as we did. I shiver, but we fellow survivors have no interest in each other tonight.

Mkimbiaji flushes a marmot the size of my fist out of the ferns, and I let him have the meal. Being sick has made him thin. Squishing a wide swath of ferns flat, he lies on his side, breathing hard. I sit near him and smile faintly for him, encouraging him to eat. Yet when he does, the sound of Mkimbiaji's jaws crushing and snapping the marmot's bones reminds me horribly of the dying forest, that world-breaking-around-us sound. The horror of it clings to me like leeches, clammy and draining me. Not wanting to dismay my tyrannosaur, I lean in and scratch above his eyes as he dips his head for another mouthful—there really are only two bites. As he lifts his head, tossing back the last of the small creature, a yellow butterfly hardly larger than my thumbnail flickers between us. My gaze follows it. It flits higher, above the ferns, above *us*, the most delicate and fragile I have ever seen. And alive—still alive. Though antlered deer and tyrannosaurs and other animals either mighty or fast have crashed to the ground and convulsed and perished, that butterfly is still alive. Maybe a butterfly can survive where a quetzalcoatl cannot. Maybe a girl and her tyrannosaur can, too. I crane my head back to keep watching it.

"Keep flying," I whisper.

Then I look away, because the butterfly has become so tiny up there in the air, and my heart saddens as I remember flocks of thousands of such yellow butterflies dancing about the high branches like sparks above a fire.

This butterfly is not thousands. It is only one. Maybe it is the only butterfly left in the whole world.

Mkimbiaji rests his head on his bed of ferns, his eyes glazed. His chest moves slowly with his breathing, then tightens as he coughs. I watch him, troubled. He sleeps for long hours now, long hours in the day and long hours in the night. And our run has exhausted him. But the run has at least reminded his body that it is alive. I curl up between his legs and his lower jaw. I am tired, too. He rests his tiny forepaws on my left shoulder, then nuzzles my cheek with his, making that low cooing sound he does, and I melt.

"Mkimbiaji," I whisper, "keep *me* safe for a while?"

He huffs a breath, warm across my face.

I smile. Our home is gone, but he is so warm, and for a moment I feel…safe.

I close my eyes, and then, despite the empty pang in my belly, I sleep.

* * *

The lapping of water against my father's boat. The whisper of the nets sliding beneath the skin of the sea. His gloves dark against the oars. I cover his left hand with one of mine, or try to. My tiny and ungloved fingers are so small against his. I glance up at his eyes—as I would never dare with Mai Changying—and his wind-weathered skin crinkles as he grins.

"You *are* getting bigger, little star." His voice is deep. "One day you'll be taller than me, and your heart as big as the sea. When you have a heart that big, use it, Nyota. With a heart that big, you can hold the whole of our people. You can hold the whole sky."

"I'm holding a tyrannosaur," I tell him. Though I am a small child in my dream, my voice is intensely serious.

He throws back his head and laughs. "That, I did not expect, little star," he says, "but yes. With a heart that big, you can hold a tyrannosaur, too."

I have never thought of myself having a "big heart." Compassion is not a value drilled into us on the station in Europa's orbit. Compassion has no value on the red sands, in the rush and heat of tyrannosaur stampede. And yet, in my months on this forest world, I have learned it somehow. And finding in my dream that it is a value my father wished me to have—that makes me feel warm inside, and…large.

I fish with my father on Titan's icy sea all night. We catch a few akin fish. And once a great mwezi, blue and bioluminescent, swims beneath the boat with its wings spread wide as the sea; I gaze down open-mouthed as its passage rocks us. My father laughs then, too, and I remember that for all his passionate intensity, for all his fire, Baba often laughed. Tears burn my eyes because in my dream it occurs to me how much, how desperately, I have missed his laughter. Mkimbiaji laughs sometimes, a huffing cough so loud I have to clutch my head, and I try to tell Baba about this. And not once during the long hours after midnight do I let go of Baba's hand.

18

Waking to the reality of injustice is like the cracking of an eggshell. Your whole world had caged you and you didn't know it. Once the cage cracks open, you can never get back inside. You are out in the cold and the weather. You can encounter a hundred new dangers. But also, you are free. You can stretch. You can run. You can bite. You can see impossible skies that didn't exist while you were in the egg.

THE GANYMEDE PROVERBS,
FROM THE FORBIDDEN BOOK
OF THE BATTLE-PRIESTS

I JOLT AWAKE and lie gasping, covered in cold sweat. It is still night. Mkimbiaji is nudging me urgently with his snout.

Two sounds capture my ear. One is a distant hiss or whisper, strangely unnerving. The other is a low whine from Mkimbiaji. It sends my heart racing, because I have never heard him make that terror-sound before. I can see the whites of his eyes.

"What is it?" I whisper, immediately alert, reaching for my spear. "What's wrong?"

I rise to a crouch, the heft of my spear reassuring in my hand. Quick glances reveal no predator approaching through the ferns. Nor do I hear any sound of approaching breath or paw, only that distant, eerie whisper which sounds as though it is *above* us.

I gaze up at the green of forest hundreds of kilometers away, just in time to see that indistinct and distant forest rip apart. A breach in the world. A tear in the green sky reveals blazing stars flying from right to left as our hollow world spins rapidly in space to create gravity. A scream rips itself from my throat. The egg we live inside has cracked, and deep night waits outside; the whisper I've been hearing is the distant wind of escaping air. The panic-surge of nanites in my cells, and I can't think over the running of my heart. Only Mkimbiaji's warm, feathered side against my back grounds me, keeps me from bolting into a run, aimless through the night-wet ferns.

"Quiet, nanites," I breathe. "Be still, nanites."

Clammy with horror, I gaze up at the stars. A tickle of warm air across my arms and face as if all the atmosphere inside our world has been stirred to movement, all of it beginning to drift toward the pull of that crack in the sky. Another sound rises, the ocean-sough of tree branches. Mkimbiaji nudges me again, nearly knocking me over. Dropping my spear, I clasp his boxy head in my arms and rest my cheek against his feathers, hugging him hard. "It's all right," I whisper to him. "It's all right, Mkimbiaji."

His whine ceases, but he is breathing hard.

So am I.

I close my eyes a moment and breathe in the scent of his feathers. "I'm sorry," I tell him, and I don't know why. The nanite song is slowing in my blood. Maybe we are about to die.

When my eyes open again, I see the edges of the rip in the sky closing like a mouth, the breach repairing itself. Maybe there are nanites in the skin of this world after all, even as there are in my own skin and veins. Those far suns I glimpse in the narrowing gap are not like the cold, unblinking stars I last glimpsed from Mai Changying's shuttle bearing us here from Europa station. No, these are the stars of my childhood, and I had forgotten how beautiful they are. *These* stars shimmer and dance, seen through the rush of escaping atmosphere. They look *alive*. Somewhere out there among them is Titan, and Baba's house by the sea, my Baba. Maybe these stars only shimmer because my eyes are full of tears.

Before the gash closes, I glimpse other flashes of light out there in the dark. My eyes widen in wonder. Those flashes and quick flares of brighter light are not stars, but ships flickering in and out of real space, ships in battle. They have to be. Beautiful, like the stars: beautiful as everything is that is lethal.

Yet the sight of them kindles a rage-fire in my heart.

Those battleships. That's what has kept Mai Changying from returning for me. Those are what sealed me in this world-sized egg, until they cracked it open again tonight. And more than that, more than that… in their flaring light I glimpse the truth. The damage to my world, the mold and the rot and the crumbling of millennial cedars, the wheeze of Mkimbiaji's breath and the days when he could ingest nothing but my blood and the heat of my own life…that damage is a *sabotage*. A violence. The *jūn lèi* Baba talked about was a weapon. Someone attacked my home. Or maybe it was like a bullet missing its target, a byproduct of whatever war is waging out there. The anger in me is hotter than fever, scorching my heart and mind. Someone out there *did* this to us. Someone with a human face, though I have never seen them.

I stand, resting my hand on Mkimbiaji's head. He must be able to feel my anger for he quivers with an answering growl. Wind has risen and it whips at my face and at my lengthening but unlocked hair. Then the gap above us closes, taking away both stars and ships. The wind dies, the whisper and soughing with it. The stillness that follows is like the silence after a sob.

Yet I tremble. The nanites surge and rush in my blood, pouring on more heat, my body ready for attack. If those unseen aggressors were here, if those saboteurs were beside me, I could hurt them, I could *hurt* them. With my fingers I could tear them open as they have torn open my world. If I could only reach them. The heat of a sun inside me bakes me with its wrath, and I hold that fury tight, my eyes wet and my breathing short, and it is a long while before I tell the nanites to cool me down again.

* * *

Mkimbiaji and I walk through the midnight ferns. He wheezes a little, but walking is helping cool the nanite burn. My skin is no longer hot to the touch. I rest my arm on Mkimbiaji's shoulder as we walk. My breaths are shallow, and I can't help but imagine the air is thinner though my mind knows that our hollow world is vast and very little atmosphere could have bled out into space before its skin healed. And there are still green, unrotted forests high above us, creating oxygen even as we walk. A breeze stirs the ferns lightly.

My anger flickers out, replaced with fear, damp and cold. Fear that the battleships might cut open our world again. Fear of the unknown war, out there, a war I can't touch, fought by warriors I can neither defeat nor plead with. Outside in the deep dark, metal leviathans burn and crack, spilling air and bodies into space like blood into water. Lights flicker out and they drift silent and massive through the endless night, while others continue banking and veering and firing at each other.

Fear of that.

And fear for Mkimbiaji and that wheeze in his breath.

I swallow and relax my clenched hands. And then I let the fear go, as I did the anger. When it is gone, only sorrow is left behind, like footprints in soft earth. My Mkimbiaji. Still sick. Strong but still sick. His nanites fewer than mine and slower at their work, perhaps less knowledgeable about his DNA. He should be cavorting in the water, splashing and hooting, a joyous young god. Instead he labors to breathe.

"Oh, Mkimbiaji." I stroke the feathered ridge above his eye, and a rumble builds in his chest. Softly, I sing to him as we walk:

Lala mtoto lala,
mtoto lala, mtoto lala.
Mama anakuja, lala,
akupe maziwa, lala.

I sing it again, and again, *lala mtoto lala*, and while I do, my voice soft in the dark, I think. I have not been trained to think, I have been trained to fight, to run, to survive, to *act*. In the arena, survival requires speed. Here, survival requires thought.

I have to keep my tyrannosaur—and myself—safe. It won't be enough to just find another nest tree, for the *jūn lèi* will spread. And I cannot access the shuttles in their sleeping caverns beneath us, nor am I certain that I'd want to. The thought of returning to Mai Changying's world of tiny cells and cold metal and memory-obliterating tea... I can't go back to that world, I *can't*.

This is my home, even if it dies.

A yearning takes me to seize a shuttle—if I could only get to one—and pilot it instead to Titan, to my father's sea. But surely the armed men who abducted me and brought me as a child to Europa Station would come for me again. Or the battleships would burn me out of the sky before I ever reached that night sea of my childhood. And what of Mkimbiaji, my beautiful tyrannosaur? Could I take him aboard a shuttle? He would not even fit through the hatch.

This is my home. Even if it dies.

I am Nyota Madaki. Here, in this place, I will always remember that I am Nyota Madaki. That Baba loves me. That I love Mkimbiaji. Inside this green world, all of that stays true. Out there, with access to the transmissions that flit invisibly across the solar system faster than pterosaurs, my nanites would rewrite me, make me into what you want to see, all of you ghosts behind the cameras. Make me into what Mai Changying expects me to become.

Who I am here—what I am—Mai Changying has not made me this.

And yet.

The fury with which I've pursued my memories, my resourcefulness and speed when I fled the dying cedars with Mkimbiaji, and the nanites written into the cells of my blood—I have a jaguar's metabolism and strength and cunning. Did I have that on my father's boat, as a child? Gently, I touch the tattoo on my breast, the roaring cat. Did I choose it because of who Mai was making me, or was this part of me before the name, before the training, before the ink? Jaguar is a performance for cameras that don't even exist on this world, and yet I, I am Nyota and I am Jaguar too.

This tattoo is mine. The nanites are mine. I have written my own name into my skin, written my own memories back into the skin of my mind. Everything that is in me—no matter where it came from, from Baba's boat or Mai's steel station spinning in orbit—it is mine now. It is me. All of me is coming together here, even as all my home is coming apart.

* * *

Three oryctodromeids leap chirping from the ferns, disturbed at our approach. Surprising me, Mkimbiaji lunges and catches one, breaking its body in his powerful jaws. So we stop walking and though my belly growls I let him devour his prey. I must eat soon also, so that the metabolic fire of my nanites doesn't burn me to ash, but I worry for him.

I wait by him in the dark, until he has stripped the last meat and sinew from that tiny dinosaur. Stooping, I lift a slender oryctodromeus legbone in my hands and crack it open. Lifting it to my mouth, I suck at the marrow. It is warm in my mouth and throat, but there's so little of it. After a moment, I toss the bone aside.

"Let's go, Mkimbiaji." The nanite fire inside me is still. I know now where to go. In my heart, I've known since we first looked out across our dying home from this high plateau.

"We're going to go to Liberty," I tell him. "But we can't go straight there. Did you see, Mkimbiaji? The rot is between us and her. So. We have to get to Liberty the long way round."

I glance up at the distant glint of the darkened microstar and at the forest sky beyond it. The long way. We stand on the interior of an egg-shaped world. If we head away from the *jūn lèi* and away from the tall stone goddess, we will eventually reach her. I can light a small fire at her feet with moss and twigs, watch her black stone reflect the shimmer of flame, and sing a prayer to her. When we sang the Liberty Prayer each night before bed on Europa station, we did not do so as our ancestors did—in supplication—but because Mai Changying taught us that anything truly beautiful and graceful must be worshipped. As we ourselves must be, once we step out on the red sands of the arena.

Perhaps the goddess does not care about one small woman and one small tyrannosaur. She cares about the races in the dinodromes, the thunder of tyrannosaurs beneath the cameras. She cares about the women who dance for her and bleed for her to screams of adulation from her millions of worshippers. So when I reach her feet, alone except for Mkimbiaji, and sing a plea to her, a plea for liberty from illness for me and for Mkimbiaji and for our forest world, she may not listen.

But traveling to her will keep us moving, will give us something to do. Something other than grow more frightened with each hour. I give Mkimbiaji a quick nod of determination. He watches me with one moist eye. "That is what we're going to do, Mkimbiaji."

I start to walk, with him beside me and a dying forest crumbling on the breeze behind me and an entire green world ahead. His belly full, he lifts his head and roars, a deep call that echoes across the plateau, and my heart lifts at it, though my own belly aches with hunger. I press my hand to my abdomen.

"Make that hurt less, nanites," I murmur under my breath. "We have a long way to go."

19

You are a paradox. You try to escape the clawed grip of your ancestors—their violence, their beliefs, their urges. Yet at the same time you reach into the past with your own desperate fingers. You resurrect beasts—giants of tooth and horn and claw—because you both yearn for what is gone and you realize that what seems gone is not truly so. The past is not gone. Fight the chains of the past as you will, you cannot break them. You cannot be free until you realize the past is not a cage to shatter, but a part of you, bone and blood and sinew, that you must master and learn to use, lest it master you. You carry the past in your blood, shaping you and driving you, as one of Liberty's daughters carries nanites: the past is in you. So decide if you will use the past or be used by it.

THE GANYMEDE PROVERBS,
FROM THE FORBIDDEN BOOK
OF THE BATTLE-PRIESTS

THE DAYS OF OUR TRAVEL are long, and the sky does not tear open again. If battleships burn and scream in the silence of space, we hear no report of it. And the things we see, Mkimbiaji and I, are the last beauties of our dying world. A migration of red butterflies just above the treetops, like a red river in the air as we crane our necks back to watch. Half the day passes before they are gone, there are so many; they bring laughter to my heart. And after that, a long aisle of still-living trees, not cedars but short flowering trees white as Mkimbiaji's feathers with a blossom scent sweeter than love or air or clear water or *anything*. Mkimbiaji carries me on his back under their boughs, and a wind sends petals swirling about us. I have some in my hair the next morning.

Later, we find a cliff of smooth black stone hidden deep in the cedars and carved into a likeness of Love, serene-faced, full-wombed, with her arms held out to embrace. A river runs down each arm and spills between her fingers in eight perfect waterfalls. Precisely placed prisms split the water into rainbows, rainbows *everywhere*, and pterosaurs barely larger than my head wheel and screech in a riot of color, sometimes fighting for a perch or a mate, sometimes dipping to the pool between the goddess's feet for fish.

We bathe in that pool and I feel clean for the first time in weeks, my skin and his feathers washed in water and refracted light. There is a snake in the pool, her scaled body larger around than I, but she is coiled among the underwater weeds and she doesn't trouble us.

Mkimbiaji hides under the water, too—so long he terrifies me—and then lunges out, his powerful jaws snapping over the wing of a pterosaur gliding near the surface. He does that until we both have enough to eat. Making a small fire on the bank, I roast mine until the meat cracks open and juices run out and my mouth waters at the smell.

At first, we travel upriver to be sure of having water and meat along our way. That is how we find the wide mesa where dinosaurs I have never seen before except in vids cross in a herd, shaking the earth with their steps. Each is larger than a shuttle, with a vast, long neck but a tiny head I could cradle in my arms. They sway as they walk, like weeds in the pool we swam in. Their grace so moves me that I sing where I sit on Mkimbiaji's back. I sing every song I can remember. Then, because I can't remember many, I just sing whatever melody my heart makes, letting it come out in syllables that have forgotten the words they belonged to, or singing Mkimbiaji's name again and again, or my own. Both my names. *Nyota, Nyota, Jaguar Nyota, Mkimbiaji and Nyota and Mkimbiaji and me*, I sing.

The breeze shifts and the immense herd catches Mkimbiaji's scent and breaks into a run, and then the earth dances. I laugh and urge Mkimbiaji to a run, as well, and we chase the stampeding brachiosaurs over the mesa until they rush in a slide down a long slope to crash into the forest below, leaving my tyrannosaur and me in a world above where the air has turned into a wall of choking dust. Laughter gone, I hide my face in his feathers until I can breathe again. But my heart still grins. Everything here is bursting with life. On this world over a thousand years the dinosaurs have become more than bones, more than footprints and traces of the past, more than measurements and stats. They have become a living, breathing present, breath and skin and sinew, even as I have been resurrected here too from my charted and measured and daily death, my unlife on the training station where I existed only as a list of integers and decimals on Mai's charts.

In the evening as the microstar dims above us, we rest against the bole of one of the mighty redwoods below. Settling against Mkimbiaji, I glance up at the mesa and see another herd, triceratops, hundreds of them: the silhouettes of placid, horned giants in the fading light. Slow and silent along the edge of the world, nothing like the bellowing stampede of horn and muscle that I have seen in vids of the dinodromes.

In the morning we wake to the nasal blaring of gryposaurs, five of them all honking together as they lumber right by us. When I stir, they hasten away. Mkimbiaji watches them go with narrowed eyes, but it is day, and he doesn't leap to his feet and hunt them.

I ride him through woods different from those we've known. There are stands of redwood here but they are fewer: the forest is denser. There is oak and ash, and the branches are lower, so that I often have to duck low and hide my face against Mkimbiaji's feathered neck to avoid being scratched or knocked off his back. Late in the day the land begins to climb and we find a dead atrociraptor against the bole of an oak, decaying and uneaten. Holding my nanite-induced panic at bay, I slide from Mkimbiaji's back and approach. With my spear, I turn the raptor's body over, examining it in the dappled forest light for any glimpse of the pale fur. There is none. I take my time checking and rechecking, even ruffling the feathers one way, then the other with the spearhead to be sure. But no. I don't know what killed this raptor—perhaps something as simple as old age—but the white rot has not come here. Not yet. It may be gathering behind us like spores on a summer wind, but we are still ahead of it.

Reassured, we find a pool deep in the wood and drink, and as I gaze down at my reflection, my body lean and strong and tattooed and mine, I think of my naked and unnamed ancestor, maker of better spears and keeper of more knowledge about forests than I could ever hope to learn. I imagine her staring back at me from the other side of the water, the other side of time's mirror.

"Thanks," I whisper to her, though I don't know for what.

Surely she never traveled on any journey like this one. More recent ancestors have, like the Earthsent who first approached Titan across the empty kilometers, fleeing a home crumbling with rot in search of liberty and love and life.

That spear-wielding woman in forests long dead—she didn't know such journeys. Yet who first wrote our courage and agility and resourcefulness into our blood, into our DNA, if not her? Mai Changying, with her training and her nanites, *woke* the jaguar in me, perhaps, but the jaguar must have slept in my father too, and in the Earthsent before him, and in so many human beings before us. I think of that first ancestor gazing up in the darkness of night not at the microstar but at a moon lifting over the sea of trees, a moon smaller than Saturn over Titan's waves but maybe just as bright. I imagine that moon reflected, luminous and vocative, in her eyes. Who gave us the jaguar, if not her?

20

Show the camera your agility, your speed, your elegance, the flash of your eyes and the flash of your hip. Show them your desire and your triumph and your anger. But never your fear.

THE LESSONS OF MAI CHANGYING

THE SHUTTLE LIES GLEAMING and immense amid the alders, but ruptured metal and wires spill from it like entrails. Behind its shattered bulk, a gap in the forest—a road of cracked and blackened trees and a furrow in the soil—shows where it came down hard. It is a wounded and silent thing, yet I hold my breath. It is beautiful.

Beautiful also—and alarming—are the small figures who stand talking with each other outside the small, aluminum-roofed shelters that glint amid the trees all about the shuttle.

People.

There are people. Here. In my world.

Mkimbiaji is napping a few hundred meters behind me, in the den he dug hastily at the roots of an alder, a scrape in the earth just large enough for him to nestle into. I have been foraging while he sleeps, spear in hand, but a sound like voices brought me toeing further than I'd meant to go. Now I peer from behind a tree and watch, with chaos in my heart.

They have been here a while; the camp has a haggard look. I can see where they pried sheets of metal loose from the shuttle's hull to make those flimsy shelters. Maybe their shuttle crashed here the night the world tore open—maybe they fell out of the battle in orbit and dropped through the rip in the world and slammed into the trees, a spacecraft suddenly fragile as a falling butterfly. The ruined shuttle has two vast, unfeathered wings, as though it is a resting quetzalcoatl, but one of the wings is snapped, its end hanging, touching the ground, the metal framework exposed. Cylindrical, metal canisters are stacked against the hull behind the broken wing. The rest of the glade is littered with detritus: metal, discarded cables, emptied food trays. I wrinkle my nose. These men are slobs. Mai Changying would have them beaten.

That's perhaps the best evidence I have that this shuttle is not one of hers—as I hoped and feared when I first glimpsed it. These are not my sister athletes returning for me. I have no idea who these people are.

They are all men. Four of them, wearing black jumpsuits. One has a pagri wrapped around his head. One is gathering sticks at the other side of the camp—for a fire, maybe. Two are arguing in low tones. The other crouches beside one of the tents, fiddling with a small, spherical device. A burst of static fills the clearing, small in my ears—but the sound rivers through my body, until my nanites are a scream of activity and adrenaline and joy. A radio. It's a *radio*. It has to be!

I have to get to it.

I could radio offworld! I could send a message out. To Mai Changying. Or no, not to Mai. To Baba. I could radio *Baba!*

My nanites shriek for me to jump up, to run down to those tents, to lean over and swoop that radio up into my arms and keep running until I am lost in the trees on the other side, and I could, I *could*, I run faster than any but one or two other human beings in existence, but Mai Changying's voice is loud in my heart—*Use your brain first, girl, then your legs*—and why invite clamor and pursuit? I hunger for that radio and I *will* take it, but I will do the smart thing and wait for dark. For them to sleep. Then I can ride down there on Mkimbiaji's back and we will take it together.

I will wait for night.

Even as I decide this, the snap of a twig alerts me—it's *close*—and I turn in a flash.

"Don't move." A woman's voice.

I am already flipping into the air, aiming to land on my feet behind her, behind the spot her voice came from. But something slams into me, pressing the oxygen from my lungs. My limbs jerk and twitch and I try to scream, and the mossy forest floor comes up hard under me and *smacks* me in the face.

* * *

Cold metal at my back and a dry, metallic taste in my mouth. For a moment, my vision is blurred, then the nanites fix it. Dim shapes stand looming over me and I try to leap to my feet, but something holds me in place. Cords, plastic cables around my wrists and arms. My mind shocks awake: I am tied to the tip of the downed shuttle's snapped wing. Men stand over me. A quick chill of fear, but my grass skirt is still about my hips and I know I haven't been touched. But I've been shot. The bastards *shot* me. My fear douses itself in a forest fire of rage.

"She woke fast." The deep voice of one of the men.

"Goddess only knows what their blood gets pumped full of." This man crouches before me, resting his hands between his knees, and I see him clearly. A broken nose in a lean face, green eyes like bits of forest beneath the cliffs of his brow. Something nearly feverish in his look, an intensity that brings back a quick gasp of fear.

"I'm not going to hurt you." He speaks slowly, as I would to Mkimbiaji if he were upset. "You're tied because Lucas is afraid you will hurt us." He touches his fingers to his brow. "I'm Asafa."

I don't answer. As subtly as I can, I am testing the bonds on my wrists. And I am listening. The shuttle is surrounded by trees. There are four men, and one woman, white, with startling red hair. She stands sentinel on the nose of the shuttle above and behind me, with a firearm, her head turning slowly as she scans the alders. It must have been her voice I heard, and her shot that slammed me into sleep.

Asafa crouches before me, two of the other men stand looming over me, and the fourth sits some distance away over a cookpit beside one of the shelters, still crouched over that small, spherical device with wires and antennae sprouting from it like tendrils. My heart races. I can see it closer now. It *is* a radio. I know it is. Nanites surge in my blood. I have to get ot that radio!

Asafa must have noticed my eyes widen. "You will not be hurt," he repeats. "We just want to know where the others are, the other daughters of Liberty who are with you. And your trainer."

"Where's your shuttle?" That's one of the other men— a great bear of a man with a bald head. Like Asafa, he wears a torn flight jumpsuit.

The hunger in their eyes is naked. I have seen people gaze on me with hunger before—the hunger for blood, for entertainment, for sex. That's how you all look at me, you behind your cameras. But this is something else. They hunger for a way out, for survival, and I am either a means to it or I am in their way. I mustn't underestimate these men who believe themselves my captors. These marooned men are not nanite-enhanced daughters of the goddess. They are weak. Yet they are dangerous. They are desperate. They *shot* me.

Yet I laugh.

I can't help it.

The laughter bubbles up in me and it bursts until I am rocking back with it, peals of helpless amusement from my lips, as Asafa and the others look on aghast. The woman sentinel gazes down at me from the shuttle's nose with horror.

Months ago, I would have been just as desperate for a shuttle.

And they think I have one.

Of course they must.

Why else would a young woman be here, alone, in the

deep forest of this hollow world? Unless she were here with her trainer and Liberty's other sacrifices?

My laughter subsides into helpless giggles that quiver through my body until I can't breathe.

The man who stands over me and hasn't spoken yet—a wiry, older man with many scars on his face—rests his hand on the hilt of a meter-long kaskara hanging from his belt, and that sobers me. I turn my attention on him, gazing up at him cooly, no giggles left.

"It is *not* funny," he says quietly.

His kaskara looks sharp.

"We will all die here," he says. His Kartic is thickly accented, but we are permitted so few vids at Europa Station that I can't place it. Maybe he's from the mining colonies in the belt or from outsystem, the listening station on Charon. He looks fast.

"Zafir." Asafa's voice still carries that sooth-the-animal tone, maddeningly calm. I decide I don't like Asafa. I like Zafir and the Bear better. If one of them moves to strike me, I will know it. If Asafa wishes to hurt me, he would do it without his eyes changing.

"We said we weren't going to threaten her," Asafa chides.

"That was not a threat. We *are* going to die here. Her, too. You saw the *jūn lèi*. It has had weeks to spread. It might be here already." He cocks his head to the side. "So tell us where your shuttle is, girl. And you can get back to riding some tyrannosaur or triceratops out here, and you can forget you were ever tied and helpless." He shows his teeth.

"I'm not helpless." The first words I've spoken.

They all look at me. Asafa is the only one whose gaze drops below my face, but that stirs anger in my blood and I wish now that I had something to cover my breasts and not only my hips. Though I had needed no such covering until this moment. But it is a momentary discomfort. Most of my mind is consumed with hot fire at Zafir's mention of the *jūn lèi*. Is it really here? And do these men know who poisoned my home in the first place? Who were they fleeing when they fell through that crack in my world, long weeks ago? Do they know who poured white rot into our forest, who nearly killed Mkimbiaji?

And where is my tyrannosaur? Does he still sleep? The nanites sharpen my ears as I begin listening to the surrounding alders.

I swallow against the dry taste in my mouth. "Untie me, and we'll talk."

Asafa covers his mouth with his hand, hiding half his face, and I like him even less.

Zafir opens his mouth to speak, but swift footsteps interrupt him. The man at the radio—Lucas, perhaps—comes running up. I glance past him at the radio where it lies in the dead leaves and my whole being is concentrated down to one thought: I must get that radio. It looks like a small thing, but there must be a repeater somewhere on the exterior surface of our hollow world that will pick up the signal and throw it further, or the men in their shuttle wouldn't have brought it here with them. I can do it. I can get that radio. I can call Baba. At last. A thousand fears and desires chase themselves through my body. I could ask him to come get me. Or I could ask him to come here, to be with me and Mkimbiaji, where he will be safe forever from the people he feared, and from the people who took me.

Except we aren't safe, even here. Nowhere is *safe*. There is the *jūn lèi*. And other invaders.

"What is it, Lucas?" Asafa's tone is still casual, controlled, but his eyes flash with impatience.

"I can't reach Sasha."

"What do you mean, you can't reach Sasha?"

"I mean she isn't answering."

Asafa curses, using a phrase I haven't heard before. "Hand me that." He nearly snatches the radio from Lucas's hand.

"Be careful. It's the only one we didn't lose when we crashed! And it barely reaches the repeater as it is."

"You be careful." Asafa jabs keys on the side of the unit with his fingers. "Sasha, reply. This is Asafa. Reply. Now."

"You're supposed to say 'End' when you're done," Lucas ventures. His face is pale and his eyes watery. I can smell the fear on him.

They all stink of fear.

Asafa ignores him. "Sasha, reply. Reply." He casts a glance at Lucas. "End," he snaps.

The radio is silent.

"Try Jabali," Zafir mutters.

Lucas frowned. "He says he hasn't—"

"Jabali, this is Asafa. Reply. End."

"I already spoke to him—" Lucas is watching Asafa hold the radio with desperate intensity, as if terrified the man will drop it or crush it in anger.

The radio crackles. "Jabali here. End."

"Have you seen Sasha? End."

"No. Haven't *heard* from her either. Almost done with my circuit, about to head back. End."

"Can you make it around to where she was supposed to be? I don't like this. End."

"She's probably been eaten," I tell Asafa, calmly. "The forest is filled with predators. And they don't like invaders."

The look Asafa gives me is hot with hate. He passes the radio back to Lucas, who takes it in sweating hands, nearly dropping it. "Tell Jabali to go find the bitch."

I stiffen at the use of the word.

Asafa jabs a finger at me. I can almost hear the electric hiss of the violence coiled inside him like hot wire. "You. Where is your shuttle?"

"I'm wearing a grass skirt," I say coldly. "You think I have a shuttle?"

That gives them pause. All four look at me.

"Fuck," the Bear mutters.

"How long have you been here?" Zafir grips the hilt of his kaskara, as if for reassurance.

I don't answer.

"They can't have sent a shuttle in here," the Bear says slowly. "The battleships are still locked in, out there. It must be months since anything civilian has gotten through."

"Definitely nothing since we dropped the *jūn lèi*," Lucas whispers.

My flicker of rage blazes up in my blood. These men *did* infect my world. These men, and that redhaired sentinel. They killed the nest tree. They almost killed Mkimbiaji. It was *them*.

"All right, all of you, shut up." Asafa is losing his mask of calm. "She's here. She got in somehow. If she got in, we can get out."

Lucas steps back and lifts the radio, speaking quietly to the man Jabali who is out there, somewhere, in the trees. I ignore him. Asafa's eyes have become chips of ice, and I am watching him, my heart beating fast. He grabs my chin, and my insides burn with hate and adrenaline. I meet his gaze without flinching.

"Now. I want you to listen closely, little bitch," he says.

"Don't call me that—"

"I'll call you what I—"

"—and let *go* of my face." My voice is steel.

His eyes narrow. Does this man think to intimidate me, unnerve me? I have faced charging tyrannosaurs and have outraced *jūn lèi* on Mkimbiaji's back, and I will *not* be unnerved by this man.

His gaze drops to my breast. Flushing with anger, I realize he is staring at my tattoo. "You're Jaguar."

Zafir makes a sound low in his throat, but I keep my attention on Asafa.

He lifts his eyes. "One of Liberty's daughters. The Empire squanders a lot of money to make you. To make this entire hollow world. So. Jaguar. You will tell me who your trainer is, how you came here, and where—"

My spittle hits him right in the eye. He lurches back with a hiss, releasing my face. I wanted to bring my leg up and dislocate his jaw or break his nose with a good kick, but I don't want them to restrain me further before I am ready. But I can spit in his smug face.

He lifts a hand and I gasp as I realize he means to strike me. Then Lucas grabs his shoulder. "Asafa! Asafa!"

"*What?!*" He almost snarls as he turns.

"Jabali isn't answering now, either."

"Damn it, Lucas. *Get* him. Keep on it until he answers, and tell him to get *back* here. We'll go out in twos, as soon as we get some answers from this one."

The others haven't heard the furtive steps among the trees. The nanites have heightened my hearing, as they often do. These men are weak, meant to loll on their benches as spectators, watching my sisters and me compete on the sands. Except they have come down here into the arena, where they don't belong.

"I am Jaguar." My voice rings out, high and clear, cutting through their bickering. "You should not have killed my forest. And you should *not* have come here."

"Tell Jabali to get back here *now*," Asafa shouts, ignoring me.

But I will *not* be ignored.

Let's do this, nanites.

With a growl that becomes a scream of effort, I wrench my wrists apart, the nanites hardening the skin until I am almost more stone than flesh, and the cables that bind me break, snapping like threads trying to hold a mountain. Great welts gouged in my flesh that will quickly heal. I rip my hands free and I am *moving*! Before his eyes even show surprise, I kick the Bear hard in the jaw. His head snaps back. Fast as a blur, I whip the kaskara from Zafir's sheath and then I am running, running as only one of Liberty's daughters *can* run, as we are trained to run on the red sand, swift and graceful and dancing never in a straight line. With a cry, Asafa pulls his gun, but I flip over the wing of the shuttle, taking it for momentary cover. And I shout to the cautious one I've been hearing in the trees, the one who has taken Sasha and Jabali, who will help me take the rest.

"*Mkimbiaji!* NOW!"

21

Most of the things we think we know are not true. So the few that absolutely are—our love for those we are joined to, our enjoyment of beauty, our need to be better than we once were—these few truths are infinitely precious. Hold them close, and near the heart.

THE WAR MANUAL OF THE BATTLE-PRIESTS

HE COMES OUT OF THE ALDERS like thunder and death, his jaws red from the kill. And my tyrannosaur's roar shakes the world. A blaze of projectile fire just past his shoulder. That isn't Asafa; that's the sentinel woman, no longer standing on the shuttle's nose but down beside it, using the spacecraft itself for cover. My body a torchfire of fury, I leap back onto the wing and run up onto the shuttle, gunfire sparks following my feet, and I flip into the air. A glimpse of the shocked sentinel below me. I snatch her hair in my hand, pulling her off her feet as I land on mine, hurling her into the ferns. Her hair like flames about her face. She brings her firearm up but I lunge in, knocking it aside with my kaskara, and before I can think of what I am doing, on fire in the nanite surge of battle and survival, I take her neck in my left hand and crush it. I will remember the terror in her eyes later, and it will make me weep and I will see it in my nightmares maybe on every night of the world, but the adrenaline is hot in me and I can't stop for thought or regret or even breath. I am already flipping back over the nose of the shuttle, spinning in the air in Liberty's dance, taking in the clearing at a glance. Mkimbiaji is crouched over the Bear, tearing a jawful of red flesh out of his belly while the giant of a man waves his arms feebly. Lucas hides behind a shelter. Asafa is bringing his gun to bear on my tyrannosaur but I scream sharply and he turns, eyes wide as I land on my feet and blur into a run, right at him.

Someone tackles me from the side and we roll across the dirt, and cold metal—a knife—slits open my face, scraping along my jaw beneath my left ear. I scream again, trying to bring my knees up between us to buck Zafir off me, but he is wiry and strong and much larger than I am, and he *is* fast, and he twists with me. So I drive the heel of my hand into his shoulder and hear it *crack*. He falls back with a grunt and rolling onto my knees, I bring the kaskara whistling in an arc toward his belly. His knife catches it but my reach is longer and my blade slithers down his knife and shears through his wrist. Clutching the stump to his chest, pouring red over his robes, Zafir hunches over and runs for the trees, only to stumble to his knees, roaring in pain and weakness, after a few meters.

Even as he flees, another sharp report cracks the air, and I am up and running toward the shelters. Mkimbiaji has left the Bear's body and is stalking toward Asafa, his head bobbing, a gunfire wound seared across his hip.

Whatever blast stunned me earlier is not enough to stop a tyrannosaur, though I can tell that Mkimbiaji is dazed. Asafa nudges a dial on the gun with his thumb—maybe to increase the lethality of the shot. I have caught up with Mkimbiaji and I grasp his neck feathers with my left hand and leap to his back, the kaskara held out to my right, scattering drops of red like dying suns falling to the ground. A battle-scream with no words in it rips out of my throat and I kick my foot against Mkimbiaji's side and he bolts into a stampede run. Asafa gets off one last shot—it goes wild—and then he bolts, weaving between the shelters. We are after him, scattering blood in our wake, a screaming athlete with a blade and a tyrannosaur furious with pain. Mkimbiaji slams into a shelter with his full weight and momentum and it crumples like a dead leaf, and he pulls free of the wreckage with a roar. Asafa is darting behind another shelter just ahead.

Suddenly the air is cracking with quick thunder, and puncture wounds appear in the wall of the shelter ahead of us. I lean to the side and Mkimbiaji veers with me, getting another shelter between us and whatever rapid-fire weapon is trying to gun us down. Lucas. It must be the one named Lucas. The shots hit something inside the shelter, and it goes up in a pillar of flame, the heat singeing my eyebrows and cheek as we barrel past. Someone is screaming, not me. We dodge and weave and roar through the shelters, and now there are flames all around us. Then Lucas is ahead of us, standing on a mount with a long-barreled weapon between his hands. As he swivels it toward us, I hurl my kaskara, the blade whistling as it spins through the air. Lucas ducks it, and the blade flies past, and before he can recover himself or his gun we are on him, a half ton of ravenous tyrannosaur and a little less than sixty kilograms of furious woman. He screams once before Mkimbiaji's jaws close over his head. With a surge of his powerful neck, Mkimbiaji snaps the man's vertebrae and hurls him away limp through the air. We haven't broken our run; just ahead of us, my kaskara stands half-sheathed and quivering in the dirt. Clutching Mkimbiaji's neck feathers tightly in one hand, I lean out from his back and catch the hilt in my hand as we roar past. My battle-scream echoes through my whole body as we wheel around the outer rim of the tents in time to catch Asafa fleeing on foot toward the alders. He casts a wild glance back at us, and I remember how he meant to strike me, and how he ogled me, and what he called me, and my blood burns hot. I know my rage is a nanite-fueled inferno, but I let them have their run of my veins. Let them burn.

We catch him in another three leaps of Mkimbiaji's powerful hind legs, and my blade carves away the top of his head and drops him limp into the grass. We run and rage to the edge of the trees and then stop. A defiant roar from Mkimbiaji shakes the alders. I slide from his shoulders, panting, turning my back on the darkening wood and gazing at the flaming shelters, bright against the falling dusk, and the silent metal bird that is the downed shuttle. The kaskara's hilt is slick in my hand, and blood drips like red rain from its blade, staining the grass. My heart still thunders.

"Hush, nanites," I whisper now. "Hush, it's done."

Mkimbiaji roars again. Then closes his jaws and lowers his head, nudging my side, his pale red eyes reflecting the flames. I hug his neck hard, nuzzling his feathers with my cheek. "Thank you for not dying," I whisper fiercely. "For not letting them kill you."

For a time, I just hold him while the nanites in the field retreat back to their fortresses in my blood cells. I listen to Mkimbiaji's ragged breathing. To the roar and fury of fire. To the faint moans of a dying man, somewhere among the shelters. Then, chilling me, I glimpse, high in the air, the spores of *jūn lèi*, like pale jellyfish, nearly transparent but briefly visible, lit orange in the glow from the fires. In horror, I watch them drift until they are lost to sight beyond the tops of the nearest alders.

* * *

We find Zafir dying in the grass. Bleeding out. Standing over him, I bring the point of the kaskara to press against his throat. "I am Nyota Madaki." My voice is shaking. "I am Jaguar and I am Liberty's daughter and I am the daughter of an elder of New Ulundi on the shores of Titan's sea. Who is *your* trainer, Zafir? Who sent you here? Who did this to us?"

Zafir gazes up at me with a look so startled it takes me aback. Then he laughs, an appalled, desperate laugh that ends with him coughing up blood. "Never told us," he coughs, his eyes wild. "Never said which of the sacrifices to Liberty and Love used to be his child. I swear, he never said."

Foreboding chills me. "*Who?*" I scream.

"I am Zafir of the battle-priests," he wheezes, his lips, chin, and throat red from the blood. Gazing down at him in horror, I know some part of what he is going to say before he speaks it. "Of the destroyers of dinodromes, the breakers of Empire, the abolishers of the evil story. And my blade, young Nyota Madaki of Titan, is pledged to Shaka Madaki of Titan … elder of New Ulundi … by the shores of the winter sea."

He lies back, barely breathing, just the tiniest rasps now in his throat. The last of the nanite-fury inside me burns itself to ash and there is only cold. Like the cold outside our hollow world. Like the dry touch of *jūn lèi*. Like the emptiness left when memories and dreams are swept from your body.

I am still standing over him with the kaskara resting at his throat when Mkimbiaji comes and nudges my side. I bend numbly and close Zafir's eyes. Rising, I feel tears on my cheeks. Sheer reaction. I can't control it. I toss the kaskara aside into the leaves and lean hard against Mkimbiaji. A breeze kicks up. Dark smoke billows past us.

A numbness in my heart and a tightness in my throat. Baba, oh Baba. Elder of New Ulundi. Fishing on the winter sea, while I sing to him and great blue mwezi pass beneath our boat, larger than shuttles, like silent worlds unto themselves. Shaka Madaki. I know his name now. I know what he has done to my world.

Kill the dinosaurs, kill the Empire. Remove any reason for daughters of elders to be abducted and ripped from their memories and trained for life on the red sands. Wasn't that what he tried to say, what he meant to tell me, that time we talked over radio years ago? That one year soon "the Patriot Days would be done," and he would be there to sweep me into his arms? My passionate Baba, with his net and harpoon clutched in one hand and his other reaching to help me into the boat. Ready to slay any beast that might threaten his family. Ready to burn the solar system away if it might mean getting his daughter back. A tickle of pride in my breast and a trickle of despair.

My chest is so tight. Lifting my face from Mkimbiaji's feathers, I breathe in great gulps of air, though it is laced with smoke and it makes me cough. We live. We breathe. And—my eyes widen. The radio!

With Mkimbiaji limping beside me, I hurry back toward the shelters, trying to get to it. Baba. My Baba. He is only a broadcast away, his voice only an hour's time lag from my ears. Baba!

My emotions are a whirlwind inside me. I must tell him—tell him everything. About this place, about Mkimbiaji, about how one of his men looked at me and how another tried to kill me. About how I love him and hate him and how he has to stop trying to attack this world, because this hollow world is beautiful and it is my home and I am in it. And he doesn't know. I have to let him know.

Mkimbiaji warbles beside me and there is pain in it. We are at the shelters, and I glance about wildly at the invaders' scattered debris. A broken gun, the ruin of a tumbled shelter wall, scattered aluminum canisters and metal pots, and there it is. Adrenaline reaction hits hard and I sway like a redwood about to die. Staggering forward, I stumble to my knees by the radio, reaching for it with trembling hands. Bullet-punctures in a line across its surface. Smoke and the reek of melted plastic. I touch its cracked screen, urging it to crackle and spatter to life, but it is twisted, battle-burned, worse than I or Mkimbiaji, shattered and useless. My hands slam against the sphere, denting it, and my scream of rage and loss echoes through the forest.

22

My heart knows many silences. Silence at a death, silence at a river of red across the sky. Silence as I sleep against Mkimbiaji's side. Silence that comes with a smile, silence that comes in tears. Silence in a cup of tea. Silence at dusk, silence at dawn. Silence is the language of my heart. The language I am trying to learn.

NYOTA MADAKI

NIGHT FINDS ME perched on the dead shuttle's wing, with Mkimbiaji curled up beside me. I have dragged the bodies into the alders so that when atrociraptors or other scavengers come, they'll feed out there rather than hunting us in the camp. While I did, I observed the alders closely. Saw the telltales of white rot in the early stages, the eruptions from the bark high on the trees. Alder bark is ghost-white to begin with, so the slow contagion had escaped my notice before.

And these trees are dry to the touch—the moisture sucked from them by something alien and malevolent. They are still shaped like alders, still bear leaves like alders, but something inside is already at work, subtly as nanites, changing them into something else.

Similarly, pale seeds have sprouted inside my memories of my father, changing them also, revealing the warrior inside the fisherman from my dreams. Now, like these trees, a threat is hidden inside the harbor that is Baba, the harbor that wears Baba's shape.

Dusk came swiftly. Flames still waver and crack among the shelters, casting garish light against Mkimbiaji's face and mine. Earlier I retrieved my spear from where I dropped it when the red-haired woman shot me, and it is propped now against the side of the shuttle. I lean back against my tyrannosaur, gazing at the green dark above us and watching for spores sailing on quiet winds. I speak softly, telling Mkimbiaji about Baba, about his boat, about Molalatladi blazing in the sky and the phosphorescence blazing in answer on the surface of the waves. I eulogize my Baba, mourning him, though out there among the burning stars he still breathes. But his men in their gleaming ships might kill me and this world too, and never know it. And I don't think I will ever see him again.

Afterward for a while, leaning against the warm safety of Mkimbiaji's feathers, I stare at my arms. *I am Nyota Madaki. Baba loves me.*

At last, unease at the advancing *jūn lèi* that has already dried all these trees into tinder—as well as hunger and the relentless urgency it gives my nanites—compels me to my feet. "Rest if you want to," I tell Mkimbiaji, with a scratch for his head. He tilts his head to watch me with one large, liquid eye, and a deep warble in his throat. "I'll see what I can find us."

I run lightly out along the edge of the wing, then flip off it, spinning in the air to land on my feet at a run. I flit from one to the next of the shattered shelters, raiding them. I find a tiny portable light; the readout on its side blinks red, so it probably hasn't much power, but I take it and switch it on anyway, using its dim flicker to explore the camp. I find a canteen with water and another with something alcoholic—despite the reek I venture a taste, then spit it out in disgust. There are two jumpsuits, one with a hole burned in its side. Neither look like they'll fit me. There is a scarf and I tuck the handlight between my chin and shoulder and run the scarf through my fingers, in wonder. It's red, and it feels real. As real as Mkimbiaji's feathers. This was *woven*—from some animal. A gift from a spouse or a sibling or a grandparent, or maybe a hobby. I try to imagine any of the battle-priests spinning wool or weaving or dyeing this thing, and I can't. I wrap the scarf around my throat. It is warm—maybe too much so for this world. But it is lovely, and I will take it with me. Otherwise it will just be eaten away by insects or time. Nothing so lovely should perish like that.

In one of the shelters, there is a second radio and for an instant my heart thunders, but this one is more smashed than the first, with parts strewn beside it and a thin layer of dust on its top revealing that the battle-priests gave up their attempt at repair long before I found them. I kick the radio out of the shelter in frustration, and it clatters across the ground.

Several rectangular trays, cracked open, reveal pouches for food—but all of them are empty. The last shelter is a wreck, and with a nanite-surge of strength that burns my reserves dangerously low, I heave the fallen plastic to the side, finding little to salvage beneath it. There's a broken firearm. I already have Asafa's, but its charge is even more depleted than this handlight's. Maybe one shot left, maybe none. I probably won't take it with us. It's heavy.

Mkimbiaji watches me from the shuttle's wing, his eyes glinting in the dark. Off to our left in the trees I can hear the night-beasts cracking the invaders' bones for marrow.

All right, then. No food out here, and not much of use except a canteen to carry water in—*that* I like. So let me look inside that shuttle.

Ignoring the door—it's closed and reminds me too much of this hollow world's unforgiving airlock—I approach the rent in the shuttle's side, touching the warped and burnt metal with my fingers. Long cooled. My handlight sends an unsteady beam into the dark within, revealing rooms of colorless, austere metal. Tiny rooms torn open yet no less enclosing. Cells. Like mine on Europa station. I hesitate. But I have to go in. There could be things we need. And my belly's hunger has me shaking, so I can't delay either. Suppressing a shiver, I slip in through the crack in the hull.

At my first touch on an interior surface, lights come on, silent and soft. I gasp. I can't tell where the light is coming from—it's just there, evenly distributed, and I can see the inside of the cell clearly. A sleeping cell—like mine, though the cell is tipped on its side, with the end of the bunk jutting down at me out of the ceiling. I set the handlight down carefully and step inside. My breathing is loud in the metal cell, and it is strangely chill in here. I am suddenly glad of my new scarf.

I jump and grasp the handle of the metal underframe of the bunk and draw myself up to reach the curving interior wall that is now a ceiling. There's a round door there, and also a shallow container set in the gleaming surface. It is palm-locked. A few slaps fail to open it. With a growl to my nanites, I hold my left hand rigid, fingertips pointed at the container. A count of four as the nanites harden my fingers, then I drive my hand forward, puncturing the metallic surface. Hissing with pain, I curl my fingers and rip a handful of metal toward me.

The container is small. I glimpse a few personal effects—a necklace, a silver disc that is probably a library, and another rolled up jumpsuit. I yank it free and unroll it. It's the sentry woman's; it might fit better, or it might not. I toss it to the ground below. Disappointment gnaws at me. I suppose no one on a shuttle carries food packets inside a container by their bed.

The cell's door is unlocked, and I shimmy up through it into the narrow corridors of the ship, though I have to fight to breathe normally. Having ridden with Mkimbiaji across open plateaus, I will never again feel welcome or safe in a tight, metal space. Yet I search the shuttle, cell after cell. There is a little circular room like a mess with an appliance that might be meant for cooking and a few tools, but the invaders have long since raided it of any consumables. In the space behind the mess is a long closet containing synthetic blankets and several small, closed trays that when opened reveal an assortment of bandages, injectors, and small vials. Medical supplies. I tuck several of the trays under my arm. There is no food, but I find several large cylindrical tanks in the back and trace their smooth surface with my fingertips, in wonder. I can't read all the words on them, but I recognize the symbol for oxygen. Air. Cylinders of air, on a hollow world that makes its own. And these others, dark and stacked tightly in a harness beneath the oxygen cylinders, these are *fuel*. Combustible fuel. The cylinders outside, stacked against the shuttle behind the broken wing, are identical to these. I know now what they are. The invaders must have dragged them out and been tapping them for fuel since the crash— for lighting cookfires easily or for powering small appliances.

Abruptly, the lights go out. I scream, startled, and drop into a fighting stance, my eyes wide in the dark. The medical trays clattering to my feet. My heart pounds and my hands go sweaty. But there is no footstep, no breath but mine. Just a distant whimper somewhere outside— Mkimbiaji reacting to my cry.

A stab of shame at my momentary clumsiness, then a furious reminder to myself that there are no cameras here and even if there are, I am crouching in complete dark. I gather up the trays quickly, making too much noise, then squirm my way back through the narrow corridors of the shuttle, trembling at the snugness of metal all around me. I want out. Oh goddesses, I want *out*.

By the time I drop through the door of the little cell, I am shaking, my hands clenched so tightly around my few finds that my fingers hurt. I leap through the gap in the shuttle wall, land on my feet, intensely grateful for the open air around my body.

"Mkimbiaji!"

My tyrannosaur leaps from the wing to the trampled ground and comes to me in rush of feathers. I run to him, too, and hug his neck, rejoicing in his warmth. He roars a challenge at the gleaming metal of the broken ship.

"Nothing's following me," I whisper to him. "Nothing wants to hurt me. It's all right. I was just scared when the lights went out."

The growl in his throat vibrates beneath my arms, and I squeeze him tightly.

"No, I don't like this place either. Let's go."

I take a deep breath, straighten. Annoyed with myself now. I didn't find food, which is what I most hoped for. Though we will be glad of the medtrays. I cast an angry glance at the shuttle, at the soot-darkened shelters, at the fuel cylinders stacked against the hull, at the mounted gun where it sits neglected now like the carcass of a slain beast. These invaders could have at least brought me food and a working radio. All they brought was a few minutes of battle and the long weeks of rot and infection.

So be it. We'll hunt, then. But I want to do one other thing first.

* * *

We take the time to be thorough. Mkimbiaji and I gather sticks, fallen branches—all so weirdly dry—from the eaves of the forest. At first my tyrannosaur watches me in confusion as I gather armfuls and make piles of kindling between the roots of trees. Silent and grim as I work. Then he tries to take up twigs in his mouth to help, and I stare at him, startled, having never considered those powerful jaws as a *carrying* device before. But I make him stop. Who knows what festers inside these branches?

When I am done, I ride him back to the shuttle and we nudge one of the great fuel canisters away from the wing, separating it from its companion barrels still stacked against the hull. Mkimbiaji rolls the canister along the bumpy ground with firm pushes from the top of his head, and I watch its roll, checking its speed with the butt of my spear, until we bring it to rest against the merged trunk of three alders that have grown into each other like lovers who share too many memories now to persist as separate organisms.

"That will do," I tell Mkimbiaji. He huffs a breath and lets out a hoot that I can feel reverberating in my bones. Chancing a smile, I scratch his feathers and we run back.

I roll up the medical trays and the sheathed kaskara inside the jumpsuit I've taken and tuck it under my arm. With my other hand I snatch up the near-depleted shoulder-rifle. The scarf stays wrapped, red and woolen, around my neck and over my shoulders. Scarf, medtrays, jumpsuit. These are useful. But I don't want to leave many other traces of these invaders in my world. Baba's fighters have done damage enough, and I would erase their debris as I have erased *them*, giving their bodies to the raptors, right down to their marrow. As I will erase the *jūn lèi* if I can.

"It's time," I tell my tyrannosaur. I grip his shoulder in my hand, toss the rolled-up jumpsuit across his back, then several long sticks. I kiss the top of his head and mount him swiftly, pulling the heavy rifle up with me. The charge blinks a pale, slow red. One shot, maybe two. That's all I'll need. "Get ready to run."

Mkimbiaji coos, and we lope away through the broken, half-melted shelters. Leaning from his back, I scoop up flames with one of the dried-out sticks we gathered, and carry fire streaming behind us until we reach the trees and I can shove the brand into one of the piles we made. The tinder catches swiftly, and flames roar up the sides of the alders, loud as my own rage, my blood burning hot as the fire. *Jūn lèi* bubbles and hisses in its fissures in the trees' rough skin. "Burn," I whisper, "*burn*."

We run along the edge of the trees, keeping the shuttle in sight. Lighting pile after pile, a flame of anger scorching my heart and my blood even as the flames lick at the treetops. The firestarting takes me around the shuttle in a great circle, until we are far from the tripartite alders where we left the fuel canister. I turn and feel the heat on my skin. There's an electricity in the air, and my hair stirs. I watch the fires—*my* fires.

I tap Mkimbiaji on the side of his snout gently, and he stops with a low, questioning rumble in his chest. Then he claws the ground with one foot and growls. Eager to be gone from here.

"Hold still," I whisper, scratching his head. "Hold so still."

It is time. This is my forest, and the *jūn lèi* does not own it yet.

Gripping Mkimbiaji with my knees, I lift the rifle to my shoulders and aim the barrel at the fuel canisters stacked against the shuttle's exterior. From here in the dark, they are just shadows against the hull, but those shadows are targets too big to miss.

I take a quick breath, listening to the ocean of my blood in my ears as I press the trigger.

The recoil nearly knocks me off my tyrannosaur's back, and the explosion is so loud my ears ring. Pieces of the shuttle go spinning past, and red fire roars high into the air. The air comes hot against my face, and I duck low over Mkimbiaji's neck as he hops backward, warbling in shock. Spores of *jūn lèi* dance and blacken to ash above us.

Even as Mkimbiaji turns to bolt, I lean to the side, take aim at the canister we set against the alders, and depress the trigger again. My sight is true and my aim is nanite-steady, and that fuel canister goes up as well. Alders snap and fragments of tree spin into the air like flaming toys; others shoot sideways through the forest, and fire roars away from us through the trees in a billowing wave of heat. A second blast of heat against my face. Mkimbiaji sprints into a run beneath me. Tossing away the rifle and gripping spear and bundle closely to keep them from falling, I bury my head in his neck feathers and we *ride* while flaming shrapnel rains down around us, fury and wrath consuming my heart. We rush into the alders opposite the fire and away into the dark.

"To Liberty goddess," I tell my tyrannosaur, though I can't hear my own voice past the tinning in my ear. "We're going the rest of the way to Liberty."

Behind us the world blazes, an inferno on the ground and flickering motes in the air as dry, cleansing flame sears the rot from alder and soil. Whatever war burns in cold space outside our world, in here I have started a war of fire and rot. My body burns with it. But as the trees go up like torches and ash falls about us like the dry corpses of a thousand brittle dreams while we run, my face is wet. As it was so often with spray on Titan's sea.

23

When we tread the road of dreams, the past, present, and future walk with us as companions, but their voices in the dark are so alike that we can't always tell one from the others.

The Lessons of Mai Changying

The night behind us roars with flame, and dark smoke billows in great drifts overhead, and we do not stop at dawn. We do not stop though Mkimbiaji's breath wheezes, though the air we breathe is dry and hot. Sparse pines replace the alders and we pick our way through them, downhill, always downhill, until we reach a slow river and drink deeply before crossing. On the other side, the land climbs again and we climb with it, but the air is less hot. Trees stand starkly outlined in the red light. These trees may not survive when the fire crosses the river, as it will. But the redwoods I love, if any are left in this world, *they* will survive. That is what redwoods do: hollow out and remain standing, though everything around them blazes. Burn out the rot, and the wood remains.

Maybe it will be for nothing. Maybe the *jūn lèi* will resist the fire. Maybe I will do nothing but reduce my hollow world to ash and smoke. But I have to try. We are fighters, we daughters of Liberty. And we daughters of Titan. Mai Changying taught me that even if you are last in the race, you don't give in to the despair. You think and you act and you do it fast: you hook a passing tyrannosaur's hip with your hook and swing yourself up and leap to a competitor's beast and sweep her legs with a kick and throw her from its back, and you keep fighting until you are first. And my father, whose house and daughter were ripped from him years ago, has kept fighting, has somehow sent people out on shuttles and warships and set them burning everything his opponents own, all they hold sacred.

I know who he is, who I am, who we are. We are resourceful as jaguars and fierce as tyrannosaurs. We are fighters.

In the afternoon, I light another fire in a heap of kindling and moss, and set the pines to burn. We ride on.

At dusk, though we are both reeling with fatigue, I gather a nest of old leaves and again I set fire to the wood. We ride on.

In the deep night, we stop. Gazing back, I find the shadows of the forest split with rivers of red. Despair is a clammy, cold thing, but my veins blaze hot. "Keep us awake, nanites," I whisper.

Mkimbiaji and I flush a few deer from a thicket, waking them to the nightmare of his jaws and my spear, and once we have eaten, I leave our cookfire burning, too. Mkimbiaiji rumbles with weariness, his eyes reflecting the fire-glow wetly, but I speak softly in his ear, telling him we can't stop, we have to go on, for a while yet at least.

The next day is almost here when we rest in an open field of jagged white rocks. I check for *jūn lèi* as best I can in the dark, but see nothing. Mkimbiaji curls up between two slabs of rock, and I rest against his feathers, gazing back across this broken meadowland, back the way we have come, watching the distant fires burn. I don't know when exactly I make the crossing from consciousness to sleep, or whether the herd of stegosaurs that pass, massive with those great plates on their backs, between us and the forest's edge are there in waking life or not. Cracks in their leathery hides begin to blaze as though each of them carries a forest fire inside its body. Then they turn to smoke and wisp away. Rising from the night forest behind them, long, pale tendrils of fungal growth wave in the air, clutching at the sky like hundreds of fingers. Some catch fire. Others dance in the wind from the flames, lovely and lethal.

I close my eyes, and for a while I rock with Baba on his boat on the sea. I try to tell him where I am, and that I and my tyrannosaur might die. But he does not seem to hear me. So I grab his shoulder, my hand a small child's, turning him to face me with the sea and the stars at his back. But—it is not his face. Not my Baba's. This face is covered in white fuzz, in squirming, rotting fur. Devoured entirely by the *jūn lèi*. I scream and lunge back against the gunwale, kicking, and I fall into the sea.

The water closes over me—but I can breathe it. For a long time I swim, forgetting the nightmare in the boat, and the whole universe is wet and deep and dark. And quiet. Blue mwezi undulate through the water, forty of them, massive, with calves darting about between them. I swim with them awhile, and their presence comforts me. It is a long time before we need to come up to breathe.

When I break the surface and open my eyes, I am no longer in the water, but seated in the branches of a high redwood, looking out across the green sea of this forest world. I can hear Mkimbiaji breathing behind me, though my waking mind would know that the branches up here are too narrow to support him, and that he can't climb. Yet he is there—his breathing, and the feathered warmth of his body—and I am comforted.

The touch of fingers on mine. I turn. For the first time since I was a child, I dare to look directly into Mai Changying's eyes. They are softer than I thought they would be, and younger. There are not so many wrinkles in her face, after all.

"When I was a little girl," she says, her voice heavy, "we daughters of Liberty were…small. Easily used and cast aside. Even as they used and cast aside the tyrannosaurs and the triceratops and the pachycephalosaurs with their ramming skulls, and all the great bulls we rode. We were nothing to them. Toys, at best. Enjoyed briefly, then forgotten. And I…I did not have the power to break the altars, burn the temples, or send all the young women home. I still do not have that power. But I could make them respect us, make them remember us. I could see how to do *that*. I could not make us free, but I could make us glorious. I could make us splendid."

Her eyes glisten.

I grip her fingers, like a sister. She does not pull away, though I can tell the intimacy is a discomfort to her.

"That was my promise," she says slowly, "and I have kept my promise."

I think about that. We sit in silence, listening together to Mkimbiaji's breathing.

"I have hated you, Mai Changying," I tell her, my voice hoarse from sleep, "and feared you. But I know you only wanted to help us survive, and I am free of you here and so I don't need to fear you anymore."

She watches me, and I can't read her face.

"And besides Baba," I tell her, "you are the only one who has come to visit me when I sleep. Thank you for that. For coming to see me. Even if you terrified me often. I have learned who I am. I...I think I would have walked through any terror to learn that."

Her eyes glow with the reflection of fire. Then I am riding Mkimbiaji through the wood, feeling his warm breathing between my legs and his feathers soft in my hands, and Mai Changying isn't here with us. The tree branches above us are not green but a cobalt blue, as though my tyrannosaur and I are running beneath the surface of the sea. Glancing down, I see instead of forest soil the broken fragments of porcelain teacups, covering the ground everywhere. In the blue shadows between the trees, I glimpse, again and again, a red-haired woman with bruises on her throat and her head at an angle and cold, accusing eyes.

"And who are you, then?" Mai Changying's voice calls to me from the blue leaves, and from the shattered pottery ringing and crunching beneath my tyrannosaur's claws, and from the air. "Who are you, girl?"

"I am Jaguar!" I urge Mkimbiaji to greater speed, because even under these ocean-dark trees, I want to feel wind against my face, wind in my hair, wind we've made together in our running. I know that when the wind burns my cheeks I will start laughing, and the laughter will feel good in me, and I won't stop until I wake. "I am Nyota!" I call out. "I am me!"

24

Others fight to stay alive. We fight to live.

THE LESSONS OF MAI CHANGYING

Do not forget what we battle for: our survival.

SHAKA MADAKI OF TITAN

LONG WEEKS LATER, beneath a redlit sky and leaving burning swaths of forest behind us, running through a world that smells of rot and cinders, we reach the goddess at last. Liberty stands half-emergent from a cliff face, like her sister Love by that deep pool we found. Carved from the original rock of this world and then polished to a black sheen, with a serene face and eyes of polished stone to watch the forest. Her figure is full and round where her sister Love is lithe. Her hair tumbles in dreads about her shoulders, concealing the source of the spring that sends water trickling down her arm to her fingers, to fall in a sweet rain into a basin carved by her side. Her toes are sunk into a bed of violets—maybe the last flowers in the world. Over a hundred meters tall, she stands poised with one foot ahead of the other, her knee bent, ready to step out and walk across the world. One hand lifts a torch high above her head; flames of glass flash and burn in the microstar's light, bright as those I've lit but purer. We are only one woman and one tyrannosaur, but she had better listen to us. I have burned entire forests before her, using an entire hollow world for her altar, kindling a sacrifice larger than any she has ever known, though she alone and not her millions of worshippers witness it. She had better listen.

We came the long way to find her, but we have arrived. We are here.

And we are not the only ones.

Atop a heap of half-chewed corpses between Liberty's feet, a pile of the grisly ruins of other beasts that sought refuge at the goddess's feet, stands the therizinosaur. Its screech when it sees our approach shakes my bones and my blood, and panic runs cold in me before I can stop it. It comes at us, its long claws like the bat-fingers of ghosts, and it is a thing of horror, white rot bursting from one socket where an eye used to be, half its feathers fallen out and great cracks riven in its hide, the white rot erupting from its emaciated interior.

Mkimbiaji roars at it. My body flinches at the memory of that beast pinning me to the ground, and for an instant I hesitate, unsure whether to flee or fight, but my tyrannosaur is nearly as large as the therizinosaur now. Baring my teeth, I crouch low over his neck and whisper, "Take him, Mkimbiaji."

He surges beneath me and my nanites surge inside me and I grip him with my legs. I hold tight with my left hand to the long feathers at his shoulders and with my right, I lift my spear high, a spike from a dead kentrosaur's tail fixed to the end, found in my foragings during our long pilgrimage here. I miss my old spear, the one with the tyrannosaur's tooth, left behind at the nest tree when we fled, but this one will be lethal enough. The invader's kaskara is in a bundle strapped to Mkimbiaji's neck in front of me, but I will need the spear's reach more than the blade's sharpness. I screech with battle-fury as we charge the therizinosaur, the sky burning behind us.

This time it will not end with me on my back and a tyrannosaur infant gnawing at the therizinosaur's hip. This time it will end with its blood spilling out over the earth.

Mkimbiaji's nanite-enhanced speed carries us to the beast in seconds. The therizinosaur's claws slash Mkimbiaji's shoulder, scoring deep, scraping along my shin. My tyrannosaur's blood gushes out over my leg, but Mkimbiaji lunges and catches the animal's other arm in his teeth, locking his jaws and jerking his head back crocodile-quick, ripping the therizinosaur off balance. I throw myself from Mkimbiaji's back as my tyrannosaur pulls our foe to the ground. The weight of the therizinosaur pulls him down too. The therizinosaur lashes wildly with its claws but Mkimbiaji dodges, his powerful hind legs sending his body hopping while his jaws remain locked on the fallen dinosaur's arm. Screaming, I rush in with my spear, driving the kentrosaur spike into the therizinosaur's belly, twenty centimeters in. The creature screeches.

Though Mkimbiaji is nearly as tall and much quicker, the therizinosaur outweighs him. The creature gets its legs beneath it, though its feet slide about on the soil as my tyrannosaur worries its arm. Bleeding from its belly, our enemy slashes with its good arm. Its claws scythe through the air, but Mkimbiaji isn't there. He has released the arm and ducked low. He seizes instead the therizinosaur's leg just above its foot, jerks his head back, ripping the beast off its feet again. It crashes to the soil like a redwood falling, and I lunge in with the spear, taking the therizinosaur in the armpit. White rot instead of blood floods out around the kentrosaur spike with a heavy reek. The creature's scream is terrible.

Suddenly I fear for Mkimbiaji. I don't know how the *jūn lèi* spreads and infects. Fleeing our redwood forest, we charged through entire clouds of it without apparent harm, but biting down on defiled flesh can't be good.

But my tyrannosaur, he is *smart*. Mkimbiaji barely breaks the skin with his teeth, using instead the power of his jaws to bend and snap bone.

The therizinosaur rolls, dragging Mkimbiaji under him, and I see the beast's hindclaws scrabbling as he attempts to hold himself upright. A foot pins my tyrannosaur as the beast once pinned me. One arm hangs loosely but the other forepaw rips at my Mkimbiaji, slicing at his shoulder and side with those obscenely long claws.

I leap to the therizinosaur's back, catching feathers in my hand and gripping my spear near the spike with the other. In red wrath, I stab the spear down, again and again, like a knife, plunging it into the gap between the therizinosaur's shoulder blades. Blood, and then an erupting spider-tracery of white tendrils that lash at its feathers, that burn like fire and venom where they whip against my arm. The pain is intense and before the nanites can block it, I have let go and am sliding down the creature's back. Its tail whips toward me, slams into my belly, hurling me into the air. I hit the ground hard on my tailbone, a gasping cry torn from my lips amid blinding pain. The spear still clutched in my hand. For a moment I can't see or breathe or think or move—just white *agony*— then the nanites do their work and the pain is gone, swift as a snowflake melted on desert sand. Panting, I spring to my feet, knowing I will pay the cost later but thinking only of my tyrannosaur, *my tyrannosaur,* who will not fight this monster alone.

Mkimbiaji is bleeding from his side and the therizinosaur from the spear wounds, as they thrash on the earth. But my tyrannosaur has twisted his powerful body beneath our assailant and his legs are beneath him. As I run toward them, Mkimbiaji surges to his feet, *lifting* the therizinosaur on his back into the air by sheer strength, and his roar reverberates in my bones. The therizinosaur shrieks and nips at Mkimbiaji's neck with its long snout, but I slide to a stop beside them, bringing my spear spinning through the air, the heavy butt-end of the wood smacking into the therizinosaur's head with all the strength and momentum of my body. It dazes the beast and he tumbles from Mkimbiaji's back. My tyrannosaur, faster than I, is on it, catching its throat now in his jaws and whipping his head from side to side, dragging the monster through the soil with it, seeking to break its neck.

But the therizinosaur, its insides swarming with the *jūn lèi*, is difficult to kill. Its breast tears open and more white, fungal tendrils lash out, a net fastening to my tyrannosaur. With a pained scream, Mkimbiaji releases the animal and rolls aside, panting. I dive in, an inferno of adrenaline and battle rage. Screaming my throat raw, I drive my spear into the therizinosaur's vulnerable belly, its breast, its side as it twists and rolls beneath my tyrannosaur. Venomous threads lash at me but I don't care; this beast hurt my Mkimbiaji. "Die!" I scream. "Why won't you *fucking die*!"

Tendrils curl around my leg and I am torn away from the therizinosaur and flipped onto my back, and I see my death, the fungal threads descending toward me like a net. I lift my spear like a bo, lengthwise across my body at arm's length, and the tendrils coil rapidly about it instead of me. Growling through bared teeth, I thrust the spear aside and roll away into a crouch. Then I am back up and the therizinosaur is, too, though it staggers to the side as if about to fall again. Mkimbiaji comes at it, but the powerful tail cracks across his face, sending him sprawling. Breathing hard, I spring, trusting my nanites to catch me if I fall. My knees hit the therizinosaur's head and I wrap myself about it, clinging like a parasite myself, digging quickly into its eye with my hand, gouging and ripping into the beast, my fingers submerged in fluids and ooze. The therizinosaur's scream is a strangled sound. Throwing my weight to the side, I try to drag it to the ground, but I am too small. Mkimbiaji lunges in, slamming his body into the therizinosaur, knocking it sprawling. I roll free, gasping, tumbling across the ground. Quick pain-flares in my shoulders and hips from the shock of hard earth and stones. Explosions that blaze briefly in my body, then are gone as the nanites rush to their own battles within me.

Then there are white feathers above me and a deep, resonant growl. *Mkimbiaji.* He is standing over me, protecting me, that snarl rising in his throat. My heart warms, and then fury-fire blazes in my blood, nanite civilizations converting my cells into furnaces of hemoglobin and adrenaline. With a shout, I grab hold of Mkimbiaji's feathers and pull myself to my feet. Climbing to his back, I reach for the bundle still harnessed across his shoulder. *Now* I need the kaskara. I seize the hilt and slide the blade free swiftly. The therizinosaur is coming at us, its eyes like small dead stones. It wobbles from side to side as it charges, trailing white tendrils like spiderwebs. Bending low over Mkimbiaji's throat, I dig in my knees and growl, "Get him, Mkimbiaji!"

We charge.

No cameras watch our thunder, but I would rather win *this* battle than a thousand on the red sands. I grip Mkimbiaji firmly with my legs and lift the kaskara, both hands on its hilt, my body burning with battle. My tyrannosaur brings us slamming into the beast's side, and as Mkimbiaji ducks to snap at its leg with his massive jaws, I thrust up and *in* with the blade. Dulled by our travels yet driven with all of my nanite-enhanced strength, my kaskara slices into the beast's gullet and carves the therizinosaur open, slicing open collarbone and belly and gut. Entrails and fungus pour out, slopping across the ground, and I fall back, retching. The therizinosaur topples, its body thrashing. A blow of its great, feathered tail knocks me from Mkimbiaji's back and sends me tumbling from through the air. The kaskara drops from my fingers, striking a stone with a sharp bang of metal. I smack into one of the few trees that remain here at Liberty's feet. My body cracks against the redwood and I slide down to rest among its roots, a patch of violets soft against my cheek.

There I lie. Panting, hurting.

I just lie there and let the nanites heal me.

This redwood standing over me, and the few I see nearby, are centuries old. Each has seen generations of tyrannosaurs, the arrival and departure of thousands of shuttles, millions of insects' brief lives. Under this soil that has gone gray as ash, their roots are probably intertwined like lovers' fingers. Lovers holding hands, wrinkled and weary, awaiting death in the night. I press my hand to my breast; my heart beats hot and fast, my metabolism quickened always by the ecosystem of tiny machines inside me. Like my sisters out there above Europa—if they're still there, amid the flash and burn of dying battleships—I live rapidly, panting from one day to the next. To those cedars, maybe I am only a flicker of color, like a brightly-hued bird that you watch for a few minutes and then forget. And now those cedars that have stood maybe as long as Liberty's statue have cracked open, fissures filled with white fuzz. And it has happened so quickly; maybe they are only just now feeling the burn of it, the pain as their bodies rot away in the long gap between one coniferous heartbeat and the next. My eyes sting. It isn't right. It isn't right that an organism that old should die like this, without grace or dignity. "I will give you a funeral pyre," I whisper in my daze. "You will have your dignity back, that at least."

Hearing a roar, I get to my feet, groaning. Whatever cracked inside me when I hit the tree has been repaired, but I feel more like a collection of bruises than a person.

The roar is Mkimbiaji. He has leapt onto the therizinosaur's body and bent his head to scream into its dead ear, a high screech of defiance and triumph. I smile weakly, then call to him, wanting him away from those tendrils that lash the air even after their host should be dead. At first he refuses, and I gasp with worry when I see him tear into the beast's shoulder with his jaws.

"*Mkimbiaji!*"

My voice is sharp. I have to call him several times, hobbling toward him, before he hops from the carcass and comes to me. He nudges my shoulder with his head, nearly knocking me from my feet.

"You absurd young thing," I tell him, hugging him desperately. The nanites are working fast to stitch him up as they have done me. A flash of rage heats me, fury at his wounds, at how near I came again to losing him. Yet the anger gives way to a strange, fierce energy. We are here. After the long weeks, we are here. Some battles, we can win.

Limping back to the redwood with Mkimbiaji following, I find the violets again. I pluck the soft-petaled flowers from the ground and weave them swiftly into a garland large enough for a juvenile tyrannosaur's neck. Lifting them toward the goddess Liberty's face, I ask her blessing, then I put the garland on Mkimbiaji. Smiling, because he lets me. And I kiss the feathers above his eye, as Madame President kisses the victor after the running of the tyrannosaurs on Patriot Day.

"You completed your run," I tell him. "And you didn't just run down forty kilometers of red sands, like the tyrannosaurs on Patriot Day. You ran around the *world*. We both did."

He coos, and I kiss his feathers again.

After a bit, I retrieve my kaskara and wipe the blade clean on a patch of trampled moss. Breathing hard, I turn my back on the beast and its rot, and my feet carry me to Liberty's great toes. Mkimbiaji plods behind me. Tilting my head back, I gaze up the great height of her body, and my heart exults because no white rot covers her. She is as free as her name, as clean as her sister Love standing in her waterfall pool.

I toss the kaskara at her feet, and it rings against the stones. Lightness fills me, and though I kneel and press my knees and hands to the trampled earth at her feet, I feel as though I might float up into the air like a bubble, all my nanites lifting me into the sky. The world behind me is hot with flame. I take a deep breath and lift my voice in the Liberty prayer.

The goddess is here, watching her world through eyes of polished stone, but everything is dying around her. I pray anyway, lifting my voice in song, ignoring the distant, punctuating crack of cedars perishing. After a few moments, Mkimbiaji joins me, cooing the melody with me.

25

My own heart beats louder in my ears than the thunder of all the suns in the sky.

NYOTA MADAKI

HERE WE REMAIN. At dawn, my tyrannosaur and I drink from the rock basin by Liberty's side, and I fill my canteen, the one the invaders of my world were kind enough to leave behind. Then I rest against Mkimbiaji's side. In the afternoon, he and I play in what remains of the meadow at Liberty's feet. At night, we hunt. We forage. We live.

The white rot is before us and behind us, but it has not yet conquered fully here at *her* feet. Maybe this part of the world is holy. We hunt in the cedars downslope. The redwoods that stood nearest Liberty—those, I have hollowed out with fire, to burn the rot from their wood. The other fires I have lit still blaze in many places up along the distant curve of the world. When there is wind, flakes of ash drift down on us like snow, and my eyes water until the nanites take notice.

On the open ground near Liberty's feet is a great heap of charred bones, for I burned the therizinosaur's body and its prey, too. Small green things—lichens and weeds—are growing now from the skulls and shattered ribs, and small furred animals den and burrow there, and I watch them anxiously, awaiting the day when I see their hides crack open and ooze *jūn lèi*. So far, the rodents are as healthy as we.

Mkimbiaji and I are gaunt but we do not thirst. Nor do we starve—not yet. A few nights ago I caught a kulindadromeus in my hands, lunging after it with nanite-enhanced speed. And though I have long since torn all the berries from the bush I found near Liberty's ankle, deer and small dinosaurs come to us here out of the infected trees, as they came to the therizinosaur before us. I chop them apart before cooking them, and if I find *jūn lèi* inside, I burn the carcass, not letting Mkimbiaji near it. The flames flicker in his eyes. But many of these animals are still clean. For now.

There are larger dinosaurs too, a few.

Today I saw tyrannosaurs moving between the last cedars. Several of them, and a juvenile younger than Mkimbiaji, though hardly a hatchling. Like us, they were thin, but they walked through the trees with powerful purpose. I laughed, watching them, and the laughter felt good in my throat.

"There are still tyrannosaurs in this world!" I told Mkimbiaji, who gazed at them, too. "One day, you'll be big enough to give a doe eggs, and then we'll get *you* a little tyrannosaur."

Though Mkimbiaji stayed at my side, he called to the passing tyrannosaurs. There was nothing mournful in his cries. Just an exuberant young call: *I see you! I know you are there! I am here too!*

My own delight filled me until I bounced on my toes. Those tyrannosaurs hooting at each other in the conifers—not everything is dead yet! Not everything. Tyrannosaurs are not easy to kill. I am not easy to kill. This *world* is not easy to kill. Maybe that is a silly hope, but right now, at this moment, I believe it.

* * *

It is midafternoon, and I am climbing Liberty. The air is chill up here, despite the ghost-flakes of ash that drift by. I am warmed by the jumpsuit, by the red scarf I've wound many times around my throat, tucking in the ends so they won't flap about my face, and by my nanites, who heat me from within. It has taken me more than an hour to ascend this high, and I have gone slowly, the nanites toughening my fingers as I seek out miniscule crevices and fissures in the sleek black rock. Up her long leg, over the curve of her hip, and across her belly and breast to her shoulder.

I reach for the next crack in the goddess's stone skin, grasp it, start pulling my self up. My hold slips, and for a brief eternity I dangle in the air by my other hand, two fingertips holding tight to a crevice just below Liberty's throat. An eternity of empty air beneath me. Wind rips at me, and for an instant I can't even feel my fingers; I am certain I am about to torn off of her and flung out into the sky.

I don't glance down.

I bring my other hand up and claw at the sheer rock. My breath comes in quick gasps. There, a tiny gap I can force two fingers into. I cling to Liberty for several heartbeats, the wind inside me louder than the wind without.

Then I climb.

One hand. A foot. Other hand. Other foot.

With a grunt, I pull myself up over her collarbone and onto her shoulder. I rest, but only a moment. Then I begin the ascent of her uplifted arm, the one holding the glass torch high over the world. I want to be up there. Where she flashes with fire and where I can see the whole world. Where I can see the *jūn lèi* and the cleansing flames and the tyrannosaurs and anything else that yet lives. Where I can see for kilometers and kilometers and kilometers—no metal cell to hold me in, not ever again. I may die here, but I will die with a far green sky above my head and a feathered tyrannosaur at my back.

The rock of her arm is smoother, with fewer holds, but the incline is gentler, too, and I find that I can almost walk up to her elbow quickly, then crawl up her forearm. Wind whips at me up here, tugging at me and blowing my unlocked hair against my eyes and cheeks and into my mouth. The wind is loud and it makes the climb perilous, but I am young and inhabited by civilizations of eager machines, and we make it up to her hand together.

I squeeze into the space between her thumb and the blinding glass of her torch. I suppose I am bathed in light from her torch, but none of you can see me. None of you ever will. The glass pressed to my back and hip has a thousand facets, and it is cool to the touch here in the shadow of her hand. I don't know if it merely reflects the microstar's light or if some light Liberty has kindled herself blazes inside it. Almost I feel that she is kindling flame like that in *me*. If I threw myself to the wind up here, surely I would soar like a pterosaur in flames. But her torch hurts my eyes, so I keep my back to it and peer instead through the gap between her thumb and index finger.

I can see *far*. The microstar looks closer here. I imagine that almost, I could reach up and touch it.

Much of my world below and above is lost in billowing clouds of white spores. In some places tendrils reach high above the ground, swaying like kelp in an ocean current— slender fungus-growths stirring in an alien tide. Elsewhere, rivers of fire flicker with soot-black forest behind, and dark smoke clings to the trees or billows along the top of the forest like something tugged along in a river current. Where I stand by Liberty's torch there is only the snap and rush of wind, but I can imagine the roar over there, where fire and rot each struggle to consume the world.

But there are still green areas, too, especially on the world's surface high over my head—forests yet untouched by the war of rot and fire. Maybe I have protected those areas by raising walls of flame. Or maybe those areas will pale and dry out and die in another week, a month, a year.

But right now, they live.

Laughing, I pull myself up to stand on the curve of her thumb with the glass behind me, Liberty's light blazing about me, cold fire from the heart of my world. The wind pushes me *against* it rather than tearing me *from* it, which helps. But even if the wind tore *at* me here, here I would stand.

Glancing down, a hundred meters or more, I see a white speck that is Mkimbiaji, and I laugh again. I wish he could climb up here with me. I wish he could breathe in this great expanse of air, free of spores and smoke. At dusk tonight, after I climb down and before we hunt, I will leap to his back and we will run together, as far and as fast as we can, just for the sheer exhilaration of movement, of being alive. And if we find evidence anywhere of the rot creeping near, there we will set fire to burn.

Once more, I lift my voice in the Liberty prayer. Letting the song fill me and flow through me and from me, giving it to the air, to the wind, to this high place that belongs only to Liberty and myself.

This is my place. Here, I know myself.

I, Nyota Madaki, the Jaguar, Liberty's daughter and daughter of Titan, I stand here. I can run fast, but I will run no more.

This is my place. My home. I may die in it, leaving my bones by the goddess's feet, but you cannot take it from me—not without taking me, too. Mkimbiaji and I, we will fight and hunt and breathe until the pale fur takes us at last. We will breathe every breath fully until it does. Whatever you are, you sickness in my home, whatever forces have unleashed you, I have seen you eat cedars, eat tyrannosaurs, eat away the moss and the soil itself, but you have yet to eat me.

Come and get me.

Come and try.

I stand on top of the whole world. I, Nyota, I stand here.

THE SCREAMING OF THE TYRANNOSAUR

1

SEE ME. See what I can do. I walk naked out beneath the cameras with my sister athletes beside me, and the heat of these pounding sands would scorch my feet, but the nanites are already at work, toughening my soles, inuring them. For seven years they have shaped me, week to week and night to night—for speed, strength, sex appeal. For this moment.

My sisters sing a hymn to Hymen, god of marriage, but I only move my lips. I feel safe in my silence. It gives me time to prepare, to look up at all your faces. Your seats look like soap bubbles to me—bubbles high above my head, bubbles containing little circular platforms with people on them. Small hovercycles zip past with cameras, projecting our faces and bodies onto screens revolving slowly in the air near your bubbles, so that you can see us and those we are here to honor. The sands curve up to the left and right, along the curvature of this steel cylinder we're inside, and there is more sand yet high above your bubbles: we are spinning in space, though we don't feel the motion; the spin is what imprisons my feet to the sand. But gravity is not imprisonment, it is illusion. In a few moments, I will dance and leap in the air, competing with my sisters, and no chain will bind me—not gravity or any other. You will see what I can do.

This is a private dinodrome, chartered for races in honor of the wedding of the Duchess Amy Mardonia and the Third Lord Leo Archibald II. Tonight's is the last of the games; the celestial couple have already wedded and departed for the Bower; it is their guests who have remained behind that I and the animals will entertain. It is said that if one of the great creatures gives its death scream at the same moment as the consummation, the marriage is to be a lucky one. Of course, these matters are timed with precision, as all ceremonies are. A radio jock stands ready to transmit the games, play by play, to the Bower station, and the couple will time their sex so that the Duchess's virginity is not taken until the first death in the arena.

Everything in the universe yearns toward perfection of form and placement; this, my trainers have taught me. All things that are by their nature anarchic, wild, hectic, must be confined within tight steel walls and the tight strictures of ritual; only in this way can the human species be made beautiful and complete. Sex is by its nature an anarchic thing. So is laughter. So is aggression. The animals that will run with me in this arena in a few brief moments—they are the ultimate anarchic impulse, the ultimate sign of the containment of uncontrollable urges and the subjugation of the wild and organic to a specific aesthetic vision.

My own body is another such sign. As I wait here, perfectly poised, with my hook and its long coil of rope ready in my hand, I can feel my breasts shifting slightly as the nanites enlarge and lift them for your view. My skin feels oily and slick, not because I have applied any ointment to myself, but because the microscopic machines inside me are preparing my skin for your cameras. Inked into my body is my tattoo, my sigil, and I permit myself a small and secret smile: because that sigil is my own, the only part of me that is not yours. The sigil is the shape of three timberwolves, one leaping from my thigh across my belly, the other two darting across my breasts. There were never timberwolves in China where I was born. But I watched a vid of them when I was nine. Wolves running in the snow: beautiful, vanished creatures. None of them alone. They moved together. They ran together, hunted together.

Died together.

I watched that vid again and again, watched the untamed perfection of their hunting, the way they turned as one, the bursts of snow from their footfalls like spray from water, their panting breath freezing in the air.

To you, my sigil speaks loudly of my ferocity, proclaims me exotic and half-feral, sexy and wild. My sigil, my nakedness, my position on these sands—all of this divides me from you, isolates me, makes me a thing to be desired, a perfectly trained and sculpted animal, and not a person. You want to watch me. You want to cheer as I move. You want to bed me. I am your Timberwolf.

But to me, my sigil is my secret, forbidden prayer.

My longing for a pack.

2

THE LOVERS are naked now, their bodies lit with candlelight – actual *beeswax* candles, from actual bees! Imagine the sheer wealth of that! They are projected over our heads on those virtual screens, larger than titans, the Third Lord grimly pleased, the Duchess looking uncertain, though flushed from aphrodisiacs. They are dancing alone beside his bed, a dance more precisely scripted than the one about to happen here below. Some of you are watching them, I know—with prurient interest, or with worshipful awe. But I will soon have you watching *me*.

The other athletes seek to draw your attention, too; they strut and poise on the sand. There are only three others for this event. It is no Patriot Day run, though you number tens of thousands, I know, and others may be watching from other stations and other habitats. Coldly, standing completely still, I refuse to look over my shoulder at any of the others. I want you to notice my disdain. I want my lack of movement to draw your gaze. I will be the woman of ice that the men among you wish to thaw, and the woman of grace and beauty that the women among you yearn to be. I have considered this performance with great care.

Anyway, I have seen the others many times in training on the conservatory world, and in the small arenas of our training cylinder above Europa's frozen sea. I have no need to look at them; I know what they are like. Hyena is leaping and spinning in the air, unworried about wasting energy because her nanites will keep her going, and I can hear her throw her head back and yip each time she lands, like the animal whose sigil she's taken. Orca's dance is more alluring. Hummingbird is kneeling with her hands pressed together and her head bowed, swaying slightly; the delicate and non-functional wings grown to her back are whirring rapidly in the air, a blur of color behind her shoulders. She wants to suggest to you something of the virgin bride, as though her performance today will uniquely honor the young Duchess.

When the trumpets call, I simply bend to a crouch, one hand splayed in the hot sand before me, head lifted, ready for a sprint or a leap. I can hear the intake of your breath. Mine is the pose that draws you, because you have been talking for weeks about seeing the Timberwolf in action at last. The media has told you that I am faster than my sisters, that I am wilder, more savage, that I might be better. Now my stance promises you that you will see it.

On the screens above me, the Duchess Amy is enduring the fondling of her much older husband, but your gaze, and mine, is on the sands. I see the grit whirlpooling down some distance ahead of me, as the first of the trap doors is opened—I can't hear it, not over your screams—but I can see the dark opening in the bottom of this artificial world of sand and heat. Then the first triceratops comes up in a rush like a whale breaching, and

267

its loud call breaks the air. I leap forward into my run, and I *am* fast, faster than you knew, tearing across the sand toward the beast, my sister athletes hurrying behind me. Others surge up behind the first, but I ignore them. My hook flashes through the air; cold metal catches the frill just behind the beast's cheek. Even as it tosses its head I spring, using the bull's movement and my own momentum to carry me to its back, landing with my legs spread wide, one hand thrust into the air in triumph. I rock on its back. The beast roars, turning in a circle, but wrenching the hook loose from its frill, I spin the metal scythe on its rope in tight circles in the air. Then a quick lash, a cut across its flank sends my bull screeching forward across the sand. All your faces above me, all you in your bubbles, as I ride the rolling bull. One of my sisters leaps into the air to my left, and there are screeches behind me, and I know my competition is in pursuit. I will outrace them all.

We charge up the long slope of the dinodrome's hull, the first of many laps vanishing beneath us. The tug of spin gravity beneath us is fierce, but the tug of your applause is fiercer; the roar of it! I could leap into the air on it and fly, only I have to stay connected to my bull. Glancing back, I see Orca and Hummingbird and Hyena, each of them mounted, Hyena yipping and laughing, Hummingbird dancing, spinning in circles, flipping and catching herself on her toes on her bull's withers, her wings becoming streaks of light and color, like flame in the air. Orca intent. Intent on *me*, glaring forward; she is the closest behind me. The triceratops are in stampede, and there are more than four. Others race between us, and to distract your attention from Hyena's shrieks of joy and

Hummingbird's acrobatics, I spring from my bull's back to another's as it nears. I spin the hook and slash, driving it fiercely on, needing whatever bull I ride to be *first*. Orca follows, leaping high—leaping *over* my head—to her next bull. Then the others.

We charge past the ribbons of light and the blare of trumpets that mark the start of the second lap. I and the others leap and spin in the air from one bull's back to the next. The creatures surge and buck beneath us, maddened. Orca is the first to miss her leap, tumbling over the frill, but even as the triceratops tosses back its head and bellows its fury, she catches the animal's horn with her hands and spins around it to power a fresh leap to its back. Seeing the opportunity, I loop the hook rope about my own beast's horn and use it to tug my creature to the side, mid-charge, and it slams into Orca's bull just as she lands, half unsettled, on its back. She glances at me in horror as she topples back over the triceratops's hips and falls on her rump in the sand. Ignoring her, I loop the other end of the rope about her beast's horn, tethering the two together, and I flip in the air, dancing back and forth between the two bulls, wrenching raucous cheers from your throats. I am showing off, and you are loving it—this is what you came to see. This is how the mating bed of the Duchess and her groom is to be honored. And despite myself, I am laughing, laughing without control or pause: great giggles bursting from me as I leap and spin. I feel hot and full of oxygen and *alive*. Watch me leap onto the edge—*the very edge*—of a triceratops's frill and dance there, fast and nimble, my bare feet tapping lightly against the rounded rim of that huge shield the creature carries on its head.

Watch me cartwheel down its snout to balance precariously by one hand on the horn over its nostrils, before leaping back to the long horns above its eyes, where I spin and flip and twirl to amaze your hearts. Watch! Watch what I can do.

3

WE ARE RACING, pursuing each other in wide circles around the interior of the dinodrome, beating down the red sand. We crash through the insubstantial ribbons of the third lap, Hummingbird first, then I, then Hyena, and Orca last. You are all cheering, and I hear screams of *Hummingbird!* and screams of *Timberwolf! Timberwolf!* and even voices raised in howling and baying, attempting to drown out the humming that has started up now like a lightship's engines, the humming of those who've placed their bets on my competitor. I grin, lost in the noise of it all, the spotlights sweeping about, washing us all in violent colors. Somewhere on screens high above, the Duchess Amy quivers in Leo Archibald's arms, but I don't care. I am the center of your universe, not they, I and three other women, more skilled, more swift, more cunning and clever and agile than any others in the universe. It is to the rhythm of our pulse that you stamp your feet, to the rhythm of our breath that you chant. One camera shows you the Duchess and Third Lord whom we honor, but a thousand cameras show us. You have placed extravagant wagers on us; you know our bodies' measurements, you have speculated about the recipes for our perfumes—

perfumes engineered specifically for each of us; you know our sexual fantasies, or what we've been told to say those are. They're nonsensical, of course; every young man among you imagines being wanted by me, but Orca is more lovely and lethal than any of you are.

Anyway boys are forbidden us. Most everything is. Not one thing we've told your cameras comes from our hearts. All of it is engineered, shaped, perfumed for your consumption, as we are. Everything that doesn't please the cameras, that doesn't please you, has been waxed away. Even our memories. Above Europa they strip away everything they can during training, dressing us in identical leotards (when we're dressed at all), forbidding us the use of any language but Kartic, mandating attendance at the shrines of the sister goddesses Liberty and Love, forbidding us outside communication, and giving us sedatives early each evening so that we do not own even our dreams.

Yet I remember some things.

I remember bamboo bending in the wind. My mother's hands holding a cup of tea, lifting it so gently to my lips, the porcelain cool and clean. Letters drawn delicately on synthetic paper as my mother sings softly in my ear. A few stories whispered at bedtime, about a past before men and women could leap between planets. A small window that, when you looked through it, showed you an actual sky. Did I have a father? Siblings? That I can't remember. Not even the name of my family, only the name Mai Changying that everyone has called me during training.

When I was eleven, I asked Orca to share a memory of hers with me, and I would share one of mine. That was a mistake. My memory became a mockery in the mess, and the others took to chanting "China Girl, China Girl," whenever I walked in. We were to have one home, one only, in which to take fierce pride: and that home is our little station above Europa, where young women are trained as daughters of the goddesses. Other women look to the stars where we glint in orbit and yearn to be as beautiful, as strong, as desired as we are.

When I was twelve, I rebelled once.

I stood in the mess as they flung "China Girl, China Girl," at me, and with tears stinging my eyes, I sang a song from my childhood, as though to say in defiance: Look! My memories are beautiful. I like them. They are mine, they are not to be scorned!

When my trainer dragged me back to my cell, she made me kneel and slapped me, back and forth across the face, six times. My ears rang with it. I was crying. "When an eagle leaps into the sky," she demanded sharply, "does it yearn for the dirt it's left? Or does it swoop and hunt and stay up high above the weak, showing everyone the sky belongs to it forever?"

I didn't try again to make friends after that.

I learned to cry silently and without tears, in my room alone, as I waited for sleep. I held tight to my memories; they were a small secret inside me that no one could touch. And when the time came, I chose the timberwolf for my sigil, and tattooed not one on my body but three, together.

Now I imagine the other women and I are a pack in a running hunt through the snow, but the snow is sand, and my blood sings in my veins that I, and only I, must be first to our quarry. Hummingbird's bull is just ahead of me.

Lashing mine's flanks, I close the distance. I draw alongside her, and however she portrays herself for the cameras and for you, there is nothing innocent or demure in the glance she casts me, only hate hot as the nuclear furnaces that once baked a third of the earth. I grin at her. Then I am past her and she is yipping at her bull, lashing it on, but mine is faster, mine will *always* be faster. I am the best.

Orca passes her, too. Falling behind has enraged Hummingbird, and she is being too rough with the animal she rides. Orca is calm, focused, as I am. Then Hyena passes Hummingbird, too, and the two of them, Hyena and Orca, are both pounding after me, one to the left, one to the right. We crash into the fourth lap, and I keep my lead all the way to the fifth, but barely. All of you are screaming, my name or the others', all of you wild with the rush of the chase. As we careen across the sands on our final circuit of the cylinder, Orca and Hyena drive their bulls toward mine from either side, as though to crush me between them.

But I am ready. My hook spins through the air, and the rope coils swiftly about the right horn of Hyena's bull; a tug at the rope and a cry of dismay from Hyena, and the triceratops digs in its toes, trying to free its horn, but its momentum tumbles it into the sand. At a sharp cry from Hyena, I glance back quickly; a pang of relief as I see her rolling aside in a billow of sand, uncrushed.

Orca slams her bull's side into mine in that instant of distraction, but my bull keeps his footing. I deliver a hard tap of the metal hook against its snout. Grunting, the bull lowers its frill and drives its scaled cheek against its opponent's shoulder. Side by side, jostling each other, the two bulls charge through the darkness of disturbed sand filling the air. Orca grabs at my hair but I duck and try to sweep her with a kick. She leaps, too fast for that. I leap to her bull's back and—watch *this*—for a few moments we each try to dislodge the other, kicking, striking; then I catch Orca behind the heel and flip her off the bull, but she catches its horn in her hand and flips about it and she is in the air spinning. For an instant I catch my breath, admiring her grace. Then she lands on the other bull, the bull I'd ridden, and I laugh, for she is now without rope or hook. I duck and catch up the rope she's lost, the hook still caught on this bull's frill. One hand pushing against the frill, I retrieve the hook, then begin lashing the bull's flank.

In moments I have left Orca behind. Hummingbird is just behind me, but the cacophony of colored lights is ahead: the end of the race, just a few heartbeats ahead. My back and my thighs itch with sweat and a thousand particles of fine sand are stuck to me, but I barely notice. My head is back and I am baying my joy, as though I *am* a wolf. I hear the panting of Hummingbird's bull just behind to my left and I wheel on my bull's shoulder, bringing the hook scything on its long rope, hoping to dislodge her. Hummingbird ducks low and the hook sweeps through the air just over her head. Then she is in the air, leaping right at me. I spring back onto my hands and my right leg comes up and the kick is *so perfect*, my foot landing right between her breasts. She crumples, wheezing, and tumbles off the back of my bull into the sand.

There are explosions of color and light all about me, and howling; I rap the triceratops's cheek repeatedly with the cold hook. He veers to the left and we halt in a skidding plow of sand, just past the lap's end. Hovers zoom overhead with hundred-faceted cameras, and other bulls charge by, several without a rider, one with Orca, and the last with Hummingbird clinging to its thigh, where she must have leapt up from the sand, digging in her hook. But I laugh as they thunder past, because the race is done. It is *done*.

All of you erupt in shouts, slamming your feet, and handlers with shock rods rip across the sands on hovercycles, sparks flying as they goad the other triceratops toward gates at the arena's sides, gates already opening like hungry mouths. In the dizziness of colored floodlights and smoke from sudden firecrackers, I glimpse Orca and Hummingbird still astride their bulls, their faces red with rage or shame. Orca's eyes are wet. Then they are through the gates, and the gates are shut and the hovercycles are zipping away, and only I on my triceratops and all of you are left. Above me, a thousand small screens show my face, flushed and sweaty, and one large screen shows the Duchess with her back arched and the Third Lord crouched over her. Her face is flushed, too, and her eyes—for just a second I see her eyes—are bewildered.

Mine are not.

This is my victory. I have *won*.

I lift my hands high, my head back, letting your applause wash over me. For this one moment, I can close my eyes. I can just stand here on the bull's back, breathing.

A scream tears through your cheers, and I gasp. No one who has ever heard that scream ever forgets it. It is like no other cry. Like metal shearing. Like a station dying in orbit. Like a rip in time. A scream older and sharper than my cry of elation or your cry of worship. A scream that sent our ancestors trembling to their burrows when our forebears were still furred and quadrupedal and small enough to hold in your hand. The scream of a wounded and lonely thing promising violence and vengeance on whatever has hurt it.

Hearing it, I know the race, the run, was only a preliminary; your thirst for blood, all of you, has yet to be appeased.

I turn to face it.

There he stands, large enough to fill a temple's interior, his jaws parted in that toothed shriek.

Tyrannosaur.

4

THE TYRANNOSAUR'S SCENT is intense, an acrid musk like things dying on the edge of an ocean. This one is a bull, and the handlers have goaded him to aggression by spraying about him, likely for the past eighteen hours, the pheromones of tyrannosaur does in season.

Yet for all his heavy scent, the animal is beautiful. I find myself staring at him. He is stronger than his prehistoric predecessors, a little taller, his forearms even smaller, his powerful back legs bred for leaping. Fifty generations of revivified tyrannosaurs have preceded him, and selective breeding has made him a fierce giant of his kind.

But he is not beautiful because he is mighty. He is beautiful because he is sad. Look at him, standing there, his head moving in tight little jerks like a bird's, his feathers lathered in sweat. He keeps glancing about for the does he smelled. Maybe he hasn't slept in a day. They have toyed with him, his handlers, making him lust and sweat and breathe heavily, preparing him to run or to battle as they wish. When the game is ended, he will probably collapse from exhaustion, docile, drugged by his fatigue, and they will come at him with a sacrificial blade and loose his blood to spill across the sand. Immense as he is, this tyrannosaur, he is more a slave than I or my sisters.

His scream tells me that. See him tilt back his head, hear his screech like metal tearing apart. That is not a mating call; I have heard tyrannosaurs' mating calls. Nor is it a challenge, this roar that makes you all quiver with delicious fear, all of you who are protected in your high seats. No, that is a panic-cry, a terror-scream. The tyrannosaur is afraid. He is a wolf without a pack, and he is afraid.

A pang of regret, and I slash my hook across the triceratops's hip, urging it forward. With a recalcitrant bellow it lowers its head, frill like a wall, horns like spears, a mammoth of sinew and muscle and ivory charging toward the tyrannosaur. I will end this quickly. A few moments ago, I had wanted to prolong everything, to make this a night that every one of you, and not only the Duchess about to receive the Third Lord, will remember until your last breath. I may die in the games soon, or be cast aside when I am a year too old, but I would have you remember my name and my sigil.

Yet at this moment, my blood and my bones no longer beat with that fevered need. I long only to stop that tyrannosaur's scream, to end its pain, keep its aeons-old loneliness from sinking too deep into my heart.

5

I EXPECT THE CLASH to knock me from the triceratops' back, and I am ready to roll and rise and leap back before either beast can trample me, but no clash comes. The tyrannosaur springs to the left, and though the triceratops bends its head as if to catch a tendon with its horns as it passes, it makes no contact. The tyrannosaur darts in once we are past, osprey-quick, lunging for the soft, unprotected back of the beast I ride—and for me.

My adrenaline is too high for terror. I tug wildly at the rope, and the triceratops veers into a circle, following the pull on its horn. With a bellow it crashes into the tyrannosaur, its right hip against the carnivore's leg. I have leapt to its other hip, so I am not crushed between them. The tyrannosaur topples under the oncoming weight and he rolls aside in the dust; the triceratops stumbles to one knee.

"Up!" I scream at the bull. "Up!"

But the triceratops is shaking its head. Something has disoriented it. These animals have little vision, and in some the olfactory sense has been artificially impaired. And maybe there are other factors: some chemical soup the handlers injected into it, now reaching the end of its effectiveness and leaving the beast dizzy and sick.

"Up!"

The tyrannosaur gets his powerful legs beneath him and heaves himself back onto his feet, impervious to the bruises that must already be forming beneath the feathers on his leg. I hold my breath. His muscles bunch for a leap. I glimpse his eyes—those dark, dark eyes—and in them no longer any panic, only rage: the need to get to his females, the fury at whatever beast stands in his path. My sorrow for the creature wells up in me.

The triceratops wallows, wheezing, another moment in the sand.

And I make a choice.

As the tyrannosaur leaps, I leap too, springing from one beast to the other, hook in my hand. I sheathe the metal in the tyrannosaur's hide and dig my heels deeply into his feathers, and I am *riding* him.

Laughing.

No athlete has ever ridden one of *these*; we ride the herbivores that do battle with the toothed beasts. But I am riding this one, and truly, not one of you will forget this night.

The tyrannosaur dodges to the side, ignoring the triceratops, his head twisting to snap at me, at this pain on his back. I dance and leap on his shoulders, beveling on the rope, avoiding the snap and close of his jaws. My heart is suddenly full of rightness, a reckless liberty I haven't ever felt before. You and I are alike, I want to shout to the tyrannosaur. We should run together!

You all know the script for the games tonight: the triceratops gores the tyrannosaur, and a triumphant woman dances on the bull's back. But I have your script in my hands and I am ripping it in two. Because there will be a tyrannosaur and a woman together on the sand, everything else dead at our feet, and then I will ride this poor bull off the sands and back to wherever he sleeps, so that he may die, when they slay him, away from all your cameras and away from all your screaming faces. The handlers will want me punished for this, but you will all be shrieking my name and pounding your feet against the hull, and not even the gods will punish a woman whose name is in every mouth of every human being on this artificial world. This is how the games will go tonight.

I slash the tyrannosaur's right flank. Without a roar, with only a huff of breath, he turns, shakes his head, and charges again—right at the triceratops still half-kneeling in the sand.

"Come on!" I cry to the tyrannosaur bull I ride. "Come on! End it *your* way! Not theirs! Yours!"

6

THUNDER IN SPACE. We make it, the tyrannosaur and I, his great, taloned feet pounding down the long meters of this arena. I am whooping and laughing on his back, and though dozens of hovercraft flash with camera lights and floodlights of a dozen colors rush about me, no one can stop me. This is my moment. Mine and his.

My bull tears flesh, bleeding and red, from the triceratops's flank, long strings of sinew, baring white bone to the flare of light. Almost I can taste it between my own teeth. He rips his head back, almost flinging me off, but I dig the hook deep into his shoulder and bevel down his back. Then he and the triceratops are circling, and I am giddy. Near vomiting, near weeping. My body is being distorted from one second to the next as my nanites multiply desperately, striving to keep pace with my exertion. This must end soon.

In the vid I saw as a child, the wolves veered across the snow as smoothly as petrels over the water. All together, in silent, irrevocable grace. I wish other tyrannosaurs were here with us—that this beast I ride was not alone. He has only me, in this metallic universe that hangs like a jewel in the endless cold. Only me. An upward glance as we circle shows me the rotating screens: a dozen times reflected, myself and my tyrannosaur in a mist of red sand, blood streaming from his open jaw like ocean from the mouth of a whale breaching. On the screen there is no screaming crowd, no space cylinder, just sand and flesh: two wild animals naked—woman and immense, feathered bird. The triceratops offscreen preparing for its next charge. As though we are in a wilderness and are not captives owned and shaped for your cameras. At those screens, I burn hot with anger. Those wolves in the vid—they were the same, bounded within some narrow sanctuary or zoo, though the screen revealed to my childhood eyes neither cameras nor fences. I know this now. They were as severed from European forests as I am severed from China, and their union in a pack was a thing both temporary and fragile. Even on the beaten worlds beneath us, farther down the sun's gravity well, nothing real remains. Everything is shaped for the cameras. Even you yourselves.

But the tyrannosaur, my tyrannosaur, is no longer screaming.

There is blood on his jaws.

He is angry now, not afraid.

Only you up there—only you are still screaming.

He pants as we circle, stirring the sand. Sweat runs over my skin. I breathe through my mouth. The triceratops drags one hind foot and snorts sand from its nostrils in explosions of breath. "Now," I whisper, and lash my tyrannosaur's flank, sending him into a run. His hunting cry is long and ululating and my whole body, marrow and bone, reverberate to it. For the briefest instant I wonder if Orca, Hyena, Hummingbird are watching me on the screens, if they can see my hair in the wind, if they can hear me whooping with the tyrannosaur bull. We close with our opponent in a crash of feather and hide.

The triceratops feints—I see it, my bull doesn't—then slams its head into my tyrannosaur's hip. I flick my hook across his cheek to warn him, too late. Two spires of ivory shear deep. My ears would bleed at the bull's scream, so near my own head, but the nanites stanch the blood before I ever feel it. Eardrums are easily repaired, more so than lungs or entrails or hamstrings, and the living galaxy of tiny physician machines burns hot and fast inside me. Not so with my tyrannosaur; no devices smaller than mitochondria inhabit or protect him. He is designed to die.

A tower of muscle and sinew, he founders.

I dance across his shoulders, but he is falling, and all I can do is spring aside to land in a blossom of sand and red dust. His crash sends a hot cloud of it at me. Still he screams as he kicks his fierce leg, throwing up more sand. The triceratops charges by me, a wind against my body. Balancing on my feet, I join my scream to the tyrannosaur's as the frilled beast slams again into his belly. There is a deeper red than the sand.

My body is hot and my breath is hot and I am cooling in a sheen of sweat, but for the fury in me there is no cooling. My tyrannosaur flails weakly in the sand. I have only a second to think and I do not use it. There is no thought, only rage. Gripping the handle of my hook, I hurl myself into the air, leaping to the triceratops, onto its shield of bone.

7

THIS DAY HAS GONE long enough without a death. Clinging with my thighs to the edge of the triceratops's frill, I spin my rope beneath and around its neck, then leap across to the bull's other shoulder to catch the hook, and as I tighten the noose, the beast gives a hoarse roar and breaks into a panicked run, clouds of red sand billowing past me like architites blowing on the wind over Neptune's second sea.

I dance grimly on its back to keep my balance, and the muscles scream in my arms. I do not care if I damage myself; the nanites will repair me. My pulse is beating hot in my temples and all I can think of is to tighten, tighten that rope.

With a gasp, the triceratops stumbles to its knees; it shakes its head as if to throw me, but I stay put. Its horns sweep past before my eyes like trees in a gust. I sit and slam my feet against its frill for leverage and I pull and *pull* at the rope. Red and purple light washes across me, garish, from the hovers, but no one interferes. All of you are watching, I can feel your lust wash up in waves against me, your yearning to see one of us naked animals down here, at least one of us, die a gory death.

I give you no gore with this one; you have had enough blood. The triceratops's tongue hangs from its mouth and its huge sides lift and fall raggedly and then are still as I cut off the last of its air. It gets uneasily to its feet, a surge of its muscled body beneath me like the whole earth moving, but then the beast beneath me tilts and it collapses onto its side, a bow wave of sand cresting away from its fall. I leap free, hitting the sand and then somersaulting back through the air to land again on its thigh, and I am pulling the ropes taut again, so taut, allowing it not one gasp. It kicks weakly, craning its head back, the great frill scooping sand before it like some monstrous shovel. I neither speak nor shout; I just strain at the rope, letting the nanites within me heighten my muscles and hyperoxygenate my veins, giving me such strength and endurance as you have only in your dreams.

The triceratops stops kicking, the death noise in its throat loud like rocks rasping together. I do not relax my hold. Then it shudders and is still, and as all of you hold your awed silence, from a thousand megaspeakers the Duchess Amy Mardonia's sharp cry pierces the air: the act of love a ceremonial refutation of the day's first death.

Numb, I slide from the triceratops's hip, barely noticing the impact of the sand against my feet. I leave my rope and hook wound about its neck. The triceratops lies lifeless behind me, of no more significance than an unnamed boulder in the hills. My fury still burns through me like forest fire through bamboo, but I no longer care about that horned beast. I give no heed to the Duchess Amy's moans or to the excited cheering of your tens of thousands that soon drowns her out. There is only one I care about now, and my eyes are on him as I cross the sand.

8

THE TYRANNOSAUR, my tyrannosaur, lies gored and dying; I walk to his head. As I bend to look into his eye, already glazed with pain and approaching entropy, the roar and rush of all your voices fades until it is nothing louder than the rush of my own blood in my ears.

It is over. I am not yours anymore to prize, or envy, or yearn for, or fuck. None of you matter.

Tenderly, I kneel by his massive head and put my arms around him. His head is warm against my breasts, his feathers soft. He makes a wheezing sound but does not move at my touch.

He has been trained and shaped, too. He has been torn from his place and time as surely as I have. And I wonder that none of you, not one of you, has thought to pity him. I can see into his heart. I make him a vow, whispering the words in Mandarin near the tufted hole of his ear. I will teach my sisters to see into his heart. Into all your hearts. As I have.

Embracing the dying bull, I sing softly to him a song of my mother's, a song of old China, words of Li Po's set to music long before I was born, in a year when there were only moons in the sky and no orbital platforms, no conservatory worlds or steel cylinders. Maybe only one moon; I think there was only one moon made by the gods and not by men.

My voice is softer than I have heard it before; tears burn at my eyes.

> *Among the blossoms I*
> *am alone with my wine;*
> *lifting my cup I ask the moon*
> *to drink with me, its reflection*
> *and mine in the wine, just we three:*
> *and I sigh, because the moon cannot drink*
> *and my reflection just mimics me, silent;*
> *no other friends here, these two*
> *alone are with me—*

The tyrannosaur murmurs low in his throat, like a child about to shift in his sleep, and I know this beautiful old animal understands the song. At least as much as I do. More than any of you ever will. Yearning takes me, to retrieve my metal riding hook and plunge it into my own breast, to bleed out here beside the tyrannosaur and leave all of you behind, all of you lost in the scream of your crowd. Because I am a wolf separated from her pack, watching my only companion die.

But I have made a promise.

As the hovers approach with a roar like cicadas at dusk, I cling tightly to my tyrannosaur's head, close my eyes, and sing softly as I weep.

FINIS.

If You've Enjoyed
These Stories…

THE PUBLICATION OF THIS BOOK—and all my fiction—has been funded by my Patreon members. Patreon is a site that empowers artists, musicians, and writers who are undertaking work that is daring and independent and difficult to otherwise fund. My Patreon members and I undertake these projects together: my members vote on the covers, read scenes before anyone else, and discuss the stories with me all along the way. It's a backstage pass.

If you've enjoyed the story, please come visit my Patreon page. Learn more about future projects, get complimentary ebooks (or signed paperbacks), and get involved behind the scenes! Membership dues are whatever you decide—even if it's a dollar a month. Come join me and the other readers; I look forward to seeing you and talking with you about what's coming up next!

WWW.PATREON.COM/STANTLITORE

ACKNOWLEDGMENTS

THESE TYRANNOSAUR STORIES have delighted my heart. Inside me there is still a young child who can't quite get enough of dinosaurs in all their majestic beauty. But going from imaginative play to writing novels is quite an endeavor—an endurance trial as grueling as the running of the tyrannosaurs on Patriot Day, if less bloody—and I owe a great deal of thanks to a great many people. To Jason Philip for always being ready to share a new paleontological discovery. To Jessy Pace for help with research early on. Any paleontological or biological errors in the novel are either my own or the result of extravagant far-future genetic engineering. To Richard Ellis Preston, Jr., who is an excellent editor; to Lauren K. Cannon, who did the cover art; to Samuel Peralta for publishing one of my tyrannosaur stories in his *Jurassic Chronicles* anthology and for loving this little world I made; to my beta readers Shoshanah Holl, Kim Klimek, Mike T. Long, and Jenna Bird, who helped ferret out many inconsistencies and rough spots in the manuscript and challenged me to make it even better. To my Patreon readers who fund my work. To Jessica my wife for vigorous encouragement—I could not have done without you. And thank you to my children, who run out on field trips with me to dinosaur museums and who share my love of these largest of all feathered birds and most intense of all scaled reptiles. Thank you all.

ABOUT THE AUTHOR

STANT LITORE WRITES about zombies, aliens, and tyrannosaurs. He does not currently own a starship or a time machine but would rather like to. He lives in Aurora, Colorado with his wife and three children and hides from visitors in the basement library beneath a heap of toy dinosaurs, tattered novels, comic books, incomprehensibly scribbled drafts, and antique tomes. He is working on his next novel, or several. You can read some of his current fiction by looking up *Ansible, Colosseums for Dinosaurs, The Zombie Bible*, or *Dante's Heart*. However, doing so may have unpredictable effects, and Stant offers no assurances that you will emerge from any of these stories unscathed. Best leave all non-essentials behind, take with you only what you need to survive, and venture into the books cautiously and ready to call for backup. Enjoy, and good luck.

Made in the USA
Columbia, SC
26 July 2023

20736750R00181